The Moon-Pool

RICHARD PARSONS

The Moon-Pool

Methuen

First published in Great Britain 1988
by Methuen London
Michelin House, 81 Fulham Road,
London SW3 6RB

Copyright © Richard Parsons 1988

British Library Cataloguing in Publication Data

Parsons, Richard
    The moon-pool.
    I Title
    823'.914 [F]
ISBN: 0 413 18490 0

Printed and bound in Great Britain
by Butler & Tanner Ltd,
Frome, Somerset

The new girl had brought in tea. Sir Marcus noticed the pale, soft hairs on her slightly sun-tanned arms. What was her name? Jenny or Judy? That was the snag about getting older. Of all the mental attributes, memory was the first to fade. It was hard to believe that he had once learned all those difficult words in Serbo-Croat and had even made a passable stab at Chinese. Now it was technique that carried him through, coupled with long knowledge of the way the world actually worked. Perhaps there was something to be said, after all, for that tiresome and inexorable rule about retirement at the age of sixty. It was best to go out like a lion, with faculties still intact.

Sir Marcus Stewart-Stibbs had become Permanent Under-Secretary in the Foreign Office, and Head of the British Diplomatic Service, at the age of fifty-two. Thin, lanky and polite, he sometimes seemed to resemble a rather nice giraffe. His elevation had surprised none more than himself. He could hardly compete in dynamic energy with Robin Compton or, in sheer intellectual power, with Graham Swinburne. Yet one had had to be content with Washington and the other with Tokyo. It had astonished the Service. But the explanation was simple. The Foreign Secretary of the day had been gifted with a rare capacity for self-appraisal. He knew he was good at the political overview but possessed only a sketchy knowledge of foreign affairs. The last thing he wanted was a bossy and demanding Permanent Under-Secretary, showing up the gaps in his own experience and insisting on urgent decisions over places with unpronounceable names. How awful to have to face the human tiger at Number Ten, or the rabble on the back benches, accompanied by Sir Robin's small Napoleonic figure or the huge, quizzical eyebrows of Sir Graham. Those formidable mandarins were better suited to pro-consular duties in some large country well away from London. For the home ranch, ministers had settled for Sir Marcus with his deferential approach, nicely cut suits and fertility in the vital arts of the cover-up and the managed leak.

'D'you take milk and sugar, sir?' asked the new girl.

'A little milk, please, Judy. No sugar.'

Sir Marcus disliked being called sir by a woman. It would not have happened once. When he had first entered the Foreign Office, the traditions of the old pre-war Diplomatic Service had lingered on. It was still a club. In the Office in London you never said 'sir' to anyone except the Secretary of State himself. Indeed, you used Christian names when the hierarchical gap was not too immense. But times had changed, and not for the better. The Service had lost its cosy élitism, ravaged by the envious breath of the Home Civil Service and the chill winds of industry. Paradoxically, this had seemed to lead to more overt rank-consciousness, rather than the reverse. Sir Marcus prided himself on his easy way with the coal-face workers. The girl had not flinched when he called her Judy. Perhaps it really was her name. It had been a snap decision. Better to get the name wrong than to appear chillingly impersonal. He had toyed with 'my dear'. But that seemed a bit old-fashioned and might even have appeared lascivious rather than avuncular. These days you had to be careful.

'Mr Gilbert is here, Sir Marcus.' That was an improvement. 'Will he have tea, too?'

'Oh yes. And cake as well. Mr Gilbert is fond of cake.'

It was one of the better moments. Sir Marcus enjoyed his conspiratorial sessions with Bernard Gilbert, discussing appointments and promotions in the Diplomatic Service. It was the only area left where he felt he had any real power. Once the Permanent Under-Secretary had seen all policy submissions before they went up to ministers. He had been the chief diplomatic adviser to the government. But nowadays the field was too wide for one brain, however agile. He had become more of a string-puller and public relations officer for the Service as a whole. In the administration of the Service he was assisted by Bernard Gilbert, one of the key Deputy Under-Secretaries, who occupied the misleadingly titled but historic post of Chief Clerk. If anyone thought that Gilbert was some lowly clerk, a latter-day Mr Pooter, they were in for a shock when they actually met him.

He bounced in now, redolent of self-confidence. A squarely built man, his ample torso, fuelled by years of good lunches, was soberly clothed in an expanse of expensive suiting. Bernard Gilbert smiled a lot. But it was the smile of an urbane and well-fed tiger. In these troubled days you did not administer the British Diplomatic Service by methods of simple kindness. Sweet reason was not the way to persuade people to occupy the nasty posts which had proliferated throughout the world. You had to use the stick as well as the carrot. Bernard was an adept with both. Sometimes, his meetings with the Permanent Under-Secretary might appear to be degenerating into mere gossip. But the gossip was about human strength and weakness, and Bernard liked to feel he was using that in the national interest, to get his pieces onto the right squares.

'You will have cake, Bernard?'

'Oh yes, please.'

It was that nice, rich plum cake again. Bernard grinned. He was a greedy man. For everything. He made no secret of it. *Joie de vivre* was an essential component of diplomacy, he believed. How else could you endure the machinations of foreigners, the bleating of ministers, the insecure vanity of members of parliament and the gnat-like buzzing of the press? Bernard always managed somehow to keep his temper. It was the safest way to climb up the razor blade of public life.

'And what have you to offer me this time?' asked Sir Marcus. They always met like this, in private conclave, before the meetings of the Number One Appointments Board. This was the Foreign Office Committee which made recommendations to the Secretary of State about the filling of the most senior posts in the Service. The responsibility, if parochial, was awesome. It involved the making and breaking of the careers of a small number of highly gifted and ambitious public servants. It might not matter much to the nation, against the background of eternity, whether Sir Gareth Griffith-Jones ended in Madrid or Mexico. But it mattered to him. And, even more, to his wife.

Chairmanship of the Number One Board was the foundation of the personal power within the Service of the Permanent Under-Secretary. A junior minister sat on the Board, as well as the Deputy Under-Secretaries. But the dominating figure was its Chairman, provided that he managed the agenda well in advance through consultation with the Chief Clerk, whose responsibility it was to make specific proposals. Sir Marcus saw to it that these were invariably to his liking. It was not that Bernard Gilbert was one of nature's yes-men. But he himself would soon need the goodwill of the PUS and the Board to secure one of the top overseas jobs for his own final post before retirement. So indeed would the other Deputy Under-Secretaries. The system was simple and worked well, provided that no one tried to rock the boat.

'There's Accra,' said Bernard. 'Leo is retiring in August.'

'Oh really?' replied Sir Marcus, consulting the invaluable Diplomatic Service List. 'But he isn't sixty until next year.'

'We persuaded dear old Leo,' said the Chief Clerk judiciously, 'to offer himself for accelerated retirement. He'd got a little past it.'

'Round the bend, you mean?'

'Over the hill. It gets noticed, you know, in these English-speaking posts. We got a blow-back from that Parliamentary delegation.'

'Hermione was back home quite recently,' said Sir Marcus. 'I met her at the French Embassy.'

'That was the trouble,' explained Bernard. 'She should never have left him.'

Sir Marcus, scenting scandal, probed further.

'What exactly has he done?' he asked.

Bernard coughed gently, as if about to lower his voice. Some appalling revelation must be on its way.

'He has gone quite native,' he croaked hoarsely.

It was a damning portmanteau phrase. British Heads of Mission were of no use once they identified too closely with the interests of the country where they were accredited. Sir Marcus took the hint and decided to enquire no further. Imagination boggled at the possibilities. He had a momentary glimpse of black breasts and heard the thin pipe of voodoo incantations. To think that Leo had been with him in the classical sixth at Harrow! He had looked quite beautiful in his cricket flannels. How strange the fortunes of mankind.

'We might get someone else to go there,' said Sir Marcus doubtfully, 'on promotion.'

Bernard Gilbert registered polite dissent.

'That would have been nice,' he said. 'People will do almost anything for promotion. But I'm afraid that Ghana will have to be kept for Martin.'

'Martin? Won't that be a shock? After Budapest, I mean.'

'It's that or premature retirement. There's nowhere else.'

'We could offer it to him,' suggested Sir Marcus. 'He might be willing to go.'

'Go?'

'Leave the Service.'

'That frankly was my idea,' said Bernard. 'His wife has money.'

It was always the same problem, a game of musical chairs. The object of the exercise, to change the metaphor, was to provide for senior officers a smoothly moving upward elevator, designed to render each posting slightly more attractive and important than the one before. But it didn't inevitably work like that. There were always the losers.

'We could try it on the Board,' proposed Sir Marcus. He liked to preserve the illusion of the Board being a rabidly independent animal, though in reality its members were almost invariably docile. At least, thought Sir Marcus, the Foreign Office was usually spared from that odious phenomenon, a thorn in the collective flesh of so many foreign diplomats from less favoured lands, the intrusion of political nominees into diplomatic jobs. Virtually all the top posts in the British Diplomatic Service were now held by professionals. Sir Marcus intended to keep it that way. The alternative was monstrously unfair. One had only to look at the State Department, whose career officers were so often doomed to hold Deputy Chief of Mission posts, under rich idiots who had contributed to party funds. That produced havoc in the promotion pyramid.

'What else have we got for next week?' asked the Permanent Under-Secretary. He enjoyed this sneak preview of the human menu. Playing God, it might almost be called.

'OECD in Paris,' said Bernard. 'Head of the UK Delegation.'

The Organization for Economic Co-operation and Development, a prestigious outfit, was mainly serviced by visiting eggheads from national Ministries of Finance. The permanent Delegation, largely staffed from the Foreign Office, had to keep them happy.

'We thought of Larry Crawford. He's getting awfully bored in Bogota. And he did once do a secondment to the Treasury.'

'Has he got the intellectual clout?'

'The Treasury have hinted that they'd prefer a lower profile next time round. The present incumbent keeps proffering unsolicited advice about the future of the world economy.'

'But that's his job.'

'Not in the opinion of the Treasury knights. The Crawfords entertain very nicely. Horses for courses, if you see what I mean.'

The meeting proceeded. Nothing really unkind was said about any of the colleagues. That would have been against the code. But the two senior officers were adept at discreetly giving the thumbs-down signal when the need arose. When they first took up their jobs, each had privately feared that he might be insufficiently ruthless for the more agonizing decisions over personnel. Neither need have worried. They had both been good at clearing out the dead wood, pruning through the tall trees. At the age of fifty-two, Sir Marcus had found himself assuming that anyone older than himself must be well past his best. As his years in the top job had slipped by, the age of senility had automatically risen for him each year. It was still one year above his own, now fifty-nine.

Bernard Gilbert kept producing options. He was undeniably ingenious. Sir Marcus felt his attention beginning to wander. In many ways it was an advantage to have a grasshopper mind which liked to hop lightly around from subject to subject. You could do some of your best thinking while some loquacious foreign ambassador was holding forth. Few elderly men knew how to be snappy. A half-hour call could usually be summarized in a couple of sentences. But sometimes you really had to concentrate. Age and a good lunch didn't make that any easier. Mental effort was needed to follow Bernard's complex human chains, each proposed appointment and promotion being dependent on the successful conclusion of the one before. Any break in the chain would be disastrous, necessitating a complete rethink.

Outside, St James's Park was looking ravishing on this afternoon of early summer. Sir Marcus relished his big, historic room on the corner of the Horse Guards Parade, one down from the Foreign Secretary himself. He tried to remember what the rest of the day had in store. Most of it consisted of receiving self-important people who insisted on approaching the Foreign Office at the highest official level. A South American ambassador was scheduled. And then there was that funny little man from the British Council. Thank God, he had declined the diplomatic receptions for that evening. How he had grown to detest them. He would walk across the park, a green thought in a green shade, and tell the official car to meet him at Buckingham Gate for the rest of the journey home to Old Church Street.

With a small stab of illicit pleasure, Sir Marcus remembered that Felicity was away for the night. She had gone down to Bournemouth to comfort her aged mum. Sir Marcus loved his wife. He was deeply conscious of her virtues. She had helped to make him. Her expansive, bubbly manner was the ideal complement to his own more arid and intellectual style. Felicity had got him the embassy in Paris. And she had performed superbly there by giggling at the snobbish locals in her awful French and beautiful Liberty frocks. But Felicity was tiring. Not exactly bossy, but terribly exhausting. A sort of psychic sponge. He needed the odd break.

As a very young man, when he had first entered the Foreign Office, the son of a successful solicitor in Norfolk, Marcus Stewart-Stibbs had been terribly lonely. He had missed the automatic, cluttered companionship of home, school and university. He could still remember those summer evenings spent wandering alone on Hampstead Heath, those solitary Sunday walks through Islington and Clerkenwell. An early marriage had saved him from all that. He was deeply grateful to Felicity. It was paradoxical now that, because for years he had been no longer lonely, he deeply relished the rare opportunities to be alone. This evening was a case in point. He would do some of the things which Felicity disapproved of so silently and so strongly. He would play *Fidelio* rather too loudly. He would have that extra whisky and soda. He might even take off his shoes and socks in the drawing-room and scratch between the toes. It was an innocent vision.

'Is that all right, then?' asked Bernard anxiously, his plummy voice cutting in abruptly on the pensive musing of the Permanent Under-Secretary. 'We liberate Bogota for Sidney. Potterton replaces him as minister in Rome. And the splendid Baxendale can be promoted into Potterton's seat.'

'Admirable,' replied Sir Marcus gravely. 'Potterton flourishes best abroad. Or so I have come to believe.'

They both knew what he meant. Potterton, currently an Assistant Under-Secretary in the Foreign Office supervising the Consular and Claims Departments and other ghastly bits of the organization, tended to be loquacious at the morning meeting of Under-Secretaries, where brevity was meant to be the order of the day.

Those confident, strident tones would be better deployed on the Tiber.

Bernard stooped to gather up his papers, well pleased with the deft ordering of his little ladders and his human chains. A little too pleased perhaps, thought Sir Marcus. It was time to stir the pot.

'What about Washington?' he asked gently.

'Washington?'

'Well, yes. It's only six months before Robin retires. He's collecting directorships already.'

It was a slightly sore subject for Sir Marcus. His own prospective non-executive directorships, with their small but solid emoluments and nourishing luncheons, were already beginning to trickle in, in advance of his retirement next year. But they still formed a modest rivulet rather than the broad flood on which he had banked. He would need those perches in the City to supplement his pension and, even more, to provide a refuge from Felicity. How awful to be stuck in the house all day. He must spend more time buttering up the bankers. Perhaps he should be devoting more attention to the *Financial Times*.

'You mean we ought to put James to the Board this month?'

'Why not? Get it out of the way. All the other big things depend on that.'

Time enough, thought Bernard. Ambassador in Washington was the most important overseas post in the Service. The embassy had always been large. Now it was bigger than ever, a complete Whitehall in miniature, staffed by the ablest officials from many ministries. The ambassador had to preside, with a firm hand and a clear eye, over this motley and opinionated crew. There was an immense range of business to transact with the American Government, on which the British perhaps now depended unduly. The representational responsibilities too were immense. Sir Marcus shuddered at the thought of those Charity Balls in New York, the clam-bakes in New England, the Mardi Gras in New Orleans, the rodeos in Texas, and those awful junketings in California. Above all, you had to act as the oil between the upper and the nether millstone, the President and the Prime Minister. The job required not only a good brain and lots of experience but also a magnificent set of nerves and a superb digestion. Sir Robin Compton, with his unshakeable self-confidence and elfin grin, would be a hard act to follow.

Fortunately, not for the first time, the Service had the right candidate to offer in Sir James Leyland. It had been understood for years that he would go to the States after Robin. Indeed, it was with this ultimate inducement in mind that three years ago they had persuaded him, the most brilliant of the Deputy Under-Secretaries, to move to Brussels as UK Representative to the European Community. That job was central to British interests, even more than Washington perhaps. But it lacked charm. James had grown weary of those all-night wrangles over the price of pig meat. He was fed up with being hunched over committee tables, listening to jabbering Continentals. His formidable presence and gift of the gab would be better deployed in the New World. There was no other serious competitor. But approved procedures could not be bypassed. His name would have to be approved by the Board, if only as a formality, for submission to the Foreign Secretary and then the Prime Minister.

'All right,' agreed Bernard. 'And then we can proceed with the rest of the chain.'

It would mean a big shake-up at the top of the Service. That was inevitable, since whoever moved to Washington would himself vacate a major post.

'I suppose it's all pretty obvious,' said Sir Marcus. 'Andrew will have to follow James in Brussels. No one else understands all the dossiers. That frees Bonn for Charles. He's been wanting to get back to Europe for years. And Gilbert can do Tokyo after Graham.'

Bernard said nothing. It was an eloquent silence.

'Don't you think so?' pursued Sir Marcus. 'There are really no alternatives.'

Bernard cleared his throat, with a diffidence uncharacteristic in so large a man.

'What about me?' he asked softly.

Sir Marcus suppressed a slight twinge of annoyance. Bernard might be an able colleague but he was not at all delicate. It was typical of his lack of finesse to throw his own hat into the ring in so overt a manner. He could not perhaps be blamed for fighting his own corner. At the end of the day, it was the last post, at the close of the career, that mattered the most. That was what you had to live with for the rest of your life. And the posting of the Chief Clerk himself did present a certain embarrassment. As head of the administration, his own ultimate destination offered a striking test of persuasive skill. A personnel chief who failed to secure a cosy niche for himself would be as unconvincing to the world at large as a toothless dentist or a bald barber. But all the more reason, thought Marcus, for operating with a certain refinement. Bernard should have left it to him.

Of course it was obvious what Bernard had in mind. The old fox had long hankered after Bonn for himself. Had he not once been Head of Chancery there under old Geoffrey Talbot? But the post was too near home. Ministers went there too often. Bernard's breezy assurance would hardly be likely to survive reiterated exposure to the Prime Minister's person. Besides, his German was none too hot. Sir Marcus had once heard it for himself at a Trade Fair in Munich, and it had sounded distinctly home-grown. It was usually a mistake, mused the Permanent Under-Secretary, to allow one's own side to listen to one's efforts with foreign languages.

'I think these Western European posts are rather overrated these days,' Sir Marcus commented, urbanely, as if he had not heard the interjection of his faithful lieutenant. 'The real action is to be found elsewhere.'

Bernard's usual high colour had begun to turn a deeper shade of puce.

'Elsewhere?' he croaked. 'I won't go to Lagos. That's flat. Singapore nearly finished us. Amaryllis was a martyr to prickly heat.'

'I was thinking of Australia,' explained Sir Marcus. 'We need a really good couple there. Not too stuffy. An outdoor image.'

'Australians live in cities,' said Bernard, rather sulkily.

'It's a whole continent, you know,' continued Sir Marcus with enthusiasm. 'Or more or less. You'll love it. And they'll love you.'

Bernard remained sagely silent. No other major post was available. He knew when he was out-ployed. At least for the time being. And now the heavily spectacled features of young Jasper Tenby protruded through the slightly open door from his own little adjoining office, as Private Secretary to the Permanent Under-Secretary.

'What is it, Jasper?' asked Sir Marcus, quite kindly. In fact,

14

desiring an interruption, he had discreetly pushed a small button under his desk. 'Is the ambassador getting impatient?'

'No, we're holding him at bay. But the Secretary of State has asked if you could pop up for a moment. Apparently he's had a rush of blood to the head.'

'How very alarming. A cerebral haemorrhage, you mean?'

'No. A brainwave.'

'Almost equally distressing. Do we know the subject?'

'Private Office say he has been staring for some minutes at a map of South-East Asia. It's a new thing in his life.'

'I'd better go and calm him,' said Marcus. 'I think that just about wraps it up, Bernard?'

Bernard nodded gloomily. He would be in no hurry that evening to return to Blackheath. Amaryllis, looking slightly like a caged tigress with a penchant for gin, would be waiting to hear the outcome of his interview with the Permanent Under-Secretary. She wanted, above all, to be somewhere near home, so as to keep a cautious eye on the children, who seemed to need more and more attention as they grew older. She would have settled for Rome but Paris would be more convenient. It was her only preference, but it had come over loud and clear. Her reaction to Australia might shatter the glass in the Painted Hall, down at Greenwich.

'There's a message from your office,' said Jasper. 'The new entrants are all lined up, waiting for you to address them.'

'To hell with the new entrants,' muttered Bernard Gilbert.

'You must excuse me,' said Sir Marcus Stewart-Stibbs. 'But I am not technologically trained. What exactly is a moon-pool?'

'It's a hole in the bottom of the ship,' explained the managing director. 'An essential component of the diving system. You can't conduct operations under water without being able to look out. With powerful lighting, you can often see the sea-bed from the ship's deck. And from a moon-pool, you can send down a flying bell. From a working moon-pool, you can even launch construction equipment. It's the latest technology.'

'But why is it called a moon-pool?'

'Well, undersea life looks rather odd when you peer out at it from the hull of a boat. You get a deep probe. It's like gazing into those mysterious craters on the surface of the moon. Hence the word moon-pool.'

They were visiting the new support vessel designed for use with sub-sea installations. It had been specially built for the North Sea oilfields. The Foreign Office had arranged for the Permanent Under-Secretary to join the party, in order to demonstrate support for the achievements of British advanced technology. It made a nice break from work at the desk, with its constant pressure. Besides, who knows? All these outfits had Boards. All the Boards had seats. And all the seats needed someone to put on them. The lunch had been rather good, too.

'Could I squint into a moon-pool?' asked Sir Marcus. It was desirable to show interest, though in fact one felt rather bemused. That brandy had been a mistake.

'Of course.'

It was a strange undersea world. Mysterious dark blues and greens were brilliantly illuminated by lights in the bottom of the ship. A tired-looking fish swam past. There was seaweed and a lot of plastic bags. But this was Sunderland, not the Caribbean. Sir Marcus could understand nevertheless the reason for the almost poetic name. The deep river-bottom, seen through the moon-pool, really did look like some weird lunar crater viewed through a powerful telescope. It was the unexpected hole in the solid surface of the ship which acted, like the frame of a picture, to encapsulate the scene. Hence the sensation of effecting a deep probe, of gazing in astonishment into the darkest recesses of the moon-pool.

'Most fascinating,' murmured Sir Marcus. 'And rather strange. Almost as if one was prying. Into things not normally seen.'

'Glad you liked it,' said the chairman of the Board. 'I was hoping you might be able to help us. With potential foreign markets, I mean. Could you manage Glyndebourne on the seventh of next month?'

'With pleasure. What is it?'

'South Koreans.'

'I beg your pardon. I meant, what will be on?'

'A group from Seoul. With their wives. Some of them speak English.'

'And the opera?'

'Oh, I'm afraid I don't know. That's all in the hands of our public relations department.'

Sir Marcus stifled an élitist sigh. He could still remember the days when those summer lawns had been filled with people who had actually bought their own ticket to hear *Figaro*. Now commercial sponsorship filled the seats. The music would be better than ever but some of the bloom had fled. In the country's long decline, it was the erosion of the centres of excellence that hurt the most.

'But we have a perfectly adequate system,' expostulated Sir Marcus. 'Sanctified by years of use.'

'And a good many sensational failures,' riposted the little man, scratching his bald head. Sir Dominic Trowbridge was not much to look at. But, as Head of the Security Service, his voice counted behind the scenes. It was he who had insisted on this meeting with the Permanent Under-Secretary at the Foreign Office. And Sir Marcus Stewart-Stibbs had known better than to refuse, though the day was a busy one, with the French Ambassador looming over the horizon. He was glad to have the hastily summoned support of Bernard Gilbert, oozing with his habitual self-confidence.

'Ministers are getting tired,' continued Trowbridge, 'of having to apologize to Parliament.'

'That's what they are here for,' said Sir Marcus.

The Head of the Security Service did not smile. Sir Marcus felt that his levity had been misplaced.

'Too many breaches of security have come to light,' snapped Sir Dominic.

'Better that than to remain concealed,' pointed out Sir Marcus.

The little man considered the point.

'I suppose so,' he at length conceded. 'But there can be no doubt about it. Our system of positive vetting is inadequate for the modern age. The Prime Minister has instructed me to devise a new one. It's not just spies we have to guard against in our midst, but people fundamentally out of tune with our whole system of government.'

'Ah, generous youth,' murmured Sir Marcus. ' "Bliss was it in that dawn to be alive." Wordsworth, you know, on the French Revolution. A crusty old Tory in age, though. He lived to lead the opposition to the railway being extended to Westmorland.'

'I don't entirely follow your drift,' countered Sir Dominic coldly. He had long regarded Sir Marcus as weedy and effete. This was the kind of cultivated amateur who had brought Britain to its knees.

'Positive vetting,' opined Sir Marcus, 'can be no more than a charade. As you know, we have a team in the Office here, working closely with your own people. Retired majors in mackintoshes, driving round Devonshire picking up references, interviewing prep school headmasters. Ponsonby-Smythe has passed for the Foreign Office. But is he sound? Was he any good at rugger? Preferred the flute, eh? Very rum.'

'It is only too easy,' said Trowbridge flatly, 'to poke fun at our investigators. Dedicated persons, working for a mere pittance. With a simple code perhaps, somewhat smacking of yester-year. But the real fault is with the system. An official who is to be entrusted with government secrets has first to be positively vetted. This is supposed to involve an in-depth investigation into his past life, his present conduct, his political opinions, his sexual preferences. The object is to root out anyone who may be tempted to commit treason, either through conviction or through vulnerability to pressure.'

'We know all that,' protested Sir Marcus. Bernard Gilbert remained sagely silent.

'The trouble lies with the limitations we impose at present on our investigators. They take up only the references supplied by the subject himself. They corroborate just the details of his past life contained on his official file. And they admit, in all their interviews, to be working on behalf of the government.'

'Well, why not?' chimed in Bernard at last. It would be a black mark for him with old Marcus if he failed to give support against this little runt.

'Because it simply doesn't work. It's only too easy at present for an unscrupulous applicant to evade our vigilance. Hence these security scandals which have gravely embarrassed the government. Only the other day we had the unspeakable Beddoes and his revelations in the *Guardian* about that terribly hush-hush stuff at Porton Down. It makes us a laughing stock to our allies. So senior ministers have accepted my recommendation that the system should be modified. In future we shan't just rely on investigating the candidate's own account of his life. That way makes it only too easy for him to conceal his private thoughts, his inner misgivings, his secret lusts.'

'What have you in mind?' asked Sir Marcus. 'Bugging their bedrooms?'

Sir Dominic's neat lips pursed up, somewhat petulantly.

'We are setting up a completely new section in my department,' he said coldly. 'A covert operation. It will operate in parallel with the traditional vetting procedure. But in areas unknown to the person under investigation. Operation Laser-Beam, we are calling it. Laser-Beam operatives will not declare themselves as belonging to the Security Service. Nor will they confine themselves to the applicant's avowed curriculum vitae. They may get to know him personally, without revealing their own status. They will certainly scrape acquaintance with his nearest and dearest. And they will probe like ferrets.'

'A sort of secret police,' commented Sir Marcus.

'You can call it what you like, Marcus. But it's about time we started to deliver the goods. At present no one admits to being a communist or a pervert. In future, we shall smoke them out.'

'Is this being announced publicly?'

'Of course not. Operation Laser-Beam is a deep secret. People must never know that we are running this parallel system. They must go on talking freely. Babbling merrily in bars and clubs. A lot of it will get back to us.'

'Just for the new entrants, I suppose,' said Bernard airily.

'Certainly not. For all levels. The Prime Minister is most insistent about that. Human weakness is all-pervasive. I am even doubtful about one or two members of the Athenaeum.'

'And what am I supposed to do about it?' asked Sir Marcus.

'Members of the Diplomatic Service,' snapped Sir Dominic, 'will not be exempt. Rather the reverse. I thought you ought to know.'

'It sounds slightly alarming,' said the Permanent Under-Secretary. 'Your great searchlight, I mean, your laser-beam. After all, none of us is perfect.'

'It's a new concept in security vetting,' agreed Sir Dominic with grim satisfaction. 'The in-depth probe.'

Bernard Gilbert swept the recesses of ancient memory. Years ago, as an undergraduate at Oriel, he had once delivered a paper on Trotsky the Seer. Might that still be in the archives? Thank God he had soon diverted to rowing. And then there was that little fling in Djakarta with that curious Swedish lady. Her activities had verged on the kinky. It was a mercy that Amaryllis had not probed. She had never cared for the wilder shores of love. One had to face it. Everyone had a skeleton in the cupboard. Some had whole grave-yards. The great thing was never to look worried. The system could hardly turn against him now. He *was* the system.

'I get the idea,' said Sir Marcus. 'I think I should call it a moon-pool.'

'A moon-pool,' countered the Head of the Security Service. 'What on earth is that?'

'You don't know?' exclaimed Sir Marcus benevolently. 'Then let me explain. It's the very latest thing.'

Jonathan Fieldhouse felt a slight, but annoying, tickle in his left nostril. A lesser man would have inserted a digit directly. But even in the London Underground Jonathan felt a need to preserve the decencies. Somebody might be looking. And who knows? It might even be an observer with the potential to influence his career. Discreetly he produced a modest, clean handkerchief. Jonathan might be young. But he had already joined the Establishment. He was a small man with a neatly trimmed moustache, dressed now in a blue sweater and jeans for an evening out. He felt already at home in the Foreign Office which he had recently entered, after taking a good degree in history at Cambridge. He had been particularly successful in the mediaeval paper, where he had displayed excellent knowledge of feudal land tenure and the development of the Wardrobe and Exchequer. The ideas of the Age of Faith had fascinated him less. He would go far in the public service. He was intrigued by the mechanics of how to get things done, not by conceptual arguments as to whether they should be done at all. In this he had little affinity with those of his contemporaries, and they were many, who claimed to be interested in nothing except everything. Not for him their swirling words and grand ideas. He would take splendidly concise minutes at inter-departmental meetings.

Opposite him sat a large black man of about his own age. Round his neck he wore a quasi-gold ornament which made him pleasantly conspicuous. Their eyes locked for a moment. Jonathan felt an instinct to give a friendly smile. But that might have seemed patronizing. He compromised by turning slightly away. People no longer smoked in the Underground but it still seemed painfully airless on an evening like this of urban summer. Jonathan began to wonder whether he ought not to have worn a clean pair of jeans. He saw too that his socks were not quite right. One of his grey pairs would have been better. Socks were often a problem. If long, the elastic perished and they fell down. If short, they tended to reveal an unpleasingly white strip where the ankles met the calves. Of course it did not matter this evening. He was only going to meet Rupert Mills, an old Cambridge friend of almost spectacularly scruffy appearance. But clothes were important to Jonathan. He needed to feel right. And he only felt really right when carried out of himself by the joy of work, drink or the company of someone exciting. Constant small anxieties, he knew instinctively, were the price he had to pay for avoiding the big horrors. It was better by far to be neurotic than psychotic. He would never go mad. In fact he had a rather awful sanity which would take him a long way. But the pressure inside him would always have to be balanced by pressures from outside, as in a man escaping from a submarine. He needed his work not because he was superior to his contemporaries, but because in many ways he was more vulnerable.

'What are you staring at me for, man?' rasped a voice.

Jonathan looked up with astonishment to see the black man opposite glaring at him in a highly aggressive manner.

'I beg your pardon?' he asked mildly.

'You giving me the gimlet eye,' shouted the black man. 'You want something, man?'

Jonathan felt distinctly uneasy. A large matronly woman beside him, no doubt a representative of the moral majority, was regarding him with marked disapproval.

'I was not staring at you,' he said. It would not do to seem too confrontational. The other man might have a knife. One had heard nasty tales about happenings on the Underground, even in the vicinity of Sloane Square.

'You was giving me the eye,' muttered the man opposite.

'My eyes had to look somewhere,' explained Jonathan, with the air of an embattled editor closing a tedious correspondence. 'If they seemed to rest on you, that was by chance. I was lost in thought.'

He was glad to make the change of trains required by the system. It had been a faintly dispiriting episode. He felt the paranoia all around him.

'Mind the gap,' boomed the loudspeaker.

It was a reference to the space between train and platform. But Jonathan felt that evening that it could have applied to the nation as a whole. The gaps were too big, too glaring, too dangerous. Fresh administrators were needed with new minds uncluttered by precedent and protocol. Young, educated people like himself.

He was glad to see Rupert Mills. His shaggy frame and merry, doubting face recalled those halcyon walks to Grantchester. With Rupert, the church clock stood still at ten to three. But Jonathan had moved on. He liked things now to be clean and new. It was hard to suppress a shudder at the disordered state of Rupert's basement flat in Highbury where he lived on unemployment benefit with his girl-friend, a dark-haired damsel of Irish provenance called Maureen. Jonathan noted that she never cooked, never cleaned, and hardly ever spoke. Her main activities seemed to be smoking and staring reverently at Rupert as if he combined rare beauty with infinite wisdom. Jonathan found her distinctly annoying, not least because he would have willingly taken her to bed himself. There at least, he suspected, she would excel.

'There's no food here,' said Maureen flatly. 'We'll have to go to the pub.'

'What a surprise,' commented Rupert sardonically. 'You wouldn't get away with that in Connemara.'

'Thank the Lord we're not in Connemara,' riposted Maureen. 'Father O'Flynn would eat you both for breakfast.'

Jonathan knew he would be expected to pay for the pub grub. Maureen too, it would seem, was without gainful employment. As the waged member of the trio, he did not object to forking out for their modest binges. But he mildly resented their bland assumption that he should automatically do so. Rupert, after all, had got a perfectly good degree. It was impossible to believe, even in modern Britain, that he could not have obtained some form of paid job. But Rupert had never wanted to be bothered with little things. They interfered, he claimed, with the free play of his mind. Besides, he had never been much good at getting up before a late lunch.

'How's the Foreign Office?' asked Rupert a shade truculently, as he accepted a pint of real ale with a mumble of muted gratitude.

'Very busy,' replied Jonathan. 'I had no idea that there would be so much to follow in Central America.'

'Tell us all about it,' suggested Maureen.

'Spill,' commanded Rupert.

'Oh, I can't do that. Official secrets, you know.'

Rupert laughed theatrically. 'You can't kid us with that one. It will all be in *Private Eye* next week.'

'Not through me,' retorted Jonathan. 'I have a duty to the taxpayer.'

'Balls,' said Rupert. 'You're thinking about your own career.'

'Well, why not? Of course I want to get on.'

It might have been a devout Catholic talking about transubstantiation. Jonathan made it sound like the central tenet of his personal creed, as indeed it was. He was not ashamed of that. There was no harm in being ambitious. If you had a good brain, you just had to use it. It wasn't possible to stop the engine. People didn't always understand that. They sneered at those who tried to make their way in the world. They didn't try to enter a mind like his. Yet it was very simple. He was avid not for money or status or perhaps even power. He simply craved to use his mental faculties on the big issues. It was a sort of chronic torture otherwise. Aristotle at least had realized that. He had defined happiness as the proper exercise of function. Ironically, Jonathan was not temperamentally well suited for success in diplomacy which depends so much, at least abroad, on a cheerful ability to sit around waiting for things to happen. He might make it to the top, holding down the big jobs in London. But his temperament could also turn very sour, if the way through the undergrowth seemed to be irremediably blocked.

'All right,' continued Rupert. 'We don't want your precious secrets. But at least tell us something interesting that has happened this week. How many prime ministers have you met? What about the Crowned Heads?'

'We had a fascinating talk,' replied Jonathan defensively.

'Who's we?'

'The new entrants. From a very senior man called Bernard Gilbert. He's in charge of the administration of the whole Service.'

'Sounds like a big cheese.'

'It had to be postponed. He was called away to cope with something really important. But we got it at last. I was encouraged to find him so robust.'

'You mean he's strongly built?'

'So confident in his attitude. He thinks that diplomacy has a great future, as well as a remarkable past. It's the web between sovereign states. More needed than ever, in a troubled and inter-connected world. There's a real idealism in a career of that sort, though concealed behind a sophisticated exterior.'

'Nonsense, my boy. It's just a glass-bead game. A way of sopping up your mental energies.'

Jonathan was conscious that both Rupert and Maureen had drained their pints. He would pretend not to notice.

'I personally found Mr Gilbert rather inspiring,' he said flatly.

'It would take more than that to inspire me,' proclaimed Rupert, as if boasting of some prized virtue. 'Some mouldy old mandarin.'

'It's about time that you got round to something yourself,' said Jonathan, feeling that he had been teased enough.

'I don't suffer from this mad urge to be active,' retorted Rupert. 'The Protestant work ethic has passed me by. Besides, I'm a philosophic anarchist. I could never take a job which required me to boss anyone else around.'

'That's not the only type of job,' pointed out Jonathan. 'You could get one at the other end of the scale.'

'I shouldn't care for that, either. The next round's on me. Are we having the same again?'

As Rupert got up to move towards the bar, Jonathan felt a surge of affection for him. Beneath his rough manner, there was a decent side to this funny old layabout.

'Actually,' whispered Maureen, 'he *is* trying to get a job. Teaching English in Japan, perhaps. But don't tell him I told you. He feels defensive when you're around.'

That was rich indeed, thought Jonathan. At Cambridge he had been more than a little scared of Rupert, whose family were rather grand and did things with horses in Gloucestershire. His own mother lived much more modestly in West Yorkshire. It was ironic that his entry into the Foreign Service had rendered him upwardly mobile, while Rupert now drew unemployment benefit. They were passing each other on the way, moving in opposite directions.

Yet up till now he had seemed to need Rupert, whose upper-class disdain for worldly success complemented his own compulsive ambition. It was all right for Rupert whose family had for long been among the tall trees of the human forest. He had never had to claw his way towards the light from that dark terraced house in Otley. Let him go on, if he wished, seeing life as a glass-bead game. He would have a shock one day when the honours were dished out.

'I'm afraid I've run out of cash,' called Rupert from among the brimming pints. 'Can you lend me three quid?'

Rupert had been his best friend, thought Jonathan. But he might not remain so for much longer.

Bernard Gilbert had braved it out with Amaryllis at breakfast in Blackheath that very morning. He had discovered by experience that this was the best time to break bad news. While the reaction raged, you could take refuge behind *The Times* and then rush out for the station, claiming an early appointment in Whitehall. Whereas a storm provoked after dinner could shake the marital bed for hours, badly curtailing much-needed sleep. As expected, Amaryllis had responded most adversely to Australia. She simply could not see the point of going so far afield when the job was not even in the top grade of the Service. It would have been worth making all that sacrifice, she conceded, for a post outside Europe, like Washington or New York, which carried promotion to the summit. But Canberra was not in that league and the family at home needed her watchful eye. Timothy showed a marked disinclination for sustained exertion, while Camilla had struck up a friendship with a most peculiar Finn. They would both go to pot while she roamed the Antipodes, out of reach of Harrods and Fortnums and everything which made life worth living. Amaryllis did not consider herself to be selfish. She was very charming, so long as she got her own way.

'Can't you change it?' she asked.

'Certainly not. It's all fixed.'

'I thought you were supposed to be in charge of these things. Aren't you the big potato? Several ladies at the Diplomatic Service Wives' Association have told me that you personally ruined their husband's career. I don't much enjoy those sessions.'

'It's been through the Board. With the other senior appointments.'

'What happens now?'

'The Secretary of State has to approve. With the agreement of the Prime Minister, if he thinks it necessary.'

'Ministers may make a change. In your favour. You told me yourself that the Foreign Secretary was seen to chortle at one of your jokes. I don't suppose he knows them as well as I do.'

Bernard smiled at the simplicity displayed by his somewhat scatty wife.

'Ministers will accept the recommendations of the Board.'

'How can you be so sure?'

'They always do.'

'Why?'

'It's part of the system.'

Mildly shattered by Amaryllis's negative reaction, but hardly surprised, Bernard sought the relative tranquillity of the Office. It was upsetting that poor Amaryllis should feel so badly about this appointment, the last of their career. She had been a loyal partner and it was sad to see the strain in those usually happy blue eyes. He sat heavily in his large chair and busied himself with reading the morning telegrams. There were always a lot of them. Nothing very exciting today. A small revolution in South America. A minister in Bonn disturbed by a British pronouncement. Scandinavian howls about acid rain. Just another summer morning in London.

But that didn't last. There was an urgent call from Jasper Tenby in the Permanent Under-Secretary's office. Sir Marcus Stewart-Stibbs needed to see him urgently. Would he please stay behind, after the morning meeting of Under-Secretaries, for a pow-wow *à deux*. There had been a development. In Foreign Office terms, most developments meant trouble. Bernard Gilbert squared his broad shoulders.

He found Sir Marcus looking unusually peeved and tense. Today he looked less like a giraffe than a well-bred bird of prey. His breakfast too had been unsatisfactory. Felicity had reminded him that they were entertaining a couple of her posh French friends that evening. They would have to go to one of those awfully expensive places in the Fulham Road. In Paris, Felicity's taste for social grandeur had been an asset. Back in London, it was merely a drain on the purse. Felicity's dukes and duchesses, with names redolent of old Versailles, straight out of the pages of Saint-Simon, seemed prone to home like pigeons on out-of-season food and the rarer wines. Besides, they would have to speak French most of the time. Sir Marcus had grown weary of foreign languages and had developed a marked distrust of foreigners. Foreign affairs would be so much more pleasant without them. He felt sympathy now with those headmasters who had never cared for the parents.

But worse than that was in store. On arrival at his office, he had found the ground crumbling beneath his feet.

'I was summoned urgently this morning to see the Secretary of State,' he explained to Bernard.

'So early?'

'He had to sandwich me in. Before the dentist. It wasn't one of our better meetings.'

'Bad news?'

'The worst.'

'Somebody dead?'

'Much worse than that, Bernard. Washington has come unstuck.'

'But the Board agreed unanimously. We put up James Leyland.'

'I do remember that,' said Sir Marcus coldly. 'My memory may not be quite what it was. But I do retain the key things for a bit.'

Rebuffed, Bernard mused clinically on the human urge to disseminate pain. Sir Marcus might be an ageing eagle today, but he was still carnivorous.

'We can blame the Prime Minister,' continued the Permanent Under-Secretary. 'The Secretary of State had a nightcap at Number Ten last night. Between them, they hatched out one of their tiresome brainwaves. I do wish they would leave these things to me.'

'James Leyland is a splendid choice. He even likes Americans. Washington was his first post, as Third Secretary. He's in with the Ivy League.'

'I know all that, my dear Bernard. But it isn't the point. Ministers have decided that, this time round, they don't want the embassy in Washington to go to a member of the Service.'

'Oh hell!'

'My reaction entirely. It ruins everything. But the PM is adamant. He needs Washington for George Craxton.'

'Craxton?'

'I'm afraid so.'

For once, Bernard was reduced to temporary silence. It was an appalling bombshell for the most senior ranks of the Service. Even without that, there would be too many of them chasing too few jobs at the very top. The loss of the diplomatic flagship would make it a good deal worse. Now James Leyland would either have to stay in Brussels, exuding articulate umbrage, or else be reposted to a vacancy scheduled for another colleague. The whole chain of senior appointments would have to be reorganized, with somebody losing out altogether. It would probably spell premature retirement for some able and ambitious man.

'Will Craxton be any good in Washington?' asked Bernard sourly.

'Probably not. But that's hardly the point. The PM wants him out of the House of Commons. And he's willing to go.'

'I'll bet he is.'

It was so unfair, thought Bernard. Washington was thought of as a convenient disposal point for an unwanted politician, whereas for a gifted diplomat it would have been the top of the tree. Political ambassadors were seldom all that effective. They might get on with other politicians, as fellow denizens of the smoke-filled rooms. But they usually lacked application in running a large embassy. The job was for an ensemble leader, not just a gifted virtuoso. And being a virtuoso was known to be Craxton's forte. He had recently left the Cabinet after a public disagreement over policy, and it was still far from clear whether he had resigned or been sacked. On the back benches, as one of the most senior members of the Party, he would present a definite threat to the government. No wonder the PM was keen to send him into gilded exile, on the other side of the Atlantic. And the opportunity to regroup in glamorous surroundings might well suit Craxton. He would no doubt plan for a triumphant return to political life at home after the next election, with the full panoply of American media publicity.

'Can't you argue with the PM?' suggested Bernard.

'I'd rather not,' replied Sir Marcus with a slight shudder. 'You know what these politicians are like. The exercise of power is what really turns them on. And they never feel so powerful as when making these personal appointments which overturn the system and cause a lot of trouble for everybody else. It has all the charm of a perversion.'

If the occasion hadn't been desperate, Bernard would have had to smile. Sir Marcus's waspish comment on the habits of politicians very aptly described his own methods, as the Foreign Office Administration had found to their cost. In the field of personnel operations, he was much given to tiresome personal hunches. Talent-spotting, he called it, in his official jaunts round the globe. What this meant in practice, thought Bernard, was that the vain old man believed he could judge ability better after five minutes' chat than the Personnel Department with their access to the confidential reports over a period of years. Reports were the true way to distinguish between an officer with real staying power and one with superficial charm and the will to please.

'Well, Bernard?' The PUS was looking at him fixedly. He seemed to expect some helpful contribution or creative idea.

'We shall have to re-do the entire chain,' said the Chief Clerk glumly. A very nasty thought had occurred to him. In the revised scheme, Canberra might be needed for some other star, displaced by the problem of seating the disappointed James Leyland. He and Amaryllis could find themselves landed with Lagos after all. He would fight that with every weapon at his disposal. And he had a good many.

'Of course we shall have to rethink all our ideas,' snapped Sir Marcus. 'I hardly need you to tell me that. What I require from you is instant inspiration.'

Bernard closed his large, brown eyes. He might have been in prayer. Then he slowly opened them again and gave a shy smile, reminiscent of a basking shark.

'There is just one point,' he said diffidently.

'Yes?'

'Craxton will have to go through the usual procedures.'

'What exactly are you getting at?'

'As a former Cabinet Minister and Privy Councillor, Craxton will already have a full security clearance. For that he will have been extensively vetted by the Security Service.'

'Of course. I don't see much mileage in that.'

'But now he's going to a Foreign Service post. In fact he will technically become a temporary member of our most senior grade. That means we have the right to check again on his security clearance. Dominic Trowbridge will certainly want to put him through the new, souped-up system, Operation Laser-Beam. We can't afford to let anything go wrong in Washington. It's the most sensitive post of all. We just have to retain the confidence of the Americans.'

'All right,' conceded Sir Marcus. 'But how is that going to help? We can hardly hope to stop the appointment in that way. These senior politicians are usually pretty good at covering up their dirty deeds.'

'Not always. I read somewhere that George Craxton had separated from his wife. That could mean a lot.'

Bernard had an immense appetite for malicious gossip. It was one of the attributes which made him so effective in personnel work.

'Well, you can try it, Bernard. It's necessary, in any case. I'd better warn the Secretary of State that the appointment can't be announced, or even cleared with the Americans, until special security clearance for Washington has been obtained.'

'That would be wise.'

For the first time that morning, Sir Marcus's thin lips trembled on the edge of a smile.

'I am beginning to like the idea,' he conceded. 'I never much cared for George Craxton. A bold, self-confident fellow. He stood on my wife's toe once at the Mansion House and didn't apologize all that nicely. It could be entertaining to see him under the deep probe. Squirming in the moon-pool.'

'Will you have some of the club claret?' asked Bernard Gilbert.

'Yes please,' replied Sir Dominic Trowbridge, 'but no more than one glass.' The Head of the Security Service intended to keep his faculties unimpaired while lunching with so wily an operator as the Chief Clerk in the Foreign Office.

Bernard gazed expansively down the long blue and gold dining-room at the Voyagers Club in Pall Mall. The ceiling could have done with extensive decoration but it was still one of the finest rooms in London, in spite of the pervasive smell of stale fish. Today it was full, as usual, of his cronies from the Foreign Office. Their presence gave him comfort, though it was perhaps just as well that none of them could hear his conversation with the diminutive Supremo of the twilight world.

'All right, Bernard,' said Sir Dominic briskly, as he attacked the potted shrimps. 'You didn't bring me here to discuss the latest play at the National Theatre. It's about Washington, I suppose.'

'Oh yes.'

'I got your letter, and I've thought a lot about it. You're quite right. We shall certainly have to run a special check on George Craxton, even though he's been a Privy Councillor for years. It will be one of the first in-depth operations under the new Laser-Beam procedure.'

'The moon-pool.'

'Call it that, if you like. Marcus is entitled to his touch of the poet. But tell me, Bernard, why are you so keen?'

'I'm always keen on security, Dominic.'

'You don't want to be stripped of your knighthood before you even get it.'

'I happen,' said the large diplomat, a shade stiffly, 'to be an old-fashioned English patriot.'

'That goes without saying,' said Sir Dominic hastily. 'Aren't we all? But you seem to be specially zealous in this case. Almost as if you were actually spurring on the hounds.'

'There is some urgency,' explained Bernard. 'Ministers are anxious to announce the appointment quickly. They hope that will dry up Craxton's oratorical floods, at least this side of the Atlantic.'

'We'll do our best,' said Dominic. 'But on one condition.'

'I see no need for a condition. You are paid to do a job.'

'What a naïve concept,' riposted Sir Dominic. 'My condition is entirely reasonable. As you know, we automatically receive copies from you of the recommendations made by your Senior Appointments Board. That enables me to flash a red light if something is obviously going wrong. So of course I know that James Leyland was your house candidate for Washington.'

'What of it?'

'I want to pop him in the moon-pool, too.'

'I don't see the point.'

'Well, for one thing, you yourself have mentioned the problem

31

of timing. Just suppose there should be anything dubious about Craxton, and I don't say there is, then it would be as well for you to have handy your own alternative candidate, recently vetted under the new procedures. Suppose, on the other hand, that something adverse shows up about Leyland, which is also unlikely, then that proves to ministers that we haven't simply been gunning for poor old Craxton. I'm sure you wouldn't want the PM to think that you had been trying to circumvent the declared wishes of the elected representatives of the sovereign people.'

'What an extraordinary idea,' murmured Bernard, looking quite shocked as he munched his steak.

'You know how politicians always stick together,' continued Dominic. 'Whatever their surface differences. So unlike civil servants. So we shall have to be careful with ministers. No vendetta against Craxton.'

'In the Foreign Office,' pronounced Bernard loftily, 'we don't go in for vendettas. We are not exactly Corsican bandits, you know. Have some more creamed cauliflower. Or, if not, please pass it to me.'

'Then that's settled. The moon-pool for both of them, Leyland as well as Craxton.'

'All right. Perhaps it will look better. But I make one counter-condition.'

'Bernard, you're being a shade tiresome. Counter-condition indeed! That's the trouble with you professional diplomats. You seem to think you're always negotiating a state treaty.'

'It's quite simple. The positive vetting of these two eminent men will be of great interest to the Foreign Office. In the unusual circumstances, we should like to be directly associated with the procedure.'

'That's never happened before.'

'There's a first time for everything.'

'Just think of the precedent, Bernard. It could mean the thin end of the wedge. You don't want to get involved in our specialized field. There would be pressure for you to go on doing so. That would be a great drain on your resources.'

'I'm prepared to risk that, Dominic.'

'What exactly do you want? A key to my interrogation chambers?'

'Something like that. I'll explain over coffee. But do have a go at the cheeseboard first.'

'I know your tricks, Bernard. You plan to snoop on the snoopers. To guard the guardians.'

'Shall we just say that I'm anxious for justice to be seen to be done? I rather recommend the Stilton. Like so much in Whitehall, it crumbles ripely.'

As usual, they were gobbling bar-snacks in the Charge of the Light Brigade, over the class frontier in Canonbury. Both Jonathan and Rupert were in truculent mood. It seemed to Maureen that they might almost have been enemies. But then Englishmen were funny. Not for them the soft voices and sudden furies of Connemara. She was content to listen, and to look at Rupert's unshaved profile which reminded her of a statue of the Archangel Gabriel.

'This time it really is on me,' said Rupert. 'I drew the benefit today. Bless the benefit.'

'Vodka for me then,' said Maureen. 'With fresh lemon. How was the Office, Jonathan?'

'Terrible. That awful man Claude Silk keeps changing my drafts. He seems to think I'm a complete moron.'

'It's better they found you out early on,' commented Rupert benevolently from the bar. 'Then they won't be disappointed later.'

'It's all so dreadfully hierarchical. So many different layers of responsibility. There's me, and the Head of Department and his Assistant, the Deputy and Assistant Under-Secretaries, junior ministers and finally the Foreign Secretary himself. No wonder my little efforts are hashed around before getting to anyone important.'

'Perhaps they need hashing around.'

'Then I wouldn't mind. I know I'm only a beginner. But that horrible Claude Silk seems to have it in for me. He gets through his own work with such effortless ease. And he's always backing horses, which inevitably win. He went to Winchester, too.'

'Do I detect,' asked Rupert, 'a small touch of envy? A tiny chip on the sloping shoulders of the lad from Otley?'

'Perhaps you do. I don't deny it. But he does look so snooty. As if I were just a bad smell. I'm sure I'm not getting a fair deal. I'm being left out of things.'

33

'Apply for a transfer then. To some other department in the Foreign Office.'

'That's just what I have done. I'm determined not to vegetate. Life's too short for that.'

'Learned self-help at your mother's knee, did you?'

He had indeed, thought Jonathan. It was all due to his mother. A teacher herself, she had introduced him to books and inspired the hope of making his way in the wider world. He revered her as much as he detested everything he could remember about his father, a feckless and apologetic semi-drunkard who never held down a job for long. His parents had curiously combined, from opposite poles, to give Jonathan a lasting hatred of laziness and inefficiency, with a profound belief in what could be achieved by human willpower. Although he would have been shocked to hear it, he was singularly lacking in compassion. Failing to realize that his own God-given gifts were well above the average, he believed that it was open to all to make their way in the world. His scheme made no allowances for human weakness or the laws of chance. He was very near to believing that the poor and unfortunate were person-ally responsible for their own condition. A section of the governing class had taken this view in the England of the mid-nineteenth century. Now it had come back into fashion in some influential circles. Jonathan was a child of the time.

He snapped back mentally into Canonbury to find that Rupert was babbling on as usual, waving his cigarette in a manner not fully appreciated by their neighbours in the crowded pub. Rupert's gestures needed space. They had seemed less inconsiderate in the water-meadows.

'I can't really understand,' Rupert was saying, 'why any sane person joins the Foreign Office today. You have to defend the country's policy. But it absolutely stinks. Take nuclear weapons, to begin with. How can you possibly justify them? The Church may still believe in the concept of the just war. But how could it ever be right to use nuclear weapons on undefended populations and entire cities? And how else could you use them?'

'You may be right,' conceded Jonathan. 'But it's still permissible to retain nuclear weapons as a deterrent, to curb possible aggres-sion. Even if you don't ever intend to use them.'

'That sounds pretty feeble to me. He would be a pretty toothless old aggressor who allowed himself to be fooled in that way. Besides, don't be too sure that we wouldn't be willing to commit mass murder. If some ridiculous American president wanted to flex his muscles, just to make sure of being re-elected, the British Government couldn't be relied upon to stand up and be counted.'

Privately, Jonathan thought there was a good deal of truth in Rupert's argument. But it was not a comfortable idea for a young British diplomat. Like some devout believer who does not want his faith to become unsettled, he preferred not to dwell on the ideological basis of his activities. It was better to concentrate on the practical side. So the German officials had argued under Hitler. It was hard to believe that one's political superiors could be capable of real wickedness, even in an evil world. He was a junior bureaucrat, not an ethical adviser.

'I mustn't stay long,' said Jonathan evasively. 'Got to be fresh in the morning. An important interview.'

'Oh, do tell us,' said Maureen.

'It's a bit odd, really. Personnel Department haven't replied directly to my application. But I've been asked to call on this tremendously senior man. The one I mentioned before, Bernard Gilbert. He's in charge of the whole administration. Personnel Department are just one of his bits. He wouldn't normally bother with anyone at my level.'

'Perhaps you're getting the sack,' said Rupert cheerfully.

'Oh, do you think so?' replied Jonathan. His confidence, never really high, dropped like a stone. He felt absolutely miserable.

'Never mind,' suggested Rupert. 'There's always the benefit. We can spend more time together, sitting by the canal and reading poetry out loud. I've still got my megaphone. And it's nice watching the barges go by.'

Even the environs of Bernard Gilbert's office proclaimed him to be a senior mandarin. There was something awe-inspiring about his ante-chamber with his boot-faced Personnel Assistant and the large coat and umbrella stand, of a monumental type issued only to officers of his rank. Entering the office itself, the trembling Jonathan almost felt that he had stepped back in time to be interviewed by Mussolini, as a mighty torso rose from a huge desk to extend a welcoming paw. The torso itself seemed to be draped in acres of expensive tailoring, which Jonathan was so busy admiring that he hardly had time to raise his lowly eyes above the huge creature's neck towards the vicinity of the double chins. Mr Gilbert had presence. Indeed he was truly terrifying to a lone new entrant, anxious to make a good impression. With a thrill of horror, Jonathan began to wonder whether his trouser zip was equal to the strain. He must resist the wild urge to make sure.

'How kind of you to call, Fieldhouse,' boomed the monster. 'I am sorry to trespass on your time.'

Jonathan gulped. Was this an example of cutting sarcasm or old-world courtesy? Would he ever get used to this brave new world that had such creatures in it?

'Do tell us, Fieldhouse,' continued Bernard with massive urbanity. 'Are you happy in the Office?'

'Well, I was glad to get in, sir,' replied Jonathan in a tremulous voice.

'Oh, please don't call me sir. We are all equals here. Well, almost. May I call you Jonathan?'

Jonathan braced himself. He had to be honest.

'I don't like my department,' he blurted out. 'I've asked to be transferred.'

'So I heard. Claude Silk is rather an acquired taste, I do admit. He was my Head of Chancery in Lima, you know. They say he doesn't suffer fools gladly. But he was usually quite kind to my wife and myself. Well, you're off the Silk route. We're giving you a rather unusual assignment.'

'Am I being transferred abroad?'

'Not exactly. But to a foreign power.'

'A foreign power?'

'I was joking, of course. To another agency, I meant. You are being temporarily assigned to the Security Service.'

'Oh. That's the snoopers, isn't it? The thought-police.'

'More the former than the latter. They're not too interested in what goes on quietly above the eyebrows. It's what you actually might do that they fuss about.'

'I thought I'd joined the Foreign Service.'

'You did. This will be only for a period of weeks. To act as liaison officer in a project of special interest to the Foreign Office.'

'That's unusual, isn't it?'

'Yes. A breakthrough. Like the invention of the wheel.'

Jonathan did not entirely care for the idea. He suspected that he was being shunted out of the mainstream. Besides, people like Rupert were always sneering at the Security Service. He had read nasty articles about them in the *New Statesman*.

'The country does have to be defended, you know,' continued Bernard. 'And the eradication of spies and traitors in our midst is a first line of defence.'

Jonathan nodded.

'It will be to the advantage of your career,' said Bernard. 'I'm looking for a very bright young man. They tell me you are one. You'll be reporting to me personally.'

Bernard did not add that Jonathan had been recommended to him as unusually immature and inexperienced. This was no job for an assured young smarty-boots. He wanted clay for his potter's hands. He explained that the special project was the security investigation of George Craxton.

'But he isn't in the government any longer,' pointed out Jonathan. Like most people in the country, he already knew a good deal about Craxton, a high-decibel, maximum-exposure politician. That florid face had graced many an evening's viewing.

'Craxton is being considered,' explained Bernard, 'for another very important government job. He's to be investigated under a new security procedure, the deep laser probe. We call it the moon-pool.'

He explained at some length. Bernard liked explaining things. It was one of his fortes, in a personality which contained few pianissimos. Jonathan visualized him as a nineteenth-century head-master, gathering his gown around him as he swept into the pulpit for a thunderous denunciation of vice. But Bernard's flow was always well controlled. He took care to say nothing about the embassy in Washington or to give any of the background explaining the intense interest of the Foreign Office. His next remark was introduced so casually that he might be suspected of a deliberate intention to deceive.

'By the way,' he said, 'there will be another investigation going on at the same time. A senior member of the Service, James Leyland, our Representative with the Common Market.'

'Are the two investigations connected?'

'They are happening simultaneously. You will be involved in both.'

'I don't really see how I can help. I'm not trained for that kind of work.'

'Your job is to keep me informed, Jonathan. You may ring Miss Johnson-Boswell any time and ask for an appointment. My door is always open to you.'

'You could get the information you need direct from the Security Service.'

'I could. And I will. But you, my dear boy, will provide an invaluable check. You see, I know I can rely on your personal loyalty.'

He could, thought Jonathan, that was the damnable thing. This Savile Row Mephistopheles had power over his future. He could get him sent to Washington or to Timbuktu. Jonathan thought with envy of Rupert, lounging on the canal bank, strumming his guitar inexpertly, no man's slave. But even he had to queue humiliatingly for the benefit. And that didn't come from the sky.

'Will the Security Service know that I'm reporting to you?'

'They will guess. My methods are fairly well known in Whitehall. But they will not be sure. I know you will be discreet. It is essential for me to be apprised immediately of all new developments.'

'I'll do my best. Where do I report? I don't even know where their head office is.'

'You won't be going there. The new moon-pool unit is separately housed. Even its existence is a top-secret. You will clock in next Monday morning at nine-thirty. They're expecting you. It's flat number thirty-seven in Bangalore Mansions.'

He gave an address in deepest Maida Vale, where once, on Church Commission property, the Maisies and Dorises had dispensed vice in the afternoon.

'Don't be put off by the name-plate on the door of the flat,' continued Bernard. 'The Corcoran Research Library. That's for cover purposes.'

'Why the name?'

'Just a little in-joke. Apparently, Corcoran was the maiden name of Sir Dominic's mother. He's their big boss. One has to try to lighten the strain. Any other questions?'

'What result are you hoping for from the investigation? I'd just like to know.'

It was too direct a question.

'We only want the truth,' replied Bernard heavily. 'Whatever is in the interest of the nation. Nothing else. But of course one naturally expects that the outcome will be favourable for the men concerned. After all, they are both held in high public repute.'

'I see.'

'You still look a bit puzzled, Jonathan.'

'I suppose I am. It seems such a funny idea. My assignment, I mean. I don't quite see the point of it.'

'You will.'

Jonathan sensed that a lot was being concealed from him. He was only to be a conduit of information, not the real motor power. But there was no point in trying to argue. People like Bernard Gilbert only left you in the dark when they intended to do so.

'There's one thing I must stress,' continued Bernard. 'You mustn't tell a soul about this special work. A leak could be very damaging.'

'I understand.'

'For the country. And for you personally.'

'Yes.'

'You see, it's a totally new approach to security vetting. Government servants have been used for many years to the overt procedure. It works well in most cases. But some damaging cases have slipped too easily through the net. The system depends too much on the person under review. He or she just has to attend interviews and give references, which may or may not suggest lines of investigation. It's all too passive, too defensive. In the moon-pool, you will be free to roam through the subject's past life in a much more aggressive way. And he won't know who the investigators are. That's the crucial point.'

'I thought I was just an observer.'

'You are, in a manner of speaking. But of course you'll have to earn your keep. I expect they'll give you little things to do.'

'Who do I report to?'

'F. Hopkins is what it says here. Probably a retired army officer. They seem to abound in those circles. Just one further point,

Jonathan. They probably won't be as clever as you are. Try to conceal it.'

'I'm not sure of the correct answer to that. Yes or No? But I expect I'll find it all interesting.'

'You know the old Chinese curse?' asked Bernard. 'May you live in interesting times.'

When the heavy door had closed on Jonathan's small frame, the Chief Clerk stood for a moment in thought, the professional smile of farewell gradually oozing out of his ample face. He hoped that Personnel Department had not made a mistake in sending him young Fieldhouse. The boy was pliable all right, as well as bright and ambitious. But he did seem awfully wet behind the ears. Brigadier Hopkins, or whatever, might just mince him up. That louse Dominic would have put one of his toughest operators onto the job. But it was too late to make a change now. He must just hope for the best. It had been tempting to give the boy a steer about the results they really needed. But that would have been too risky. Young people these days seemed allergic to these Byzantine processes, so necessary to keep the ship of state afloat.

The telephone rang. It was his wife. Amaryllis sounded in sprightly mood. The disappointment over Canberra still rankled but her normal high spirits had carried her through.

'Sorry to bother you, darling,' she chortled.

'It's all right.'

'Are you doing something important? Or just fooling around?'

'Just fooling around.'

'I was thinking of coming into town today to do a little shopping.'

'I'll bet.'

'I thought I'd pop in and place the order for our new visiting cards. And the invitation cards, too. For Australia, I mean. They have to be ordered well in advance.'

'I shouldn't do that if I were you.'

'You mean we might go as a Sir and Lady.'

'Well, that's a distinct possibility. But I wasn't just thinking of that. You see, everything is rather in the melting-pot again.'

'I'll have a vodka,' said Maureen.

'How did it go?' asked Rupert.

'What go?'

'Your talk with the big tomato. Sir Bernard or whatever.'

'He's still a Mister.'

'Can't be all that big, then.'

Jonathan searched the blackened ceiling of the Charge of the Light Brigade for inspiration. He found none.

'It went all right.'

'What did he want?'

'He gave me a job to do.'

'What sort of job?'

'Oh, shut up, Rupert. You know I can't tell.'

'Precious friend you are. No little titbits. Nothing to sell to the gossip columns.'

'I've signed the Official Secrets Act.'

'He's leaving us, Maureen. He's swum far beyond our ken. Into the world of titles and nuclear weapons and real money. He will be Sir Jonathan before long.'

'Stop teasing him,' said Maureen. 'You're only jealous. What about you? Going home to Mummy and Daddy for the weekend.'

'I have to be on parade. My sister's birthday. A house party for the young things.'

'You won't look right,' said Jonathan, eyeing Rupert's shaggy locks and scruffy denims. Small boils had appeared on his chin, where he had used an old razor blade owing to the collapse of his electric razor. Yet Maureen still gazed at him with the eyes of love. Oh, the body's hunger, thought Jonathan, the soul's desire. Did anything else really matter?

'I shall look all right on the night. I've got to get there a day earlier. Mummy is going to clean me up. She uses the same disinfectant on the horses.'

'You haven't invited me,' said Maureen in rather a small voice.

Nor me, thought Jonathan. But he didn't say it.

The flat in Bangalore Mansions proved to be unusually spacious. In fact, at the back it consisted of two flats run into one. The ceilings were high and the doors had fine white mouldings around them. The effect was decidedly monumental, verging on the funereal.

41

'I have an appointment,' Jonathan told the elderly male door-keeper, 'with somebody called F. Hopkins. Colonel Hopkins perhaps. Or Major?'

After showing his Foreign Office pass, which was carefully scrutinized, he was shown into a small room at the rear of the apartment. It contained two desks, at one of which a young girl was sitting. Jonathan noted her with approval. She had long, fair hair and piercing blue eyes which might have been made from Dresden porcelain. As she got up to greet him, he was glad to see that she was shorter than he was. He had quite decided now that Hopkins must be a colonel. This must be the colonel's secretary. A potentially useful ally.

'Hello,' he began cheerfully. 'I'm Jonathan Fieldhouse. From the Foreign Office.'

'I know.' Her voice was slightly squeaky. It wouldn't sound too adult on the telephone. He liked that. It was hard to be fond of anyone who was quite perfect.

'I've been told to report to a person called Hopkins.'

'You can call me Fiona.'

'Thank you. I'm Jonathan.'

'You said that before. Why don't you sit down? That's your desk.'

Jonathan was not best pleased to have to share the small office with a secretary. Presumably the colonel or, perhaps, brigadier, had a huge room next door. But it would not do to appear snooty. The Foreign Office already had a reputation for that.

'And where,' he asked, 'is this Hopkins person?'

The girl laughed.

'Not far away,' she said.

'Well, I should like to get to meet the boss.'

'I am the boss,' said the girl.

'I beg your pardon?'

'My name is Fiona Hopkins.'

Jonathan registered the idea in stunned silence.

'You look surprised,' she said.

'I am.'

'Perhaps you object to working under a woman?'

'Oh, I don't think so.'

'That's just as well.'

'But I thought you would be older.'

'And uglier?'

'Yes. That too,' said Jonathan.

'It does seem rather odd, you being senior to me.'

'I started earlier. I didn't go to university. So I've had four years already in the Service. Though I've only just moved into this new, super-secret unit. Got one promotion in the process.'

'Well, you'd better show me the ropes. I'm all attention.'

'You already know what it's all about. The work requires close attention to detail. I'd better warn you of that. Women tend to be specially good at it. This is no place for inspired hunches, unsupported by facts.'

'My mother knows everything that's happening in Otley.'

'Let's hope it's a hereditary talent. We're starting on the Craxton probe. You must have heard a bit about him?'

'Oh yes. He's not exactly a shrinking violet, is he?'

'There's a lot more to know. Some of it is in those files. You'd better try to memorize them pretty quickly. That should keep you busy, even if you are one of those academic whizz-kids.'

'I say, you're not chippy, are you?'

'What do you mean?'

'Not bitter and twisted. About not going to university.'

'Not in the least,' replied Fiona calmly. 'It got me my seniority. Which will be very useful in keeping you under control. Now, you'd better get on with these files. I have reading to do, too.'

'Do we just sit here and read?'

'Of course not. But you've got to know how much we already know, before you try to push forward the frontiers of knowledge. Then you can start with interviews of your own.'

'Don't I get to meet anyone else here?'

'In due course, you will be admitted to the presence.'

'Whose presence? The supreme pontiff?'

'More or less. Major Glossop. Valentine Glossop. Late of the Royal Halberdiers, a regiment known to the upper classes, I understand, as the "Plums".'

'The Plums?'

'A reference to the colour of their lower garments, when in full dress.'

'Is he awfully grand?'

'He is a tremendous swell. And very senior here. So senior, in fact, as to be my boss.'

'It's a relief to hear you have one. I thought you might be working direct to the Prime Minister.'

Fiona ostentatiously put on a small pair of spectacles, nattily framed, and started to read.

'Do you really need those?' asked Jonathan.

'No. Actually, they're plain glass. I only put them on to make me look older.'

'You shouldn't give away your trade secrets. Or, at least, not so easily.'

'It's my sense of the ridiculous. It keeps betraying me. Perhaps I should point out that we rather discourage idle chat during office hours. There's so much to do.'

'Are you allowed to fraternize with the hired hands?'

'What exactly have you got in mind?'

'When lunch-time eventually comes, we could have a sandwich together. There must be pubs round here.'

'It's possible.'

'It's going to be rather rum. Sharing an office with a girl.'

'You won't be sharing an office with a girl, Mr Fieldhouse. Let's get that quite straight from the start. You will be working under a woman.'

They looked at each other and burst suddenly into laughter.

Felicity had reminded him that morning, over the toast. They were due that evening at the Coliseum for the new experimental opera, the one with the electronic effects and the chorus wearing masks. The British Council had asked them to escort a minister from Indonesia. Sir Marcus Stewart-Stibbs blenched at the prospect. The day was quite tiring enough already without adding a little extra torture. The annoying part was that Felicity would be fresh as a daisy, after a pleasant afternoon watching Wimbledon on the box. She might even, unlike him, enjoy the late-night supper at the Savoy. What one did for the nation! At least Felicity could be relied upon to keep the conversation going, like some verbal Niagara of potent natural force.

Now the new girl popped her pleasingly curly head round the door. That would mean that Jasper Tenby, his Private Secretary, must be temporarily out of the office. He was going to classes to brush up his Arabic. So Judy, somewhat timorously, got direct access to the monster. Sir Marcus could afford to think of himself in jocular terms, knowing that he was, in fact, rather liked. Was it Judy though or Jenny? It had become almost a disgrace not to remember. After all, she was hardly a new girl any longer. Sir Marcus could scarcely recall when she had not been around.

'Yes?' he asked, with an avuncular smile, designed to reassure.

'It's a Mr Craxton, Sir Marcus.'

Craxton, thought the Permanent Under-Secretary, a little peevishly. Who on earth could that be? Was that the name of the persistent Chelsea neighbour with the wispy beard, who was trying to form an amenity society? Then of course the penny dropped. Who could forget the eminent politician, the household name who had designated himself for Washington? Privy Councillors expected you to be readily available.

'He wants to come and see you,' continued the girl. 'He says it's urgent. We could fit him in this afternoon before the Bolivian Ambassador.'

'Oh, all right.'

George Craxton seemed almost as overbearing when housed on the back benches as when he had been one of the stars of the Cabinet. His great height was encased in a smart summer suit, while his craggy, fleshy face disseminated an air of superlative confidence. One could easily understand, thought Sir Marcus, how he had made his first million before he was thirty. Sir Marcus disliked such people but he was clever at disguising his feelings. He would not otherwise have become the professional head of the Foreign Office.

'Good of you to see me,' boomed Craxton, 'when you must always be so busy.' It came over as a perfunctory apology.

'I understood it was urgent,' said Sir Marcus, a little coldly.

'Well, I wanted to get away to the country,' explained the politician, a bit shamefacedly. 'I'm opening Sweetladies for charity.'

'Sweetladies?'

'My house, you know. Inigo Jones. He did so little in Suffolk. It takes a lot of keeping up. I have to supervise the topiary work myself.'

Sir Marcus looked suitably awed. Craxton had done well from a modest beginning in the wrong part of Muswell Hill. The dull mottling of his jowls suggested that he had lunched expansively, presumably at Greens, the posh club at the right end of St James's Street, to which he had recently been elected after a strenuous campaign among the more gullible members. It was reported that Craxton had offered a generous anonymous donation for the redecoration of the smoking-room. He was well known for his anonymous donations.

'You must come down one weekend,' continued Craxton graciously. 'Bring your wife.'

'That would be nice.'

Privately, Sir Marcus resolved that wild horses themselves would not succeed in dragging him down to Craxton's country seat. There would be loud men talking about politics, middle-aged ladies with dubious pasts, and Portuguese maids who kept losing your socks. Doors would slam in the night. Different people would be there for breakfast. He would say nothing to Felicity, since she would surely long to go. He himself preferred to spend Sundays pottering around Chelsea. Nowadays it was the only decent day in London.

'We shall be working a lot together,' said Craxton with his boyish grin which exposed a lot of expensive dental work. 'From now on.'

'I suppose so,' said Marcus.

'Mind you, I wasn't keen to take Washington at first,' boomed the former Cabinet Minister. 'It will be a great wrench to leave the House. Such wonderful friendships there. But the PM was very persistent. You know how it is, over at Number Ten.'

'Yes,' said Sir Marcus wryly. 'I do.'

'It appears that I'm the only one who can do the job,' continued Craxton. 'It seems unlikely but the PM seemed quite sure. The Americans are being difficult, as usual, and they want me to manage the President. Put like that, it was hard to refuse.'

'I understand.'

Sir Marcus boiled inwardly. It was the only way he could boil. External manifestations of intense feeling had been ruled out by the exigencies of his profession. It would never do to reach out and smack George Craxton on those plump cheeks, redolent of expensive aftershave. And yet the man was extremely annoying. Here he was, walking into the top job that the Service had to offer and

46

brazenly proclaiming that he was the only one who could do it. Was he so stupid as really to believe that? Had he never tried to enter the massive mind of James Leyland, perhaps the best First in Greats since the War? Was Craxton unaware of the carefully constructed pyramids of promotion he was carelessly kicking away for other people? And did he really think that he would ever be allowed to spend all that much time with the President of the United States? The Kennedy-Harlech epoch had long since gone. Did he really know how ambassadors actually occupied themselves these days? He was in for a rude shock.

Sir Marcus did have some friends among British politicians. He liked a handful whose personal eccentricities and misplaced humour had denied them the highest office. But, as a whole, he detested the class. He could not abide their egotistical belief that they had a unique contribution to make to Britain and to the world. Admittedly, creative artists thought in the same self-centred way and were equally difficult. But then they at least had some degree of talent. He objected to the bland assumption of his political masters that they had some kind of world overview, to be serviced by the colourless, humourless bureaucrats. It was so often the other way round. Who was this self-assured popinjay to brag about managing the President? Sir Marcus felt even better now about popping him in the moon-pool. They would see how he looked under the deep laser.

Sir Marcus satisfied himself that none of these emotions showed in his bland face. When he disliked people, and he was surprisingly good at that, he was always especially courteous. It was due to the training.

'When can I start drawing the money?' asked Craxton.

'The money?'

'The pay. The allowances for Washington. I've made some enquiries already. It doesn't sound too good. One of your little men, a fellow called Gilbert, came over to brief me. In my room in the House.'

Sir Marcus resented inwardly the implication that he might have offered to do the same. But this was outweighed by the joy of hearing the portentous Bernard Gilbert described as a 'little man'. He must remember that.

'The Foreign Office system seems most unfair to ambassadors,' continued Craxton. 'You work out how much we need. And then you top up the pay with allowances to make it all possible. But you don't leave us with any cash for private purposes.'

'The system doesn't allow for private purposes,' countered the Permanent Under-Secretary. 'I expect you'll feel too tired.'

'We really work for nothing,' wailed Craxton.

'We did try to make a change,' said Sir Marcus with deceptive mildness. 'But the Treasury were adamant. You were a minister there at the time.'

George Craxton gave him a long, hard stare. He did not wholly care for the unwavering glance of this lanky mandarin. Would it be wrong to suspect in him a tiny flame of incipient mutiny, of dumb insolence? He knew these senior civil servants only too well. There had been people like that in the Treasury. They tried to patronize you, with their expensive educations and good degrees. And yet they were as poor as church mice, had a dreary life-style and had never been heard of by the public. How many of them could have stood up in the House when it was baying for blood, or faced a dithery Cabinet on one of its bad mornings? In one serious respect, Sir Marcus had underrated Craxton. Like most people in show business, the former minister made it his business to assess audience reaction. Beneath a rather coarse exterior, he had almost feminine powers of intuition. He had sensed quite easily that Sir Marcus resented his appointment to Washington and that he had even begun to dislike him personally. It was a feeling that Craxton reciprocated.

'Well, if the money is inadequate,' continued Craxton, 'all the more reason to start paying me soon. I shall have a lot of expenses. And I'm taking a big drop. I was offered some important director-ships when I left the Cabinet.'

'You might be able to have an advance of allowances,' conceded Sir Marcus, 'when your appointment is actually announced.'

He never ceased to marvel at the pertinacity shown by rich men in laying their paws on yet more money. Presumably that was how you became rich and continued to be so. It was a strange passion, when there was no mechanism for taking it with you at the end of life.

'Let's make the announcement now, then.'

'That won't be possible. There are still processes to go through.'

'What processes?' asked Craxton suspiciously.

'The Queen's informal approval. Seeking the *agrément* of the American Government. Then the Queen's formal approval.'

'It sounds a real rigmarole.'

'I can only say,' retorted Sir Marcus coldly, 'that the whole procedure is sanctified by tradition.'

'I'll bet. Like everything else in the Foreign Office. Life isn't always like that outside, you know. It only took a phone call to put me in the Cabinet.'

'An internal appointment. An ambassador is the Queen's Representative abroad.'

'Well, for Heaven's sake, get on with it, Marcus. May I call you that? I'm spending a fortune on Sweetladies. Then there's the house in South Eaton Place. Not to mention my wedding. It takes a lot of cash to get married. We may honeymoon in the Galapagos.'

'Your wedding?'

'Certainly. My divorce from Sally has come through at last.'

Sir Marcus remembered her in the file, a quiet, dark-haired woman from the north who had been conspicuous recently by her absence from political and social circles. It was rumoured that her father, an estate agent in Newcastle, had advanced the young Craxton his first five hundred. No doubt she had outlived her usefulness.

'Who are you marrying?' he asked politely.

'Martha Freeport. You know her?'

'Only her pictures. Congratulations.'

Sir Marcus recalled a well-groomed though hard-looking blonde, backed by an almost infinite supply of Texas oil money.

'Martha knows everyone in Washington,' said Craxton. 'And in New York and Dallas, too. She'll be the most tremendous asset. She used to have her own breakfast chat-show.'

Sir Marcus shuddered inwardly. Breakfast chat was hardly in his line. It was the moment of the day for husbanding one's fragile resources. Martha sounded even worse than Felicity when it came to sapping one's vital energies. It was typical of the pushy Craxton to have got himself engaged to a rich and influential American, in preparation for his mission to Washington.

'It will be just a small affair.'

'Your affair?'

'My wedding, Marcus. A few choice friends, if I get my way. Though I suppose the tenants may demand something bigger at Sweetladies. You know what tenants are like. One has to try to please everyone. But we need the announcement first. People have got to know what I am going to be.'

'It will take time.'

'You keep saying so. But I don't quite see why. I'm not exactly unknown in the Palace. Or in the White House.'

'I suppose not.'

The Bolivian Ambassador, thought Sir Marcus, would be waiting. Time was so precious in this job. There was often somebody waiting. But his talk with the opinionated Craxton could not be rushed. It was too important. Besides, it had moved on to danger-ous ground. Sir Marcus could sense the danger. One false move might be very tricky. It was through the ability to feel danger in advance, denied to some of his ablest contemporaries, that Sir Marcus had got on.

'You forget, my dear Marcus,' continued the booming voice of the professional politician, 'that I'm not exactly a beginner. I've been on the inner track for years.'

'So what?' the Permanent Under-Secretary wanted to reply. But it seemed more prudent to remain silent.

'Let's cut the cackle,' said Craxton. 'I'll ring the Queen's Private Secretary today. He's stayed at Sweetladies, you know. I think we put him in the tapestry room. Tomorrow Martha can call the State Department. She's not exactly unknown there. They sent a limou-sine for her last time she went to Washington. The Secretary needed help with his image. Back to the Palace on Friday. An announce-ment that afternoon. Just in time for in-depth articles in the heavy Sundays and exposure on the weekend box.'

'It seems theoretically possible.'

'Theoretically?'

Craxton's hackles were beginning to rise. This shilly-shallying was typical of the outmoded, fuddy-duddy methods of the Foreign Office. It was high time that he blew the chill winds of change through the Washington Embassy. They would not forget him and Martha in a hurry. The dead wood would be on the return plane soon enough. The flagship on Massachusetts Avenue was due for a short, sharp shock. He could hardly wait to get his mitts on the place. Just so might some Viking warrior have leaped from his curved prow at the sight of a fat, unguarded village on the Saxon shore. In his innermost being a natural bully, Craxton detested the undefended weak. But he had underestimated the Foreign Office quite as badly as they underrated him.

I must be careful, thought Sir Marcus. He will know all about positive vetting. After all, he's been in the Cabinet for years. It's the moon-pool that he must never be told about. That was the new super-secret, which some might say made the country almost a police state, but which had become essential to fight terrorism with its own methods.

'All right,' he conceded. 'There is *one* further element in the procedure. And it's not something you can do yourself with telephone calls to the top.'

'The tailor, you mean,' said Craxton brightly. 'I've seen to that already. My little man in Sackville Street has measured me for new tails, new morning coat. I gather I shan't need diplomatic uniform. Rather a pity. But I'm taking sailing and hunting rig.'

The fellow's as vain as a peacock, thought Sir Marcus sourly.

'Security clearance,' he snapped. 'You'll need a fresh one.'

'But that's absurd. I've been positively vetted for years. Ever since I entered the government.'

'In the States you'll have access to some specially sensitive material. It has to be done again.'

'Well, you'd better hurry up about it,' blustered the big shot. 'The Prime Minister pressed me to take Washington. I accepted, after some thought, for the good of the nation. But I don't expect to be messed around now by petty bureaucrats.'

'There is no special hurry,' countered Sir Marcus with dignity. 'The post does not become vacant until the late autumn.'

'We could accelerate that. I'm sure the present man could do with a nice rest.'

'Sir Robin Compton has never had a nice rest in his life. He was born on the hop. He won't expect to move until his sixtieth birthday.'

'What's so special about sixty?'

'That's the system.'

'It's Martha, really,' said Craxton simply. 'She wants people to

51

know. The public announcement means more to her than actually getting there. It's like a first pregnancy.'

'Well, I'm sorry. But, in any case, it's not fair to Robin Compton to announce his successor's name too far in advance. And especially such a famous name. It might make him seem like a lame duck. You'll just have to be patient.'

Craxton's large features began to crumple. It verged on a confession of human weakness.

'Martha's already had one disappointment,' he confessed. 'She thought I'd be taking a peerage for Washington. The poor lamb's a bit vague about these English things. Lord Craxton of Sweetladies, she suggested. But of course I can't go to the Lords. My enemies would be delighted. I must be free to return to the Commons.'

'A knighthood could, no doubt, be arranged. That would at least make her a Lady.'

'Well, you know, it's a bit – How shall I put it?'

'You don't want to be mistaken for a provincial Alderman?'

'That's one way of expressing it.'

'You might just seem,' said Sir Marcus, a shade nastily, 'like a professional diplomat. Somebody who has worked his way up.'

'I think I'll stay a Mister. Like Mr Pitt, the Great Commoner. She can be Martha Freeport-Craxton. Though that's a bit long for the cover of *Time Magazine*.'

'We'll keep in touch,' said Sir Marcus.

'So kind of you to spare me your time. Your valuable time.'

'Judy will show you out.'

'It's the park door I want. The Rolls should be there by now.'

'Let's hope the police haven't towed it away. Security is so tight around here.'

'I hope I haven't seemed over-exacting, Marcus.' The politician gave one of his mock-modest grins which seemed to photograph so well in the constituency. 'I do realize that I'm not the only onion in the stew.'

It had been a fairly satisfactory interview, thought Sir Marcus. He had avoided calling the fellow 'Craxton' or 'George' or anything else. There was something a bit strange about the man, something faintly unreal. He had never noticed it before. Larger than life, less than human. And he had certainly reacted when mention was made of security clearance. That petulant display of bluster wasn't simply due to understandable impatience. The annoyance was too sudden, too strong. Sir Marcus felt pretty sure of that. He had detected a slight whiff of fear. Craxton wasn't all that keen on having his private life investigated. Well, who was? Most people trembled inwardly as they approached the Customs. It might mean nothing. But you couldn't be quite sure. It would be interesting to see how he got on in the moon-pool.

The girl was back, offering tea.

'Did Mr Craxton get away safely, Jenny?' he asked, mainly for something to say. You had to keep contact.

'Oh yes. A man was waiting there for him. With a bicycle. And bicycle-clips.'

'It must be his exercise afternoon. Perhaps he got confused. We all do.'

'There is just one thing, Sir Marcus. I hope you won't mind. Me saying it, I mean.'

'What's that, my dear?'

'Well, you see, my name's Lucinda.'

'Just thought I'd pop in,' said Sir James Leyland.

'Delighted to see you, James,' replied Bernard Gilbert.

He was not at all delighted. The emergency arrangements for Beirut had still to be worked out before the Foreign Affairs Debate that afternoon. But Leyland was one of the most senior men in the Service. He could hardly be denied access to the Head of Administration. And Bernard had worked out that it was actually easier to get rid of people quickly if you gave them a hearty welcome.

'I'm over from Brussels for the day. I dash across every week now. So many people to see, so much to do.'

The UK Representative to the European Community carried a crushing burden. As Head of the UK Mission, he represented all Whitehall Departments over an immense range of work, much of it being of great importance to the national interest. Other British ambassadors abroad might have significant duties in the way of projecting the British standpoint, calming foreigners and promoting trade. But only Leyland had to negotiate almost daily with wily Continentals, intent on robbing Britain of its money and securing unfair advantages for themselves. The old, fierce wars of Europe continued to rage in this apparently more peaceful forum. Leyland was still mentally on the battlefields of Ramillies and Blenheim, of Oudenarde and Malplaquet. He was very much the commander in the field.

'Glad you could spare the time,' said Bernard dishonestly, 'to visit my humble nook.'

Bernard was under no illusions. Leyland had probably sandwiched him in between two Cabinet Ministers. It was not a social call. He was not the man to waste a moment. Only one subject would have been sufficiently important to warrant this unexpected visit. James Leyland's own career. James had always been a little like that, ever since those very distant days when they had started together in the Third Room, or lowest rung, of South-East Asia Department. Apart from losing most of his hair and taking to even thicker glasses, James had not changed all that much in appearance. He still had that wizened face, sparkling with intelligence, those sharp eyes with their crinkled lids, and that cut-glass voice with its impressively precise delivery. Bernard and James were both grand. Bernard was magnificent with his massive frame, expensive tailoring, booming voice and monumental self-confidence. But James, in his shabby suit and scuffed brogues, bore the unmistakable imprint of pre-eminent mental power, of a mind that effortlessly played with concepts, minced up arguments and paraded the relevant facts. The only trouble with James, thought Bernard, was that he was far too clever for most of the jobs the Service had to offer. It could be almost a handicap to have so huge a mental machine. You couldn't simply shut it down. And, unharnessed to a distributing system, it might just blow up.

'I shall be glad not to stay in Brussels much longer,' said James. 'It's really the devil of a job.'

'I suppose so.'

'I'm looking forward to the transfer.'

'I can well imagine.'

This was proving worse than Bernard had feared. He had not had time to clear his line with the Permanent Under-Secretary. What on earth was he to say to this ambitious colleague with his domed skull and immense expectations?

'It should all be quite straightforward,' continued Sir James. 'Robin's retirement date is a fixed point. Charmian and I would like to be well installed before Christmas. We're hoping that Tess will come out. She got bored with Brussels.'

'Tess?'

'Our daughter. Quite a big girl now. There's a lot of work to do. Settling in. Charmian has ideas for the ballroom.'

'The ballroom? Where?'

'In Washington, of course. Where else do you think we might be going?'

'Oh, yes.'

'Bernard, what on earth is the matter with you? You don't seem at all your old self.'

'Never very strong in the morning.'

'You ought to put it to the Board. My appointment, I mean.'

'We have,' replied Bernard faintly.

'Oh good.'

It was the moment James Leyland had been waiting for, the climax of a great career. It seemed but yesterday that he had gone to Washington, his first post, as Third Secretary. It had been a simpler capital then, still getting used to the reality of American power, largely innocent of the arts, unencumbered with the hideous requirements of modern security. Jefferson's America, with its splendid vision for mankind, had not seemed all that distant. Famous statesmen still walked their dogs on the leafy streets of Georgetown on summer evenings. Eminent pundits sang in the Verdi 'Requiem' with the Cathedral Choir. He had mixed a martini for Mr Dean Acheson and once had done the washing-up with Mr Justice Frankfurter. He had entertained, in his bachelor apartment at the Anchorage near Dupont Circle, before the exclusive Dancing Class, so exclusive as to be now defunct. The best of young America had lapped up his duty-free whisky.

Above all, he had been in love. That was long before Charmian. It still caught him by the throat to remember how impulsively they had snow-balled each other in the wintry garden of her parents' place in Virginia, how touchingly vulnerable she had looked at the Bachelors and Spinsters Dance, gossamy in her long gown on the staircase of the Sulgrave Club. He could hardly bear, even now, to recall those dark curls framing the smooth, delicate face, the soft American voice. It was the vision that came, unbidden, every time that stupid people tried to generalize about 'Americans'. How could he feel anything but love for a country where he had known so intensely what his beloved Plato would have called the desire and pursuit of the whole? It was Plato who had made Socrates describe it in a nutshell. Love is the only subject that I understand.

Washington would have greatly changed. But not its colours. There would still be the cherry trees and the white marble, autumn leaves a riot of red and gold in Dumbarton Oaks, crisp winter mornings in Rock Creek Park, those blue horizons stretching distantly from the Skyline Drive or the Shenandoah. And, even better, the welcoming American voices, the tinkle of ice in Bourbon, the laughter of uninhibited kids. For James Leyland, it had all the magic of a happy first post. It was the land of lost content.

And now, at last, he was going back. He could almost have hugged that pompous old Bernard. At least he had delivered the goods.

'We ought to celebrate,' said James, shedding temporarily a quarter-century of intense mental effort. 'I'll stand you lunch.'

'Celebrate?'

'The Board.' Really, Bernard was being unusually obtuse this morning. Now he seemed to be giving a gulp.

'I'm afraid I have some bad news for you, James.'

'What do you mean?'

'The Board did indeed recommend your appointment to Washington. But ministers turned you down.'

Sir James went ashen-white.

'Turned me down?' he croaked.

'Yes.'

'But why?'

'They may want to make a political appointment.'

'The bastards! The Secretary of State promised me himself. He's mentioned it several times.'

'There's been a change of plan. Quite recently. Direct intervention from the Prime Minister.'

'In favour of Craxton, I suppose.'

'How did you guess?'

'It could only have been him. I keep my finger on the pulse.'

'I'm awfully sorry, James.'

'It's hardly your fault, Bernard.'

'Marcus would have told you himself. It ought to have come from him. But you reached me first. And I couldn't lie to you.'

'Of course not.'

'We've still got some months. We're trying to salvage your appointment. Keep this under your hat. It's bloody for the Service, for the promotions chain.'

'I know. We're on the same side.'

James was behaving with great dignity. But it was a shattering blow. Bernard could guess how badly he was hit.

'What will you do?' asked Bernard. 'You know how highly we think of your work in Brussels. You could always stay on there.'

'Certainly not,' snapped James. 'I'm fed up with the working breakfasts, the brainstorming lunches, the drafting dinners. I detest the Council of Ministers, the jabbering parliamentarians, the solemn owls on the European Court. I loathe getting instructions from the bloody Treasury and every damned ministry in Whitehall. I feel faint when I see the antics of those gesticulating Continentals. Have you ever tried to co-ordinate policy with a Greek?'

'Then what will you do, James?'

'You might try blowing me out of the mouth of a gun. Like those rebellious sepoys at the end of the Indian Mutiny.'

But the sudden display of bitterness did not last. As he calmed down, Sir James began to think more lucidly. He might go for a College. Oxford preferably or, failing that, Cambridge. Wasn't Belial coming up soon? It had a nice Master's Lodge. It might be wise to dine again soon at All Souls. They always had the hot scoops there.

The Foreign Service had never been quite right for him. He could see it all too clearly now, when he had apparently been pipped at the post by this grotesque politico. His old philosophy tutor had been correct all along. He should have stuck to Plato, the first and greatest love of his intellectual life. Man had so inherently this vision of the beautiful, the just, the eternally true. Christian theology had trivialized it with the anthropomorphic concept of an Old Man in the Sky. People could not take that any more, and they were floundering. They had tragically thrown out the greater concept of the immortal soul. To work on Plato and show his relevance to modern theology with its starting-point of the Absolute Being, that would have been worth doing. It was through philosophy that the real limits of the mind could be reached. There might still be time. Charmian would miss the Residence on Massachusetts Avenue. But she could have the Lodge instead and they could keep the cottage in Iffley as a bolt-hole.

Sir James Leyland was famous for his resilience. He even made it clear that the lunch invitation was not cancelled, once the Chief Clerk had sorted out the problems of staffing in the Lebanon. Bernard remembered, too late, that the Athenaeum was not noted for its food. Over the brown Windsor soup, James was careful not to tell him about his own academic ambitions. Let the Service stew in their own juice. He would not let them off the hook too lightly. So he acquiesced gravely when Bernard reminded him that all was not yet lost, and he might still become ambassador to the United States. It was Bernard's aim to keep all the elements in play. His own juggling act depended on that.

'I don't believe that this Major Glossop of yours exists,' said Jonathan. 'A figment perhaps of your spirited imagination.'

'Nonsense,' snapped Fiona. 'He's very much all there. And all here. Except last week. He takes days off for Wimbledon.'

'The price of liberty,' remarked Jonathan sententiously, 'is eternal vigilance.'

'You work better,' explained Fiona, 'with the mind and body refreshed. At least they do in the Plums. Major Valentine is brimming with the regimental spirit.'

'I'd like to meet him.'

'You will. I'll prepare him for the treat.'

Major Glossop was deep in the *Financial Times* when Fiona entered. His office had once been a large back-bedroom, looking out onto the Paddington Recreation Ground. Lace curtains had concealed some fairly curious diversions there in the old days. It was amazing what Maisie knew. But no ghosts appeared now to haunt the retired cavalry officer, who had been specially selected to direct the moon-pool under the personal eye of Sir Dominic Trowbridge. Even seated, Major Glossop looked magnificent. He was tall as a lance, straight as a ramrod, as if the iron had entered into his soul. It was hard to believe that he could be completely real. He could have passed as some huge action-man, a giant doll designed for the amusement of little boys.

'The dollar is moving again,' said Major Glossop. 'And the yen.'

'I haven't got any yen,' said Fiona.

'I often wish I had nothing,' said Major Glossop. 'It would be so much easier.'

'Not in my experience. You enjoyed the tennis?'

'I go mainly for the strawberries. How's the new boy?'

'Jonathan?'

'The bright spark from the Foreign Office. The lightning-conductor.'

'Why do you call him that?'

'It's his function to lead the shock away from us. These investigations are potentially electric. If anything went wrong, we could end up in the history books. That's why this Jonathan lad has to become deeply involved. To commit the Foreign Office up to the hilt.'

'He's just longing to be involved.'

'A sure sign of inexperience. Make sure he continues to see himself as a worker, not simply an observer. I am good at delegation, you know.'

'So we noticed.'

Major Glossop was no fool. That attitude of disengagement was no more than a pose. He had left the Regiment as a major not because of lack of ability to rise higher but because he had a large farm in Somerset and did not care for his colonel. It suited him to be underrated. In his circle, it was socially the kiss of death to be thought of as too clever by half. His desk was empty of papers because he remitted enquiries down the line, and then fell on the results with the eye of a swooping hawk. He had been the best adjutant in the history of the Plums.

'I miss the club,' said Major Glossop.

'For lunch?' asked Fiona.

'Even with the tube at Warwick Square, it's usually too far away. I never expected to be out-housed like this, in the provinces. An uncle of mine died suddenly in Randolph Avenue, you know. Took a lot of explaining to Aunt Winifred.'

'I can imagine your aunts.'

'Aunt Winifred was a lady to her fingertips. Though not, I believe, further in.'

'I think you should see Jonathan Fieldhouse.'

'Admit him to the presence.'

Jonathan blinked when he saw Major Glossop. He seemed to be sitting so very still. There was a coiled tension in this wax-like figure. It was almost a relief when it uttered in a mellow baritone.

'Welcome to the mess,' said Major Glossop.

'The mess?' Jonathan had a mental vision of Guest Nights in Simla, old silver, horse-play in the garden.

'The mess. The confusion. The human muddle.'

'I feel at home already.'

'Fiona is great at that. She's very welcoming. Like the spider and the fly. You expected somebody older?'

'You look quite old to me.'

'Fiona, I mean. Our little Miss Hopkins. Your boss.'

'She keeps reminding me.'

'She's quite scared of you. A young man from the Foreign Office.'

'She conceals it pretty well.'

'Of course. That's part of the game. There's a lot of concealment here. It's a top-secret establishment.'

'I've only been allowed to read files so far.'

'Don't worry. Your turn will come. I shall give you the leads. And then you start running. I used to back greyhounds, you see. More civilized than you might suppose. They feed you quite well at the White City.'

'It's all a mystery to me, Major Valentine. Is that what I'm supposed to call you? I used to know Blues, but never the Plums. What exactly is my role here? Do I call on the old schoolmasters, the family referees, the friends of childhood? They must be terribly old by now.'

'Oh no. The Service has people for that. Men in trenchcoats. Withered crones. In the moon-pool we are far more sophisticated. Nobody is going to associate *you* with *us*.'

'Thank you.'

'You are personally going to get to know both George Craxton and James Leyland.'

'How on earth shall I manage that?'

'I shall arrange it. We old Plums have a tremendous network. It's called the Orchard.'

'And they won't know what I am up to? The victims, I mean.'

'Of course not. That's the point.'

'I shall feel a bit of a stinker.'

'You will be.'

'Almost an Iscariot?'

'The end may be less catastrophic. As far as we know, they're both clean. You want to get on, don't you?'

'Yes, of course.'

'Nobody has ever suffered through working for me, Jonathan. You'll find the Regiment distributed throughout the corridors of power. Oyster-chef at Greens. Barman at Annabel's. Head Door-man at the Ritz.'

'That wasn't quite my aim.'

'I was just working my way up. We have done wonders for the officer class too. We happy few, we band of brothers.'

'But I'm not a Plum.'

'You could become an honorary Plum. I mould men.'

Jonathan did not like the sound of that. There was a martial glint in Major Glossop's pale blue eyes. Was he wholly sane? Jonathan had embarked on what he believed to be a safe career, leading gradually upwards, like a well-oiled escalator, towards an eventual knighthood and then a pension. He had not bargained for his special relationship with the slippery Bernard Gilbert or for the dubious rewards offered by this semi-crazed military magnifico.

'Now you must excuse me,' said Major Glossop. 'I have to telephone my broker. He wants to get me into titanium. I think drink is safer.'

'How did you like the big cheese?' asked Fiona.

'I thought him very odd.'

'Isn't he beautiful to look at?'

'I'm not that way inclined.'

'So deliciously statuesque. He stands at parties lost in thought. Like patience on a monument. They have to prick him with forks to make sure he's still breathing.'

'I thought I was a bit junior for that.'

'I like that humility,' said Fiona. 'It's very becoming in one so young.'

'You have a very pretty nose.'

'This is a harassment-free zone, Mr Fieldhouse.'

'Let's go somewhere else, then. It's time for the Rialto Bridge.'

Named for its comparative proximity to Little Venice, the Rialto Bridge was a consciously quaint pub. Twenty years ago it had been brassily modernized. Now, at great expense, it had been re-Edwardianized, with red velvet and imitation gaslights, to attract the foreign tourists. Major Glossop had a point about the financial benefits associated with the provision of alcohol.

'I buy the first drink today,' said Fiona.

'All right. You're certainly an improvement on my friend Rupert.'

'I shall have to meet him.'

'You will.'

'He's your alter ego, isn't he? The other side of you.'

'He's quite different from me.'

'That's what I meant, Jonathan. You're complicated, aren't you?'

'Isn't everyone?'

'Major Valentine is very complicated. I hope you do realize that. He only pretends to be cut out in cardboard.'

'I don't like what he's going to make me do. Snooping for spies, I mean.'

'It isn't a question of spies,' expostulated Fiona. Jonathan liked the excited way she waved her glass. 'The real threat,' she continued, 'is not from the sellers of information. There aren't many secrets left. And you probably wouldn't understand one if you saw it. It would be written in algebra on a computer.'

'So why security?'

'To weed out the agents of influence. The people who might be tempted to destroy us from within. The enemies of the system.'

'Rupert's an enemy of the system.'

'Not in that sense. If he was, you'd have to cut him out.'

'You're very bossy, Fiona.'

'I have a clear, simple mind. Perhaps because I didn't go to university.'

'Not that again. You're extremely attractive.'

'That's another handicap.'

I mustn't let her know, thought Jonathan. At least not yet. It would be a disaster. The truth was that he had fallen in love with the wretched girl. He didn't want to, but he had. He had been tremendously attracted to her from the first. Shakespeare was right about that. Who ever loved that loved not at first sight? And now she obsessed him. All day he kept stealing glances at her. In the evening, when they were usually apart, it was worse. Her little face came creeping in on him. Somehow, he knew that he mustn't tell her yet. She would take unfair advantage. The one who loved the most was inevitably the weaker.

Rupert must meet her soon. Rupert would know what to do.

In the basement flat in Highbury, Rupert was in bed with Maureen. This was by no means unusual. They spent a lot of time in bed together. Rupert liked to see Maureen sprawled over the white sheets, her dark hair on the pillow, her shadows and her soft places. Although scruffy and tousled on the exterior, naked they were both surprisingly white and clean.

It distressed Rupert to feel as he always did after the climax. Sadness would not be quite the right word, but it was getting on that way. As passion mounted, he felt so loving, he said such sweet things, he kissed so fondly. Could any girl be blamed for believing that this was the real thing, the intertwining of two souls for which the mind and body craved, the healing of the separated heart? And yet, afterwards, with the anticlimax in the most literal sense, a lot of the intense love seemed to have drained away. He still cared for her, he was grateful, but she was no longer the object of his heart's desire. In fact she was lying rather heavily on his left arm and making it feel a bit stiff. And she was nibbling on his ear, which he did not much enjoy, at least not afterwards. That was the trouble with girls. They seemed to cool down at a different rate. They took literally what you said to them in moments of intense excitement. And then, most unfairly, they accused you of deceit. Perhaps it would be different if you were deeply in love. He had not yet had experience of that.

'Darling,' murmured Maureen. 'I do adore you.'

'Me too,' said Rupert with facile grace.

'We'll always be together.'

'Oh, yes.'

'You're sure?'

'Of course.'

Women were never sure. They kept needing to be told. It was part of their charm. And yet it could become exhausting. Take now, for instance. Maureen wanted to stay lolling in the bed for hours, her body curled round his, trying perhaps to arouse him again. Rupert, however, had now had enough of their golden swoon. The summer afternoon sun was beginning to set. So, temporarily, had his lust. He intended to spring up to take a shower, and totter round to the Charge of the Light Brigade for a noggin and a sausage. Maureen, if he insisted, would do the same.

It was quite a good way of life, thought Rupert. Not perfect, but enough. At home last weekend for his sister's party, they had shaken their heads. His father, the brigadier, had taken him lightly by the arm and steered him across the lawn. Sad-faced, he had asked the inevitable questions. Wasn't he going to try to make something of his life, to take advantage of his expensive education, to justify the hopes of his family? With his mother, it had been worse. Putting on her brave demeanour, she had assured him that they still believed in him, still trusted him. She had patted his hand, had she dared she would have patted his tufted cheek. With both he had been polite. Inwardly he had resented their pressure. He had not bothered to explain. They assumed he was Bolshie, anti-Establishment, alienated. In fact it was only personal freedom he cared about. After years in boarding schools and university, he had a thing about being no man's slave. He wanted to range at will, watch the clouds racing across the sky on Hampstead Heath, hear the ducks quacking in Regent's Park. He was like a man recently freed from prison. Would he always be like that, he wondered? He really did not know. But one thing was certain. He was lazy, too. Deeply and physically idle, with an ingrained allergy to effort and sustained struggle. The motive force was lacking. Nobody had ever been able to persuade him that it was all worthwhile.

It made him see Jonathan as a sort of freak. He found it fascinating that his friend should actually want to go to an office every morning and spend the day ministering to the vanity of his superiors. He enjoyed the thought of all Jonathan must have to put up with. It made his own unencumbered days seem all the sweeter. Watching the long barges go by, he would wonder what Jonathan was doing at that moment. In this respect, he needed Jonathan almost as much as Jonathan needed him. How could the joys of idleness be savoured without an occasional glimpse into the tyranny of work?

Maureen had taken his hand and was trying to press it into her less public places.

'I'm hungry,' said Rupert.

'Hungry for what, my darling?' Her Irish lilt had always slightly irritated him. He suspected it of being a bit artificial. What did she really know of the rain-washed shores of Connemara with their coral strands and blue, enchanted hills?

Rupert bounced brusquely from the bed as the doorbell pealed. Wearing only a small towel, he opened it to admit Jonathan and a neat, fair-haired girl who was introduced as Fiona. The newcomers stood self-consciously in the hall, gazing around at the squalor in mute disgust, while banging and bumping sounds emerged from the bedroom and bathroom where Rupert and Maureen were now getting washed and dressed.

'I hope it's not a bad time to call,' shouted Jonathan through the thin wall. It was amazing how effective Rupert was in making him feel he had done the wrong thing. It had always been like that. And yet he, Jonathan, was the more estimable of the two.

'Of course it's a bad time, you old stupid,' whispered Fiona. 'That's obvious. They've been having it off.'

'Time is no object to us,' sang back Rupert. 'That's the charm of it.'

The ill-matched quartet moved to the Charge of the Light Brigade. Jonathan bought the first round.

'I'll have a vodka,' said Maureen. 'To celebrate.'

'Celebrate what?' asked Jonathan.

'The joy of it all.'

Fiona gave a slight sniff. She didn't think she was going to like Maureen, too consciously the Celtic charmer.

'And how do you two know each other?' asked Rupert in his direct way. 'Did he pick you up, Fiona? Jonathan was known in college for his wolf-whistles. They called him the Beast.'

'We work together,' said Jonathan with dignity.

'Oh, I see,' proclaimed Rupert. 'She's your secretary then. Your personal assistant. In the Foreign Office, one becomes frightfully grand at a tender age.'

'Certainly not,' snapped Fiona. Then she noticed the mute appeal in Jonathan's anxious face. 'We are – colleagues.'

'Like Maureen and me.'

'No,' replied Jonathan firmly. 'Not like Maureen and you.'

'There's only one Rupert, my wild, darling boy,' said Maureen, 'in all the wide world.'

'Let's hope so,' muttered Jonathan. 'How was your weekend, Rupert? How were Daddy and Mummy and the horses, the beagles and the giant marrow?'

'He's going to take me another time,' crooned Maureen, 'for the hunt ball and the harvest festival. I'm going to be Queen of the May.'

'It's not nearly as exciting as you two make out,' said Rupert evasively. 'Spare us the class aggro. Well, why don't you ask me the usual question, Fiona? What do I do?'

'I know what you do, Rupert. Or don't do. That's why I'm not asking.'

'Very tactful. I suppose I feature in young Jonathan's mythology. The wastrel friend. Tom Rakewell, on his way to perdition.'

'Nonsense,' said Jonathan.

'That makes me the Bearded Lady,' pointed out Maureen.

'As a matter of fact,' said Fiona, 'Jonathan thinks very highly of you. Though he would never admit it. Attraction of opposites, I suppose.'

'Don't you lead our Jonathan astray, little Miss Fiona,' said Rupert.

'Me?'

'Yes, you've got him by the short and curlies, I know. He was a nice, unspoiled boy when he joined the Foreign Office. Full of simple ambitions like a desire to be rich and famous. Don't let him loose in the rat-race. It won't do any good. At the end of the day, your sort of top people are still slaves.'

'What do you mean?' asked Jonathan.

'He knows what I mean,' said Rupert to Fiona. 'He's heard it all before. The real rulers in these isles of ours are the masters of economic wealth. In huge slabs of property and land. They call the tune. Civil servants, even the eminent ones, are only their agents.'

'All right,' conceded Fiona, 'there may be something in that. But the country still has to be run. And work is a joy. And a necessity.'

'Not to me,' said Rupert flatly.

'Nor me either,' echoed Maureen.

'Some people have these needs,' admitted Rupert loftily. 'These inner cravings. One has heard of these unsavoury obsessions. But I can manage without work. In an era of mass unemployment, it's the way I make my little personal contribution.'

'Me too,' said Maureen, twisting the end of her long, dark hair and dipping it, unhygienically, into Rupert's best ale.

'Isn't it a moral issue?' asked Fiona, led on by Rupert's teasing dialectic. 'Give and take, I mean. You can't just accept things from people and then offer nothing in return.'

'Oh, can't I?' growled Rupert darkly. 'I don't feel in the least out-ployed by you in the morality stakes. You two don't do your work out of duty. You do it because you like it, and because it gives you a good conscience. Bully for you. But I happen to get my kicks in other ways.'

Maureen seemed to regard this as an invitation to insert the tip of her tongue into Rupert's ear. It was not a sensation that he had ever enjoyed. He frowned at her, causing her to respond with a suggestive giggle.

'You are awful, Rupert,' said Maureen with satisfaction. 'There's no point in arguing with such a dreadful, darling man.'

'What *is* your work, in any case?' pursued Rupert. 'This famous activity that fills your days. Jonathan used to give us regular bulletins, when he first joined. But now, quite suddenly, he's shut up like a clam. It sounds fishy, if you ask me.'

'We're in Personnel Selection,' answered Fiona promptly.

That was the agreed cover, not too remote from the main work of the Foreign Office or from their real activities, if any enquiries came home to roost.

'You have to be completely ruthless in that field,' opined Rupert. ' "Be absolute for death." '

'For death?' shrieked Maureen.

'It's a quotation, my lovely.'

'My cousin was in the Royal Ballet School,' said Maureen. 'Such a gorgeous girl. But they chucked her out. Said she was growing up lumpy. They were ruthless enough.'

'Quite right,' remarked Rupert. 'Are you without compassion, Fiona?'

'We have to do our best. For the public service. But we don't mind them growing up lumpy.'

'People will take anything,' opined Rupert. 'Even summary dismissal. If you are totally straight.'

'How do you know, Big-Mouth?' asked Jonathan.

'I just sense it,' replied his old friend. 'Hereditary lore. I was born, you know, into the master race.'

Jonathan stole a glance at Fiona. He was not at all sure how she was taking to this strange couple. He was even less happy, after the bar-snacks, when Fiona elected to walk back to the flat with Maureen. He had never really been able to tolerate the pseudo-Irish girl, except for the sake of his friendship with Rupert. You had to accept them together as a package deal. He and Rupert followed at a slight distance, savouring the sounds and scents of this Islington in high summer.

Rupert wasted no time.

'You're mad about her,' he said.

'Is it that obvious?'

'Plain as a pikestaff. I'm surprised you didn't split your pants.'

'It's much more than that, Rupert. I really think about her all the time.'

'That's what I said.'

'But not just in that way. With the mind and heart too.'

'Poor Jonathan. You *have* got it bad.'

'What do you think of her?'

'Nice enough girl. But she's not in love with you.'

'I didn't think she was.'

'But you hope?'

'Of course.'

'Don't hope too much.'

'Why not?'

'There's something about her. I can't quite put my finger on it. I think she could be hard on a man.'

'*La Belle Dame Sans Merci*?'

'Something like that.'

'And no birds sing.'

'Cheer up, you old fool. You should be like Maureen and me. For us, it's just a romp in the hay.'

'It is for you, Rupert. Not for her.'

As if to demonstrate this, Maureen, out of earshot, turned round and blew a theatrical kiss towards Rupert.

'You've got big trouble coming,' continued Jonathan.

'So have you.'

'Trouble is my business.'

'That may be true,' agreed Rupert. 'I don't quite like the way you're shaping.'

'What on earth do you mean?' asked Jonathan.

'You can't deceive me. I'm your best friend. Do you know what I think?'

'No?'

'I think you've got into something that isn't quite straight.'

Jonathan's heart almost missed a beat. He suddenly remembered an incident in his childhood. He had managed to pay a half-fare on the bus in Otley by fraudulently pretending to be under fifteen or whatever the age was. Foolishly he had boasted about this over their high tea. That was a big mistake. His mother had taken his meal away, as a lesson. He could see the untasted food, to this day. Honesty, she had shouted, was an absolute. You had to be completely straight.

It was disturbing, thought Jonathan. Having this conscience. He hoped it would not hold him back.

'Do you mind if I squat here?' asked George Craxton with unwonted humility.

'Not at all,' replied Major Glossop in his pleasant bass-baritone. Sitting so straight and silent, he did look uncommonly like some huge military dummy, perhaps a cut-out for target practice. At the long central table in Greens, any member can seat himself next to any other. It is part of the ethos of the club, a thoroughly democratic institution once you eventually secure election and reach the sanctum. Craxton had naturally not spotted the Major's artful trick of deliberately going into the dining-room just ahead of him, and then selecting a spot with spare places, one of which the former Cabinet Minister was likely to wish to occupy. It suited Major Glossop to let Craxton believe that their proximity came about by sheer chance.

'Craxton's the name,' said the politician. Considering that television had been bringing his fleshy face for years into almost every home in the land, it was a modest gesture. He had been warned not to throw his weight around in Greens, where they were not slow to award wounding nicknames.

'Glossop,' growled the Major. 'I advise against the vol-au-vent.'

It might be imagined that the nationally unknown retired officer would be flattered by the propinquity of the famous political figure. But, in the closed society of Greens Club, the pecking order was curiously reversed. Craxton was a mildly dubious new member, lucky to be elected at all. The Glossops, however, had been members of the club since the early eighteenth century. Indeed, the one-eyed Colonel Julian Glossop had breakfasted there on champagne and oysters after his notorious duel with the Bavarian minister in Lincoln's Inn Fields. It was part of the history of the institution. Even today a fair sprinkling of the more influential members had been officers in the Plums. Here Major Glossop was on the inner track.

'The soup's safe,' he volunteered.

'Thank you. I see you know your way around here.'

'Ought to by now.'

There was something rather magnificent about the man's posture, thought Craxton. Like some inspiring monument on the Nile at sunset. It would go down well in the States. Perhaps it could be imitated for chat-shows and appearances on Capitol Hill. One must cultivate the manner of a commander born to rule. That's what they liked in the new, confident America.

'I'm a new member,' said Craxton meekly.

'I know,' commented the Major. 'Have coffee afterwards. Tell you about the club port.'

'Is the dinner equally good?' asked Craxton later, when they were installed in elderly leather chairs with seats so uncomfortably long in the base that they must have been constructed for giants of the past.

'Better,' answered Major Glossop. 'But stick to the saddle of mutton and the cheeseboard.'

'I ask because it could be handy some evening. My fiancée's away at the moment. Seeing her folks.'

'Her folks?' Glossop managed to make the noun sound like some bizarre obscenity.

'She's American.'

'Oh.'

'I shall be glad of the Parliamentary recess,' said Craxton affably. 'Then I can get away to Sweetladies.'

'Really? What does your fiancée think about that? But perhaps she is one of them herself?'

'My house,' explained Craxton rather less pleasantly. 'We open the grounds for charity in the summer months.'

'You politician fellers must have a helluva life.'

'It's tough. Being always in the public eye. But we survive. As a matter of fact, I'm in a bit of a limbo at the moment. I'm taking up a rather interesting new job.'

'Oh really?'

'It's all settled. I had a very nice chat about it the other day with the Prime Minister. It's just a question of getting the announcement out.'

'Some delay?'

'You know how it is. These little civil servants. Tiny minds.'

'Yes,' said the Major. 'I know how it is. There's not the discipline these days.'

'We believe in discipline,' commented Craxton. 'In the Party, I mean.'

'We tolerated no dawdling in the Plums. Once an idler was sighted, I had his name and number taken. That made him jump.'

'How terrifying. Are you still in the Regiment?'

'Retired. Just pottering around. Have another glass?'

'It's my turn now. My uncle was in the Royal Army Educational Corps.'

'Never mind.'

'But he always had the highest admiration for the Royal Halberdiers.'

'So I should imagine. We do turn out some pretty fine young fellows these days, thoroughly licked into shape. It's rum what happens now. There's one regimental family that I happen to take an interest in. Father was an old Plum corporal, voice like a raging bull, thick as two planks. The son got himself an education and is now in the Foreign Office, of all places.'

'How praiseworthy,' mused Craxton. 'It's just the kind of upward mobility we have tried so hard to encourage. The governments, I mean, of which I have had the honour to be a member.'

'It was easier in the old days,' growled Glossop. 'People knew their places.'

'As a matter of fact,' continued the former minister, 'I'm keeping rather closely in touch with foreign affairs these days. I have to. My new job will be in that area. The trouble is, it's such a huge field. I thought of asking to see the Foreign Office telegrams. After all, I'm a Privy Councillor and entitled to know about state secrets. But there are just too many of them. What I need is some handy system of regular oral briefings.'

'No trouble about that, I suppose,' said the Major.

'Oh no, I'm well known at the top of the Office. In fact I was with Marcus Stewart-Stibbs only the other day. I could go direct to him again, I suppose. But I don't want to seem troublesome or self-important.'

'Some informal arrangement, perhaps?'

'That would really be better. Approved by the top brass but not actually laid on through them. That would avoid setting a precedent. They won't want to oblige all the ex-ministers in the Party in the same way.'

'This young man I mentioned,' said Glossop, 'might be able to help you. The son of the old Plum. A bright lad, they say, and now working in London. He could pop across, every so often, and give you the hot scoop.'

'That's rather a good idea.'

As Craxton began to entertain the notion, he found it increasingly attractive. It would be useful to have a direct line to the Foreign Office, just to make sure that the mandarins did not try to short-change him. At the same time, he would be making a friendly gesture towards this fossilized ex-officer who seemed to wield considerable, if local, influence. That was obvious from the way that other members kept passing him with friendly *badinage*. In his constituency he had always been good with the minor Party workers and their awed consorts. George Craxton had little doubt that any young man in the Foreign Office, and especially the offspring of a humble corporal, would find it an honour and a pleasure to come into regular contact with him. He would, after all, be in the history books. And there was more to come.

'Jonathan Fieldhouse is the chap's name.'

'You know him personally?'

'Oh yes. Knows how to hold a knife and fork.'

'I hope he's not a smarty-boots. You know what these young diplomats can be like.'

'He's OK. Very inexperienced. But bright. And keen as mustard.'

'Well, tell him to give me a ring. Ask for my secretary at the House. Of course we'd have to get official clearance.'

'There would be no trouble about that.'

'How do you know?'

'I just do.'

Glossop had seemed mysteriously assured. Perhaps he was engaged on some kind of secret work. If so, it might be prudent not to ask. The man certainly had a sort of magisterial demeanour. People who were really just pottering about didn't usually put it quite like that.

'And now excuse me,' said the Major, rising to his massive height, like some well-sharpened pencil. 'I have to go and phone my broker.'

The former Cabinet Minister felt dismissed somewhat abruptly. It was an unusual experience, except with the Prime Minister.

'Is something special happening?' he asked.

'Equities have lost their lustre.'

'Martha is heavily into leisure. That's my fiancée. Her broker says it's going to last. He's specially keen on the sunshine belt. But Martha herself has always been mad about Europe. I think she'd find this place awfully quaint and scenic.'

'No doubt. She would only be able to dine at the ladies' end.'

Major Glossop decided that, in the light of this successful outcome, his lunch at Greens might be construed as an official expense. He treated himself to a taxi back to Bangalore Mansions, where he passed on the good news to Fiona and Jonathan.

'This is brilliant,' exclaimed Fiona. 'One of your brightest efforts, Major Valentine.'

'I thought so myself.'

'How often am I to see this Craxton?' asked Jonathan, feeling somewhat bowled over by this turn of events.

'That depends on him. And you. Don't push it. My guess is that he'll go for you.'

'What exactly do you mean by that?'

'Craxton is between women. He's lonely. He needs a friend to confide in. He'll tell you a lot.'

'But I'm so junior.'

'People often confide more to their juniors. They think it's safe.'

'And isn't it?'

'Not in your case.'

'I shall feel a bit bad,' said Jonathan.

'You'll get used to it.'

'I don't want to hear his secrets.'

'But we do. In the moon-pool. That's what it's all about. You'll have to be careful with Craxton, though. He's no fool. Of course you know nothing about his appointment to Washington. Or about his positive vetting.'

'I'm not a complete idiot,' expostulated Jonathan.

'I didn't think you were,' said the Major coldly. 'But human relations aren't simple. If he starts really talking to you, you won't find it easy to belt up. It's a natural reaction to repay a confidence. You'll have to stifle your instincts.'

Jonathan felt increasingly uneasy. Instincts were often a sound guide about the decent way to behave. He was being asked to live life against the grain. Once again, he wondered whether he had got himself into something that wasn't quite straight. But it was too late to back out now. His career was at stake.

'There's another thing,' continued Glossop. 'You'll have to mug up the regimental history of the Plums.'

'Why on earth?' asked Fiona. 'You are a devious old thing.'

'I had to say that Jonathan's father was a fellow Plum. Craxton was instantly impressed.'

'I don't see the need for that,' said Jonathan.

'How else could I explain my interest in you? I manoeuvred Craxton into thinking he was doing me a good turn.'

'It's most awkward. The Plums are a posh regiment. How on earth shall I sustain it? You know I wasn't even at a public school.'

'Oh, don't worry,' laughed the Major. 'I said your old dad had been one of our corporals.'

'I see.' Jonathan felt rather deflated.

'That's not very nice of you,' said Fiona. 'Jonathan's father could have been an officer.'

'Hardly, my dear. Let's be realistic. Horses for courses, you know.'

Jonathan frowned at the put-down. He was getting tired of the old Plums and their luxuriant Orchard. When he had come south, he had thought that sort of class snobbery was being swept away. But it wasn't. People like Glossop would never give up until they faced a firing squad. But that wasn't a very constructive thought. It was certainly not the way to get on.

'Give him a ring tomorrow, Jonathan,' said the Major. 'At the House. And make sure you hit the right note from the start. A combination of whizz-kid and idiot boy.'

'I am content,' said Craxton, 'to be judged by history. My resignation from the Cabinet, in spite of almost frantic pleadings from the Prime Minister, will be viewed as a stand of principle.'

'What principle?' asked Jonathan.

'The right of the individual to stand up and be counted. Even a Cabinet Minister. I'm so glad you don't smoke. Martha will have to go on a cure.'

'Martha?'

'My fiancée. A most wonderfully warm person. She's going to be the most fabulous asset in my next job.'

'I'm afraid I don't know what that is.'

'It's a secret, my boy. A deep secret. I wish I could tell you. But I can't.'

Jonathan had prepared for this encounter with some inner anxiety. After all, it was the first time he had met a Cabinet Minister, whether past or present. There had been none in Otley. He had decided on his best white shirt and the tie with blue spots. And he had brought a special cloth in his brief-case to give his shoes a final shine just before approaching the policeman at the entrance to the House of Commons. It was all a great strain. But the Right Honourable George Craxton had given him an affable welcome and even a broad smile. Craxton had long years of practice behind him in putting nervous constituents at their ease. He was only alarming when he wished to be. To his surprise, Jonathan had almost begun to enjoy the conversation. It was at least a new experience to be cooped up with this almost legendary figure in this tiny, hot room, relieved only by an occasional gust of river breeze.

75

George Craxton was much nicer to the youthful Jonathan than he would have been to a more senior official. That was because he did not feel threatened by him. With Sir Marcus Stewart-Stibbs he would have been waspish. A brief chat had shown him that Jonathan was too inexperienced to be of much use in general briefings on foreign policy. But he could still be helpful on certain specific subjects. Anyway, the main point of the exercise was to have a personal nark in the Foreign Office. This young man would be the very thing. Craxton knew from experience what a lot the young would do for him in gratitude. It was highly flattering to a beginner like Jonathan to be the recipient of his professional charm. It always worked. Craxton had spies everywhere.

'However, I can say,' boomed the politician, 'that my new appointment will be a very important one in the field of foreign affairs. That's where you can be so useful to me. Before each of our meetings I shall ask you to come prepared with the latest information about official thinking on a specific subject.'

'Oh, all right.'

Jonathan thought hard. Of course he could not tell Craxton that he was no longer working in the main building of the Foreign Office, that as a result he had no automatic access to the daily distribution of confidential guidance telegrams. But the problem could be managed. Through Bernard Gilbert, he could get briefed regularly in the Office on what to pass on to the ambassador designate in Washington. It was an odd procedure but not improper.

'In two weeks' time, for example, I'm making a big speech on arms control. I need to know more about policy on chemical warfare and nuclear testing. I'm familiar with the broad outline, of course. Haven't sat in the Cabinet for years for nothing. But I'd hate to get caught out on the details. Some of these disarmament fanatics will stick at nothing.'

It was odd, thought Jonathan, that the former minister spoke about the control of the arms spiral as if it were just one interesting topic out of many. Whereas to people of his own generation it meant nothing less than the continuation of the human race. Couldn't the wrinklies begin to see that? It had taken countless thousands of years for humanity to evolve even as far as it had. And now the future lay, so far as the West was concerned, with an

American president of spectacular mental vagueness. Sometimes he wondered whether Rupert might not be right. But these were rebellious thoughts which should be stifled at birth.

'Of course I am in favour of disarmament,' continued Craxton, almost as if he had read Jonathan's thoughts. 'Who isn't? But it must be mutual. It was Byron, I think, who said that in one of his marvellous letters. He hated anything that was not perfectly mutual.'

'I imagine he was thinking of something else.'

Craxton grinned.

'Well, life is not all politics,' he conceded. 'Tell me about yourself. Where do you come from?'

'Yorkshire.'

'I know the north,' said Craxton softly. What is he thinking of, thought Jonathan? He himself had read Craxton's file in detail. It was embarrassing to know so much more about this important man than the man realized. He hoped he would never betray this knowledge, but it would not be easy.

'Yes,' continued Craxton, 'we used to have holidays in Northumberland. Such a grand country.'

Inevitably Jonathan thought of the politician's first wife, the ditched Sally. Where was she now? He imagined them in youth roaming the fir forests of Kielder or watching the screaming gulls on the sands of Lindisfarne. Had Craxton ever really been in love? Had they hoped to share a whole lifetime together? Perhaps she was the not unusual type of political wife who failed to keep pace with her husband as he progressed relentlessly upwards in the power struggle? No doubt Martha Freeport would be more useful to him now.

'And what about your life in London?' continued Craxton. That was the secret of man management, to show a genuine interest in the workers. He had once lectured on the topic at business seminars. 'Do you have a girl-friend?'

To his inner fury, Jonathan felt himself beginning to blush. It was horrible to be so young. He certainly had a friend. He was with Fiona all day now during the week, and quite a lot after work in the Rialto Bridge. And she was indubitably a girl. But he had never quite been able to bridge the divide, to confess to Fiona that his whole life revolved round her.

77

'Not really,' he replied. 'Not yet.'

'Women are important,' said Craxton sententiously. 'For a rounded career, I mean. You'll have to choose very carefully. They say that behind every successful man stands an astonished woman.'

Jonathan found the older man's attitude unattractive. He might have been talking of carpets or curtains. Was the politician lacking, for all his bland manner, in genuine human warmth? Beneath the smooth exterior, Jonathan began to sense a deep, inner vacuum.

'I don't think of politics just as a career,' continued the statesman. 'The urge, in my case at least, is to serve the nation. It is, I think, the highest way in which to serve. The word idiot comes from the ancient Greek expression for a private citizen not involved in running the state. Though I don't say that in public speeches. Just look what has happened to those unfortunate countries where the best people haven't gone into politics.'

Jonathan privately wondered whether modern Britain might not be included in the category. But it seemed more prudent not to say so. He was getting used now to biting back the incautious remarks which rose unbidden to the lips. The Foreign Office was full of deeply cynical people. But they didn't get on by making it too obvious.

'I went into politics,' boomed Craxton, 'because I felt I had something to contribute. An individual point of view that was essentially George Craxton. Tough but tender, you know. That's absolutely necessary for success in public life, a conviction that only you can save the nation. Unfortunately the nation doesn't always recognize its saviour when it sees one.'

Jonathan was beginning to suspect that gifted people might be rather difficult. Some seemed to combine a flattering assessment of their own gifts with an inadequate appreciation for those of their competitors. It was not, he guessed, the best way to be happy. Happiness required a higher degree of acceptance. Men like Craxton would never be totally at rest. He wondered how hard it had been for Sally, the lass from Tyneside.

'Mind you,' said Craxton, 'I'm not denigrating diplomacy. That's enormously important too. As we get weaker, Abroad gets bigger. Foreigners need the most skilful handling, some of them are so peculiar. I saw a good deal of British ambassadors during my ministerial visits abroad. They rather tended to unroll the red carpet for me. One little fellow in Paris used to stay up specially to offer me my usual nightcap of malt whisky. Some were rather too easy to use as pillar-boxes. But the job has enormous potential. A great ambassador, with delicate antennae and charisma at the podium, could do a marvellous job for Britain. Just think what the States mean to us now. Too much perhaps. We must try to influence them more.'

'Like the Greeks getting their own way with the Romans, through superior culture?'

'Well, perhaps that was always a rather arrogant analogy. It's not one I should care to use publicly these days. But it's certainly the sort of thing I had in mind.'

'I should like to get posted to Washington,' Jonathan said innocently. He must not forget his posture as an idiot boy.

'I'm sure you would, my lad. Who wouldn't? But I mustn't say any more. Secrets are a part of the trade. When I was hotting up for my budgets, I used to retire to study the calculations in the boiler-room at Number Eleven. Now I mentally associate changes in tax thresholds with the most ghastly gurgles. Didn't want to risk a leak.'

'In the boiler?'

'No, in the budget.'

Jonathan hoped that Craxton would not try to make too many jokes. He was not very good at them. Perhaps, as a younger man, he had been advised that humour was a necessary part of the armoury of the aspiring politician. His whole personality gave the impression of an artefact put together by a conscious effort of will, rather than the product of organic growth. It was not entirely convincing.

'I'm hungry,' said Craxton. 'Let's have tea on the terrace.'

As they munched, the former minister provided some informative commentaries on their neighbours. All seemed to be on their way down. One had been taken in adultery, another had made an unfortunate joke about the Prime Minister's family, and at least four were dying of drink. This did not prevent Craxton from giving them all the most cheery waves. Perhaps he was trying to console the lesser breeds.

'This is the most wonderful club,' said Craxton with a beam. 'In spite of our political differences, we have this deep camaraderie. I shall miss it terribly.'

'Miss it?' asked Jonathan.

'In the fullness of time,' replied the statesman hastily, recovering himself with aplomb. 'When I'm an extinct volcano. That's when they'll pop me in the House of Lords.'

Later that night, Jonathan mentioned to Rupert that he had met George Craxton, though without revealing any details.

'I've seen him often on the box,' said Rupert.

'So have I,' said Maureen. 'And he's a fine, great chunk of a man.' Jonathan wished that she would stop eating the ends of her long, dark hair. It was one of her most disgusting habits. But he could hardly say so. You couldn't tell people when to stop.

'There's something wrong about Craxton,' said Rupert in his confident way.

'What exactly?' asked Jonathan. He really did want to know what Rupert thought.

'It's the eyes. They're false.'

'You mean they're made of glass?' asked Maureen.

'No, silly. But they don't reflect the soul. He doesn't want them to.'

Fiona, it was understood, lived with her Aunty Mary in Wimbledon. She showed no inclination to invite Jonathan down. He got the impression that Aunt Mary might be rather frail and perhaps a bit crotchety. It would be better not to intrude.

'And what about you, Jonathan?' asked Fiona. 'Always so nattily turned out. Do you roost on windowsills, like some bird of the air?'

'I have a tiny flat above a shop in Brixton,' replied Jonathan defiantly. 'Don't want to get too far from my class origins.'

He took her there shortly afterwards. She enjoyed the walk from the tube. Some old-fashioned Cockney people might feel affronted and frightened by the flamboyant atmosphere. But Fiona, like Jonathan, warmed to the sight of the tandoori take-aways, the rasta records, the Bamboo Palace and the Coconut Grove. All human life was here, the Third World come to Europe. It was the wave of the future. In Brazil they had, more or less, bred out their colour problems. There was no point in trying to set back the clock.

'But you're cheating,' protested Fiona. 'You live in Tulse Hill. And there are signposts to immensely respectable areas, full of Tory activists. Dulwich, Streatham.'

'I prefer to think of it as Brixton,' said Jonathan.

Brixton was ethnic and interesting. He had not risen all the way from Otley in order to live in the lower reaches of Streatham. These things mattered. They walked on, in the summer evening, to Brockwell Park, not far away. The park was impeccably maintained, to Fiona's surprise, with a marvellous display of flowers.

'The council are wildly socialist,' explained Jonathan. 'They believe in full employment and high rates.'

'Poor ratepayers,' commented Fiona. 'Lucky flowers.'

On a bench, among the fading roses, he took her hand. It was absurd that it should have taken so long for such a minimal step. But their relationship was unusual. Most of their time together had been spent in the office, where the silly little thing ranked as his nominal superior. You couldn't try to bed your boss in Bangalore Mansions. And there, though constantly in contact, they talked too much. Here, in Brockwell Park, he didn't want to talk at all. He just wanted to be with her, to feel intensely the proximity of every inch of her small body.

Intellectually Jonathan knew that he was undergoing an extremely common experience for a young man. It was as old as time, nature's tender trap for repopulating the world. But emotionally it came to him as a unique revelation, as if he himself were pushing back the frontiers of knowledge. The thing was so damned mysterious. It was physical attraction that he had first felt for the girl. He wouldn't be sitting here with her in the park if he didn't long for her smooth skin, her mysterious places. But that wasn't all, not by a long chalk. He was held too by her mind, by her slightly high voice, by those shafts from the soul that sometimes pierced through her blue eyes, even by her defects and her mistakes which made her human too. He longed to know everything about her, to share her every thought, to be familiar with the whole of her body, above all to unite with her in the only act that could join together the separated soul. It was a constant ache now, this longing of the body and the heart. And the experience was so shattering. It was hard to remember that it had indeed happened to a great many other people too.

'You're very silent this evening,' said Fiona.

'I was thinking.'

'Don't strain the brain.'

Why couldn't he just tell her all this, thought Jonathan. She wouldn't laugh at him. He knew she liked him. But did she feel the same way about him? It seemed highly unlikely. In spite of the intensity of his own yearning, common sense told him that, whatever vibrations might be emanating from Fiona at that moment, they were probably not of a violently amorous nature. That was what held him back now, he thought: the lack of a response equal in any way to his own creative love. If he made a fool of himself now, she might just laugh at him. And it would be damned awkward tomorrow in the office. Fiona might even request a transfer from Bangalore Mansions. He imagined her asking coldly for a private word with Major Glossop. Everyone would know. He cursed the inhibitions that prevented people from being just simple and overtly loving with each other. It must have been much easier in a primitive society. People like Rupert managed well enough, of course. He had got Maureen to bed on their second date. But Rupert, most unfairly, had that tremendous confidence. Jonathan did not think he could bear the pain of rejection by Fiona. He would suffer almost anything to avoid that. You could always hope, it was better than knowing the worst.

'There are some very odd people in this park,' said Fiona. 'I love to watch them.'

'Perhaps they love watching you.'

'Look at that old boy over there with the bag. What on earth is he collecting?'

'I haven't the vaguest idea.'

Jonathan felt extremely tense. He longed to snap out at somebody, just as a way of relieving his feelings. It was unfair of Fiona to remain so placid, cucumber-cool, with every hair in place. She looked at him sharply, turning towards him to see if something were wrong. The gesture was too much for poor, starved Jonathan. He put his arms around her, pulled her down towards him and started, almost violently, to kiss her soft cheeks.

'Oh, do be sensible, Jonathan,' said Fiona quite calmly. 'You're messing up my hair.'

He had to have bodily contact with her. The urge was too strong to resist. There was a point when you had to go beyond words. Well, it hadn't worked too well this time. She had failed to co-operate. But it wouldn't always be like that.

'I do like you,' added Fiona. 'But not in that way. Not here.'

'We could go back to my flat.'

Jonathan's brain was spinning. He'd made a mess of it. He had failed to get in a packet of those things. It wasn't pregnancy you had to worry about these days. There were horrible new diseases. Well, they would have to be content with what the Americans quaintly used to describe as heavy petting.

'No, thanks,' said Fiona. 'I have to get back to Wimbledon. Aunty Mary will be waiting.'

'With your evening cocoa,' suggested Jonathan with an almost Byronic sneer.

'Not quite,' laughed Fiona. 'Mary prefers brandy. The truth is that I'm deep in this awful book. You know, the block-buster, *Battle of the Dinosaurs*. About the two rival candidates for the job of Archbishop of Canterbury. I can't put it down. One has just got Durham and now his hated enemy is hoping for Winchester. And they've discovered that at Oxford they were once in love with the same girl. A gorgeous flame-headed enchantress who has now become a Reverend Mother and does popular religious programmes on the telly.'

'It sounds perfectly idiotic.'

'Of course it is. But I'm enjoying it immensely. I do so love a good read. It's the perfect way to spend the evening, don't you think?'

Jonathan did not think so at all. They had not talked like that in old Verona. He felt deeply frustrated and disappointed, as he saw her to the tube through the exotic streets. He did not like the sound of that possessive Mary. It was almost insulting that Fiona should go placidly home and read some silly bestseller. How could she, when they had been so close in Brockwell Park? He himself would not be able to sleep for hours, he was far too wound up. He would climb on past leafy Dulwich, pound the summer pavements, sing a bit and recite verse. To hell with what people thought. You couldn't be a Foreign Office official all the time. Sometimes you had to be young and a man in love.

*

'What's wrong with you, Jonathan?' asked Fiona. 'You seem to have a black eye. And perhaps other things, too.'

'I was punched,' replied Jonathan with dignity. 'In Pollard's Hill.'

'Is that some part of the anatomy? It seems quite possible. You could have a stone in the pollard.'

'It is a remote suburb. Beyond Norbury. I arrived there shortly before dawn. I was giving them the bass part of "Unto Us A Child Is Born". We have a fine tradition of choral singing, you know, in West Yorkshire.'

'You must have woken them all up.'

'That's what the big man said. Just before he delivered the blow.'

'Poor Jonathan, you are an old silly. Why on earth didn't you go quietly to bed?'

'I couldn't sleep.'

'You should try a book at bedtime. The Reverend Mother is thinking of leaving the cloister. And a bit of masonry has fallen off the cathedral at Winchester. It just so happens that the Bishop of Durham was standing below at the time examining the buttresses. He missed death by inches. There's a wonderful amateur detective from the Church Commission, Adrian Cranmer, deeply grounded in Byrd and Palestrina. He too proves to be an old friend of the Reverend Mother. In earlier days it seems she had a lively social life. She's been trying to atone for it ever since.'

'Oh, do shut up,' said Jonathan petulantly. 'I believe you're making the whole thing up, just to tease me.'

'You think I tease you?' asked Fiona.

'You certainly do.'

'Teasing is a form of affection.'

'It's not the only form.'

'It's my form, Jonathan. You must take me as I am. Don't try to build me into some kind of ideal girl.'

'I loved being with you last night.'

'Yes, I know.'

He longed to go further, to tell her that he adored her. But not here. Not now. Besides, it must be obvious. If you felt as strongly as that, it must show through. Real feeling always came across. There was no need to say anything. Words were inadequate, they spoiled things.

84

'Why don't you come and stay over the weekend?' he asked suddenly. 'In my pad. There's room.'

'I'm afraid I can't, Jonathan. Aunty Mary is taking me to Bath. She says it's a lovely town. I would be free on Thursday, though.'

'Oh dear, I'm on duty that night.'

'On duty?'

'Yes, old man Craxton is taking me to Glyndebourne. I shall have to ask Major Val for the afternoon off from the office.'

'My word, you are going places. That costs a bomb.'

'I think he's a bit lonely.'

'He must be desperate,' said Fiona. Then she saw the young man's face fall. 'Only a joke,' she added hastily.

'Glyndebourne,' said Major Glossop, a little later. He had just progressed into their room, stiff and stately. His looming carriage made him look more than ever, thought Jonathan, like the Statue in the last act of *Don Giovanni*.

'What's the opera?' asked Glossop.

'*L'Incoronazione di Poppaea.*'

'The Coronation of the Poppy, eh?'

'Well, not quite.' Jonathan had little time that morning for this military philistine.

'It's time to rescue that poor Monteverdi,' added Major Glossop, with a slight gleam in one of his beady old eyes, 'from that dubious 1962 version by Leppard. I'm an early-music man myself.'

'The poor Koreans didn't feel too good in the helicopter,' said Sir Marcus Stewart-Stibbs. 'The company might have done better to ferry them down by road.'

'We made a lot of dust when we landed,' said Felicity Stewart-Stibbs. 'Beyond the ha-ha, of course.' She gave the happy giggle which had seen them through the years in Paris. Glyndebourne looked delicious on this summer night.

'I enjoyed coming in the helicopter,' commented the Permanent Under-Secretary. 'It made me feel important. As if my time was valuable.'

'It is valuable, dear,' said his loyal wife. 'Remember who you are.'

The official papers, thought Sir Marcus ruefully, were not inclined to let him forget. It had been a rush to get away to the heliport in mid-afternoon, so much earlier than his usual time for leaving the Foreign Office. He had just got up to put on his dinner jacket when Jasper Tenby had come rushing in with the draft of the Cabinet paper with the new Middle East proposals. They simply had to be with ministers in their overnight boxes. Peeved and rattled, he had managed to de-gut the document very quickly and then dictate a brief comment for the Secretary of State to that new girl. Was she Lavinia or Laetitia? There was never time these days to ask anything. He had been suffering ever since this spurt from the worst of gastronomic ailments, mental indigestion. But Felicity had been keen to accept this invitation from the business firm who seemed to find their presence useful. One had to do things sometimes for Felicity, who was such a good sport. And it was all for free. There would be more time for these not unpleasant cavortings when he had moved over, with a peerage perhaps, to his little crop of non-executive directorships.

'Our bus, described picturesquely as a land-cruiser, took the Brighton road,' said Sir James Leyland. 'It is supposed to be faster. But I missed the scenic route via East Grinstead.'

'You wouldn't have seen a thing, you old goose,' said Charmian Leyland. 'You were reading those wretched documents all the way.'

'I had no choice,' protested her husband. 'Tomorrow in Brussels I've got one of those regular lunches with the Permanent Representatives. We can't afford to be outflanked.'

'I'm sick of Brussels,' said Lady Leyland. 'All that eating and boozing.' She was a thin, intense woman who had got a First at Somerville.

'Daddy works too hard,' interjected their daughter, Tess. 'My boy-friend says it's not at all necessary.'

'I don't think your boy-friend knows much about work,' said her mother acidly.

Sir Marcus was not sure that he entirely approved of Tess Leyland. Her table manners left much to be desired. But it had been a nice idea to include all three Leylands in this agreeable freebie, which fitted in with one of James's regular visits from Brussels. Marcus was glad to do something for this difficult but gifted colleague who was also an old friend. He felt bad about that sad business over the Washington appointment. And the commercial company were pleased to introduce their Korean guests to Sir

86

James as well as Sir Marcus. Now they were enjoying dinner in the Nether Wallop Hall during the long interval.

'This is rather good wine, Marcus,' said James cordially. 'Did you choose it?'

'Oh yes. Our kind hosts agreed that we five should have this table to ourselves. The Koreans have asked for special food and are having a picnic on the lawn. We have to chat with them afterwards. A junior man from the company is supposed to be looking after them.'

'You should have offered your services as a geisha, Tess.'

'Very funny, Dad.'

'Your father is practising his *badinage*, dear. It will be needed in his next job.'

There was a grain of truth in that, thought Sir Marcus grimly. Dear old James's massive intellect, well allied to that of Charmian, was usefully deployed in his present post with a complicated multilateral organization. But it might seem almost forbidding in a bilateral relationship with a single country, however large. Of course, such mental powers would have been useful in mastering the complexities of the American scene. But alas, the poor man wasn't going to get to Washington. Surely he had accepted that. So there was no need to practise his persiflage or generally improve his social skills. It was all quite pointless.

'I think conversation is so important in our life,' chimed in Felicity. 'And so hard. In Paris, you know, I used to tuft.'

'Tuft?' asked Charmian, always keen to improve her knowledge. 'What on earth is that?'

'Jumping from one tuft to another. In the talk, I mean. As if you were crossing a marsh and could only stand on the bits of firm ground. The little scraps of conversation you could actually understand.'

'I see,' said Charmian coldly. Marcus, amused, guessed that this redoubtable lady had never had to do much tufting. She would understand everything only too well. But had she been any more useful to the Service than his own deliciously scatter-brained Felicity? Foreigners preferred you not to be too clever. It was a lesson that the Leylands had still to learn. Not everyone wanted to play literary scrabble after dinner.

'I thought we weren't supposed to talk about Dad's new job,' said Tess.

'Quite right, dear,' said her mother. 'But tonight we are all in the know. I think I shall concentrate on the intellectual side. I look forward to symposia at Harvard and Princeton. James can do the Hill quite well without me.'

With a thrill of horror, Sir Marcus realized that poor James must have lacked the courage to break the news to Charmian that their appointment to Washington had been blocked. It was painful to hear her burbling on like this. James too was looking rather pink.

'I shall embarrass you,' said Tess cheerfully, 'by bringing over my sleazy friends. There are lots of cheap charters to New York these days.'

'Spare us,' said her mother. 'That boy-friend of yours sounds quite awful.'

'You've never even met him, Mother.'

'Is he ever out of bed for us to meet?'

Sir Marcus sometimes rejoiced inwardly that he and Felicity had never been blessed with children. Diplomatic offspring seemed to present rather a problem these days. Many of them had turned against traditional values, spurning the gentilities of the chandelier belt. He suspected that Tess might be one of these. The Leylands, with their austere intellectualism, would not exactly have been cosy parents. Nor, as a family group, were they proving ideal guests. A spat between mother and daughter would be only one shade less painful than those unfortunate references to life in the United States.

'Has everyone finished?' he asked brightly. 'Then we might go out on the lawn. To chat up the Koreans. Got to sing for our supper, you know.'

It was lovely on the lawn, with cows still grazing on the hills, the men in black and white looking like penguins, soft trees around the lake, singers warming up in the dressing-rooms. At Glyndebourne they never tried to hide the mechanics. It was part of the unique charm of the place.

'Where are the Koreans?' asked Sir Marcus. 'I hope they haven't got lost.'

'Good evening, Marcus,' said a familiar voice. George Craxton, complete with red carnation, came massively into view. Jonathan

Fieldhouse stood modestly behind him. The former Cabinet Min-ister naturally knew James Leyland too. Introductions were made to the wives.

'And this is one of yours, Marcus,' said Craxton. 'Jonathan Fieldmouse, a brilliant young man whom I have borrowed for the evening from the Foreign Office.'

Jonathan flushed as he shook hands with these very senior officials from his own Service. It infuriated him not to be able to retain his composure better. He was all right when he knew people, but it was hard to control his nerves when he first met them. The truth was that they frightened him. It was not that they were intrinsically alarming. In fact they were rather mild and polite. But he was apprehensive of what they might do to his career. Because Jonathan was afraid of failing to make the grade, he often did best with people he didn't really care about.

'It's good to take time off,' said nice Lady Stewart-Stibbs, with a smile of approval to young Jonathan. 'All work is no good.'

'The same can be said,' cut in Charmian, 'of all play.'

She looked round for Tess, in order to give her a meaningful glance, to rub in this sally.

'Where on earth is our daughter gone?' she asked.

'She disappeared after dinner,' said Sir James. 'Walking round the lake, perhaps.'

Lady Leyland would have liked Tess to meet Jonathan. He looked like the sort of highly motivated young man of whom one could approve. Tess was always so coy about her friends. They seemed a dubious bunch. And now the silly girl had skipped off, just when she was needed.

Sir Marcus did not realize the significance of meeting Jonathan with George Craxton. But then Bernard Gilbert had not thought it necessary or desirable to give him details of how the moon-pool was operating. He was therefore unaware of Jonathan's special status as a laser-beam operative under deep cover. He doubted whether he would be able to remember Jonathan's name, though he ought to do so. After all, he was Head of the Service, the father of his flock. But new names were so difficult nowadays. His long career had been too many names, just as, for the weary emperor, Mozart's music had been too many notes.

'I don't feel we are doing our stuff,' said the ever-zealous Sir James. 'With the Koreans, I mean.'

'News has just come through,' said Sir Marcus. 'The poor boy from the company is distraught. At the start of the long interval, the Koreans thought it was the end of the opera. They went out to look for the helicopters. Now they are being rounded up on the Downs.'

'Oh, the joys of commercial sponsorship,' said Craxton lightly. 'Of course they are all for it in the States.'

'We have a lot to learn from the Americans,' said Lady Leyland. 'In almost every field.'

'I agree,' said Craxton. 'And they from us.'

'Do you go there a lot?' asked Lady Leyland.

'I expect to see a good deal of the place from now on.'

'Oh good.'

'Why do you say that?'

'Well – er – we shall be meeting.'

Both Sir Marcus and Sir James found this conversation extremely painful. But neither dared intervene directly.

'I think special talents are needed in Washington,' said Charmian. 'Not a lot of silly socializing. There's been too much of that already. We must tap the finest American minds. They don't go to cocktail parties.'

'Nor do senators,' said George Craxton. 'Choice little dinners are more the thing. For top people.'

'I shall hope to see you, Mr Craxton,' said Charmian mysteriously.

'Me too, Lady Leyland,' agreed the politician. Each thought they had discreetly invited the other to the embassy in Washington. For Sir Marcus, it was a moment of nightmare.

'I thought the intermezzo went rather well,' he interjected at last. 'The one between Valetto and Damigella.'

'I was feeling a bit peckish at that point,' said Craxton. 'I'd like to see the Glyndebourne opera more often in the States.'

'There are great opportunities there for British artists,' agreed Charmian. 'Under the right patronage, of course.'

'Now we have an interesting new bit,' interjected Sir Marcus rather desperately. 'Nero, elated by the news of Seneca's death, drinks himself insensate.'

'You can see that any evening in the House,' said Craxton. 'No need to come down to Sussex.'

Meanwhile, Jonathan was doing his best to sustain a conversation with the daunting Sir James. He was delighted to meet him like this by happy coincidence, since Sir James was to be the next target for covert investigation in the moon-pool. Major Glossop would regard it as a most fortunate break. Heaven must be on their side.

'What exactly do you do?' asked Leyland. His tone suggested that he didn't really need to know.

'Well, I've been in Central American Department,' replied Jonathan, praying that he wouldn't be asked any current questions.

'With Claude Silk?'

'Yes,' answered Jonathan with a slight shudder.

'One of our best. Takes his work seriously.'

'So I have noticed.'

'It's good to have a hard task-master. At least when you first join. Helps you learn to draft lucidly.'

'I suppose so,' said Jonathan with false enthusiasm. He wondered what the missing Tess would be like. Everyone around him seemed so old.

'That's the bell,' said Sir Marcus. He felt that the interval had lasted too long already.

'We never talked to the poor Koreans,' said Felicity. She was a kind-hearted soul.

'They've been taken to the stables. To get their pumps pumped out. It seems that they fell into a dew-pond.'

'Opera in the country,' Craxton boomed heartlessly, 'seems to have its hazards.'

'Oh, there's Tess at last,' said Charmian, 'somewhat the worse for wear. Where on earth have you been? I've managed to produce a respectable young man for you.'

'We'd better hurry,' said Sir Marcus. 'They close the doors and then you can't get in.'

'This is Jonathan Fieldhouse,' said Lady Leyland. 'From the Office. My daughter, Tess.'

Jonathan looked at the girl in astonishment. She started to giggle. Then he lost his cool.

'Maureen,' he said angrily. 'What the hell are you doing here?'

*

'Major Val,' said Jonathan next morning. 'I had rather a lucky break last night.'

'So had I,' snapped back Glossop. 'It's a great help to be able to use the Special Branch.'

'I spent the evening with both our special targets. And neither suspected me.'

'Suspected you of what?'

'Being from the moon-pool.'

'I should hope not. Put it all in writing. I've got an assignment for you. A thrilling away fixture. In drinking hours this evening I want you to be in Canonbury – gentrified part of Islington. Once full of city merchants, now stuffed with Eurobond dealers and BBC producers.'

'I know it.'

'Pub called the Charge of the Light Brigade. James Leyland's daughter Tess goes there a lot. We'd like to know more about her. She's often there with two young men, one scruffy, the other tidy but odd. The tidy one buys all the drinks. He's got rather a mean, hatchet-like little face with a silly moustache.'

'Oh, do you think so?'

'I'm only quoting from reports. There's no point in running a moon-pool unless you do it in depth.'

'Why are you so interested in her?'

'A man's Achilles heel is often his family. Just think of Hamlet, King Lear, Othello. Diplomatic children present a special hazard. If you've met the father, you may be able to spot the daughter. Pale face, dark hair, somewhat intense.'

'Irish accent?'

'I shouldn't think so. Why should she? She went to Cheltenham Ladies College.'

'Can I put it on expenses? The cost of the drinks, I mean.'

'If you get receipts.'

'You can't ask for receipts in a bar. It would arouse suspicion.'

'I'll see what I can do. If you deploy the old laser-beam to good effect. Keep an eye on that hatchet-face little runt. He could be from a foreign embassy.'

'I think you're prejudiced,' protested Jonathan. 'Just because he's small.'

'Big men do tend to have a certain magnanimity.'

'I'm small.'

'Yes. But you're from the Foreign Office. You have the backing of a great Department of State.'

'How was Glyndebourne?' asked Fiona, next door.

'Very pretty. I scored two bull's-eyes. Made some useful contacts.'

'The music, I mean?'

'I was too wound up to concentrate on the music.'

'You are a Philistine, Jonathan. I must broaden your education.'

'I wish you would. Have a good weekend in Bath.'

'Aunty Mary says I am to take walking-shoes. It doesn't sound like a rest.'

'I don't care for that Aunty Mary. She'll run you off your feet.'

'I really wanted to concentrate on my book. Curled up on a sofa.'

That presented a luscious mental image to Jonathan. He longed to give the girl a squeeze. But they frowned on that sort of thing in Bangalore Mansions. It was agony to have her so near and yet so far. Surely she must know how he felt. Had she ever been in love? There seemed to be some spark missing, at least on her side. Love was such a bloody thing, a dreadful unsatisfied ache.

Jonathan found Rupert opportunely alone in the Charge of the Light Brigade. He wondered which of the loafers at that bar came from the Special Branch. Could it be that moon-faced man sipping the vodka-tonic? Or that homely lady on the bench who seemed to be doing some advanced knitting? Could she, in reality, be a Girton graduate who represented the country on Interpol? Anything was possible in modern Britain, a land straight out of the Arabian Nights.

'Where's Maureen?' asked Jonathan.

'She had to go and look after her old mother.'

'I didn't know she had one.'

'Lots of people have mothers, Jonathan. It's part of the human condition. The venerable crone is paying a visit to our metropolis. She'll be going back soon to Galway.'

'Galway?'

'Or the Arran islands. Somewhere on the edge of Europe. She lives in a smoke-blackened cottage, it seems, gently crooning Gaelic sagas and distilling illicit whisky.'

Jonathan remembered Lady Leyland, the epitome of intellectual perspicacity. He was getting tired of these grotesque charades.

'Have you actually met this old creature?' he asked nastily.

'I don't need to. Maureen has made her live for me. That girl has wonderful powers of description.'

'I've never noticed it.'

'She only talks in bed.'

'How well do you know Maureen?'

'How well can one know anybody?'

'I suppose you realize that she's not Irish at all?'

'Anyone can choose to be Irish, Jonathan. It's a state of mind.'

'Her name is Tess Leyland.'

'Don't spoil it.'

'Did you know that?'

'She's Maureen to me. That's how she wants it. I respect her decision.'

'It would frighten me.'

'It doesn't take much to frighten you.'

'I think she's disturbed.'

'You have problems too, Jonathan. You can only live in the here and now. Maureen has willpower and imagination. She doesn't care for her background. So she's simply renounced it. She's invented a new one.'

'Are we supposed to believe in it?'

'Only if we want to. There's an element of satire.'

'But when Mummy and Daddy come over from Brussels, she has to rally round?'

'She doesn't have to. But she's not without family affection. Oh, Jonathan, you are a literal old thing.'

'I can distinguish between fact and fiction.'

'How limiting.'

'It's the safest way to keep out of the criminal courts.'

'I don't know how I put up with you. It's an awful reminder of what might have happened to me. If I'd taken a job.'

'I don't know how you can bear to live off the state.'

'What do you think you're living off, Jonathan? How's your affair with Fiona progressing?'

'It's not an affair.'

'You only say that because you've not managed to get her into bed yet. People think it's a love affair, if you do. And, if you don't, it's only a friendship.'

'It's the usual distinction.'

'It's an unreal one. The French know better. They speak about *"une affaire blanche"*. That's a love affair that is realized only in the mind. They can be the most passionate kind. There's no feeling of let-down, no morning after, no anticlimax. Dante and Beatrice.'

'I don't think I can bear it. Not indefinitely.'

'Try making it up. If the real world's too tough, you have to take refuge in fantasy.'

'I feel I've known her long ago. On some other shore.'

'You're coming on, Jonathan. Welcome to the world of fiction.'

'In the Foreign Office,' said Jonathan, 'we don't approve of fiction. Our prose may not be exciting. But it does have a certain element of reality.'

'How was your day with Tess?' asked Sir James Leyland. He and Charmian, both back in Brussels, were taking their usual Sunday afternoon walk in the Bois. Behind, at a discreet distance, ambled the plain-clothes police. Security was such a bore these days. But Belgium was a dangerous place for British diplomats.

'Not too bad,' said Lady Leyland. 'We went to the Academy. And then, in the evening, to the Cottesloe. I'm afraid she can be very irritating.'

She had stayed in London especially for a day after Glyndebourne, leaving James to go back to Brussels alone. It was time for another determined effort to get a grip on Tess. But the girl had been as evasive as ever. Charmian wished she could like Tess better. Surely one ought to be fond of one's own daughter? People expected it. But Tess, though outwardly polite, remained implacably sealed off from all human emotion. At least that was how it seemed to her mother, who did not know the depth of the girl's feeling for Rupert. What on earth had made her go so sour? Perhaps she had been sent away to school too young? But they'd had no alternative in Santiago. The Foreign Service might produce great external rewards. But it was not all beer and skittles. They had lost their only child in the process.

Charmian sometimes wondered whether the loss had been sudden or gradual. After all, Tess had been a delightful small child, cuddly and almost too affectionate. What on earth could have transformed her into this scowling alien? Lady Leyland could not help remembering that first holiday in Chile. The girl had arrived tired and unwontedly subdued after the long flight. Two days later she had persuaded her mother to take her for a picnic in the foothills of the mountains. Charmian never cared for the Andes. They had no real birds and were too big for the human scale. But she had humoured the child. Tess had poured her heart out, sobbed forth her hatred of the school, her loneliness and fear, her longing to be back home with Daddy. It was the reference to James that had really stung Charmian. He never bothered with the child and yet she had this insane affection for him. It was unfair. In her usual calm, polite voice, for she believed in courtesy to children, Charmian had rejected Tess's request. Of course she could not leave school. It was just not feasible. When Tess grew older, she would learn that in life you often had to put up with things you did not care for. That was character-forming. It was good for you in the end. You just had to keep cheerful and not distress other people with your little problems. Meanwhile, Tess might like to have another piece of the currant cake. As they got back into the Range Rover, Charmian felt she had handled the situation rather well. Glancing sideways at the girl, she was surprised to see a look of pure hatred on the tense young face.

And now, years later in Brussels, when James was eminent and most people treated them with deference, Charmian felt an element of gruesome replay as she described to him her abortive approach to their own daughter, no longer a tear-stained child but an unduly controlled and buttoned-up adult who had mentally abandoned them.

'Did you meet the boy-friend?' asked James Leyland. He knew that Charmian would never get on with Tess. The two were irreconcilable. It was written in the stars. Women could be so cruel to each other. Perhaps he might have had a better chance. Girls were supposed to be fond of their fathers. Tess had loved him once. He should have stayed behind in London and had another shot. But the timetable in Brussels was so horribly crowded. Even another day out of the office would have severely interfered with the programme. He was a slave, lashed to the treadmill.

'Oh no,' replied Charmian. 'He's always kept well away. In spite of all my hints. I suppose she realizes he isn't very presentable.'

'Perhaps it's you.'

'Me?'

'The one who isn't very presentable.'

'I never thought of that,' sniffed Lady Leyland.

Poor Charmian, thought her husband. She means so well. But let's face it, she isn't exactly sensitive.

'At least,' said Charmian, 'I got her to talk about him. In fact she was good about describing him. It seems he's some form of Irish layabout. He's called Rory and is very dark with blue eyes. That Celtic colouring. His family are tinkers. A polite word for gypsies. They mend old cars and play the violin rather badly.'

'Oh dear,' responded James. 'Irish. I hope they are not politically undesirable. We don't want him in Brussels.'

'You're not getting either of them.'

'Just as well, perhaps. Why did that young Foreign Office man behave so oddly at Glyndebourne? He seemed all right otherwise.'

'What do you mean, James?'

'He knew Tess already. That was obvious. But he kept calling her Maureen.'

'Some silly joke, I suppose. I don't understand young people these days.'

'It's the generation gap, my dear.'

'Gap indeed? More of a chasm, I should say. We were never quite like that in my day.'

James remembered Charmian as a young woman. Rather severe, with that straight, corn-coloured hair, but with honest, hopeful eyes. He had been a frequent visitor at the comfortable house on Boar's Hill, dominated severely by her father, the Professor. That was where he had learned the pencil and paper games that they still played after dinner. Charmian's memory was accurate. She had always maintained a civilized, if strained, relationship with her own parents. Estranged children like Tess were new phenomena in the family.

'We shall lose touch with her completely,' continued Charmian, 'when we are in America.'

Sir James Leyland drew in his breath with a sharp hiss. This was awful. Poor Charmian, he had let her make such a fool of herself at

Glyndebourne. He could hardly imagine what that odious Craxton must have thought on that painful occasion.

'We mustn't talk about America,' he said feebly.

'At least we can think about it,' said Charmian. 'I suppose we shall be inundated with visitors. I shall breakfast alone in my room. That man Craxton seemed to think he would be coming.'

James Leyland stopped suddenly. Charmian looked at him in surprise. His face looked unusually set.

'I've got something to tell you,' he said.

'What's that, dear?'

'I think we've lost Washington.'

'What do you mean? We were promised! Ages ago.'

'Only by Marcus. The Prime Minister has decided to make a political appointment.'

'Who?'

'George Craxton.'

'Christ! I thought he was behaving oddly. But the laugh was on me. I made a perfect fool of myself.'

'I'm sorry, dear.'

'I can hardly believe this. How very unfair. Are you quite sure?'

'It's not absolutely certain. Various enquires are being made. But we have to be prepared for disappointment.'

'All right, James.'

'Are you dreadfully upset?'

'I am for you. You would have been so good.'

'I don't know about that.'

'I want you to have scope. To spread your wings. Otherwise you'll be impossible to live with.'

'There would be a lot of social life. Every night. Neither of us really enjoys that.'

'You must do something, James. The machine can't just be stopped.'

'I thought of Oxford. A college. I believe Belial is coming up.'

'Daddy never really enjoyed dining at Belial. He considered their taste in claret unsound.'

'Your father knew nothing about claret.'

'That's why he wanted his hosts to do so.'

'The Lodge has a certain charm.'

'It needs the ivy clearing away.'

'But you'd come?'

'Of course I'd come, James. I did follow you to the Congo. Didn't I?'

A foreign wife would have made such a fuss, he thought. On these occasions, there was a good deal to be said for English reticence. It carried you through.

'How was Bath?' Jonathan asked on the Monday morning.

'Oh, we didn't go,' Fiona said cheerfully.

'You didn't go?' Jonathan sounded incredulous.

'We couldn't be bothered in the end. The weather seemed a bit problematical. I had a lovely time with my book. There's an awfully exciting dénouement in Lambeth Palace.'

The heartless bitch, thought Jonathan. I could have been with her, all the time. She could so easily have let him know. It was obvious now that she didn't care about him, that she never could. The spark just was not there. You could do nothing about that. He felt a strong urge to burst into tears.

'There's a message for you, Jonathan,' said Major Glossop, bearing in upon him like some stately galleon. 'A number you have to ring urgently.'

Jonathan looked at the scrap of paper without interest. There was only one person he wanted to ring. And she was standing at his side.

'I know who it is,' said the Major. 'We had it checked. Bernard Gilbert of the Foreign Office. No doubt he wants to know how the investigation is getting on. We keep tabs on everyone. And he keeps tabs on us. You'd better not keep him waiting. You've got to think of your future.'

It had not been one of Bernard's better breakfasts. The walk across Blackheath had failed to restore him to his usual equanimity. Amaryllis was in one of her states about the children. The house-master, Mr Watts-Dunton, had telephoned discouragingly about Timothy. The boy showed a strange ability to be serenely happy without doing a stroke of work. He had even given up cricket and brushing his teeth. It would not end well. From Camilla the news was even worse. Her Finn was fading. He threatened to go back to his pine forests unless a sauna was constructed for him in their squat. Who ever heard of a sauna in Potters Bar? Camilla, on the telephone to her distraught mother, had been loquaciously lachrymose. Amaryllis had been too upset to do bacon and eggs. In the long run, thought Bernard morosely, he himself was always the chief victim. Who on earth wanted children anyway?

'And now you order me to go to Australia,' Amaryllis had wailed. 'How on earth do you expect me to run a problem family from the other side of the world?'

'I don't order you to go to Australia,' Bernard had explained patiently. 'It is fate that drives us there. That's the trouble with a diplomatic career. The top of the pyramid is so very angular.'

'I'm tired of perching on a pyramid,' said Amaryllis. 'It doesn't feel at all comfortable. I wish you were in commodities instead. My cousin's husband has made a killing out of October cocoa. I'll bet it's less effort.'

Miss Johnson-Boswell at the Office also seemed to be in a stew.

'Lucinda telephoned twice,' she said with a sharp intake of breath as he entered. 'From the office of the Permanent Under-Secretary. Sir Marcus is keen to talk to you at once.'

'I had a nasty little brush with the Prime Minister last night,' said Sir Marcus down the phone. 'Got caught at the State Dinner. The PM can't take Craxton much longer. He's been giving insolent stares in the House. It's making the front bench wriggle. Number Ten want to announce the fellow's appointment to Washington as soon as possible.'

'You explained about Robin Compton?' asked Bernard. 'About the months he still has to go.'

'The PM couldn't be less interested in that aspect. There's just this tremendous urge to put the Atlantic between the House of Commons and George Craxton, with his fleshy jowls, his self-satisfied smirk and his plummy voice.'

'Oh dear.'

'So it really is urgent, Bernard. A result from the moon-pool, I mean.'

'I'll look into it, Marcus. We have an excellent team on the job.'

'Well, be careful, Bernard.'

'What on earth do you mean?'

'How you look into the moon-pool. Don't overbalance and fall in yourself.'

Was this some kind of warning? Bernard felt a tiny twinge of fear. Was he under investigation too? No one was ever wholly clean. Or was that just one of Marcus's nasty little jokes? Beneath his usual urbanity, the PUS sounded in a peevish mood that morning.

'You too, Marcus,' said Bernard heavily.

'My life is grim indeed,' said Marcus. 'Felicity is dragging me tonight to a Charity Ball at the Savoy. I've just discovered, too late, that the damned thing is fancy dress.'

Bernard suppressed a disloyal chortle.

'What are you going as?' he asked politely.

'Jasper has gone off to try to hire a costume. What a waste of official time. I thought of going as Jack the Ripper. It will suit my mood.'

'Well, keep away from the press.'

'The trouble with Felicity is that she doesn't take me seriously. Or my work.'

That was true, thought Bernard. But it was no bad thing. Old Marcus had needed his laughter-loving wife who constantly teased him, in spite of his elevated posture. She had prevented him from getting too stuffy. This had been the making of him, though he failed to realize it. Alone, he would not have come so far. His own wife, Amaryllis, was a splendid support in her own different way. He really must try to save her from the kangaroos. Marcus was right. The moon-pool just had to produce results quickly. He would debrief the boy Jonathan and then check his story with Sir Dominic Trowbridge. You had to trust people, but you didn't have to trust anyone completely.

'I'm afraid we haven't got far,' said Jonathan, hastily summoned from Maida Vale.

'That's for me to judge,' replied Bernard Gilbert, almost severely. His usual *bonhomie* seemed to be under eclipse that morning of high summer. 'Just tell me everything you've been up to.'

'. . . So you see,' said Jonathan, almost breathlessly, a few minutes later. 'It doesn't amount to much.'

'On the contrary,' opined Bernard, 'it adds up to quite a lot.'

'What have I discovered, then?'

'You are penetrating into the real depths of personality. You know now that George Craxton is inexplicably lonely. And that James Leyland's daughter harbours strange resentments.'

'Does that matter?'

'It could. We shall see.'

'It's only the end of the beginning.'

'Or the beginning of the end.'

'I don't like it. Worming my way into the confidence of these people. Under false pretences. They have no idea that I'm an agent of the screening process. It's just not fair.'

'Fair, Jonathan?' Bernard looked at his most avuncular. 'That depends on how you look at it.'

'Don't I owe them loyalty?'

'You owe a higher loyalty to the nation.'

Jonathan wondered what Rupert would have made of that. No doubt he would dismiss it scornfully as one of the oldest tricks in the power game, one of the feeblest excuses for totalitarian tyranny. But it would not do to argue too long with this senior mandarin. What he had already said might prove to be unwise. But the little outburst had come unprompted. He had not been able to contain it.

'I'm sorry,' said Jonathan, deflated.

'There's no need to be sorry. You are obviously a very decent young man. I respect you for it. But sometimes, in this imperfect world, we have to use devious methods to protect the state. You will come to understand that. In a career which holds great promise.'

Bernard saw the gleam of ambition in Jonathan's eye. It was all right. He wouldn't be making any trouble.

'Bangalore Mansions could be a stepping-stone for you,' continued Bernard seductively. 'Perhaps to a minister's Private Office. I'll see what can be done about that, in due course. Ministers are happier with realistic young people, who understand how the world actually works. It makes them feel better.'

'I love this time of year,' said George Craxton as they sat on the terrace at Sweetladies. 'A touch of summer sun. Parliament in recess. And the shooting season begun.'

'That doesn't mean much to me,' said Jonathan.

'But you shoot, of course? Tomorrow we'll flush out the home coverts.'

'I don't shoot.'

'You must ride? I'm thinking of taking up polo. Golf, billiards?'

'I don't do any of those things. There wasn't much opportunity where I was brought up.'

'How odd. Well, how do you fill your weekends?'

'I usually sit around. Mostly in pubs.'

The Foreign Office must indeed have changed, thought Craxton. It was taking in a different type of new recruit these days. In a way, it was rather comforting. He felt thoroughly at home with Jonathan, an engaging young man whose social origins were not so remote from his own. The million he had made in his twenties, by a little judicious asset-stripping, had opened new worlds for the ambitious Craxton. But it had cut him off from his own modest roots. And it had made him eternally false. It was quite a strain to be always striving to belong to the ruling class with their expensively simple wardrobe and exhausting outdoor pastimes. How delightful to be like Jonathan, just sitting around in pubs. But Craxton was too old to change his personality now. It was artificial but it was the only one he had. Although he had been in the Cabinet for years, he still could not quite get over the feeling that he didn't belong anywhere.

'I find it important to shoot,' said Craxton.

'Why? Is the country grown so dangerous?'

'It's the way to keep up contacts. We're off to Bolton Abbey next weekend. And then they want us at Castle Howard.'

Craxton was a bit pathetic, thought Jonathan. Did he really think he was fooling anyone? Even his vowels were suspect. But the weakness was part of his charm.

'It's good for Martha, too,' continued Craxton. 'A chance for her to get to know the great estates. Of course she knew lots of fascinating people when she was married to Orson Freeport the Second. Two-generation wealth on that scale makes you an aristocrat in the States. And her chat-show made her many influential contacts. But they were mainly in America. I want her to be thoroughly integrated in top British society before we proceed to our next job. I keep forgetting, you don't know what it is.'

Jonathan wondered how Martha would get on with the duchesses with their dowdy tweeds and old brogues. Martha was apparently always dressed up to the nines, as if she were just going out for cocktails. Jonathan had first seen Craxton's experienced fiancée the evening before, as she descended the great staircase at Sweetladies in an ineffably chic little black dress, discreetly cut with the simplicity that costs the earth, and a necklace of small, perfect pearls. No one could accuse Martha of vulgarity. Her financial resources had been used to employ the best talents in hairdressing, haberdashery and *haute couture*. In fact she had cultivated a rather awesome gentility, like the late Duchess of Windsor. From a distance, her blonde features projected the prettiness of a porcelain shepherdess. Only at close range did her jaw look rather too hard. Her voice also, though not over-accented, carried with it the slightly too imperious tone of a rich, powerful woman accustomed to being obeyed. Jonathan did not know much about British society but he doubted whether it would really take to Martha. She was just too well groomed, too sophisticated, too anxious to please and to be pleased. It was not the English way. If the ambitious Craxton wanted a high-profile partner, he had indeed obtained one. Jonathan could not help wondering how much good it would do him.

'I've heard about you, Jonathan,' Martha had said, extending a beautifully manicured paw. 'George says you're one of the most effective aides he has ever had.'

'He's more of a friend,' Craxton said hastily. 'I mean, he isn't on our payroll. Jonathan works for the Foreign Office.'

'What an honour,' riposted Martha politely, in a voice that had a slightly metallic edge. 'To work for the British Foreign Office, I mean. Orson always had great admiration for you Britishers. He kept a permanent suite in the Dorchester for years.'

'You must know London well, then,' said Jonathan.

'With Orson it was only the insides of plushy restaurants,' replied Martha. 'He was always on the job, adding to the pile. If he sent red roses, they were tax-deductible. I was expected to go alone to the art galleries and the symphony concerts.'

'That won't happen any more, dear,' said Craxton affectionately. 'You'll be happier from now on.'

'I sure hope so,' said Martha decisively. She looked to Jonathan like the sort of woman who would expect happiness as a natural right and would not suffer its absence in silence.

He remembered reading about Orson Freeport, whose death in a private plane crash en route for Palm Springs had aroused considerable media interest. Certainly he had been indecently rich. Oil had gushed from his father's ranch in the early days of the Texas boom. But he had gone on to manage and enlarge a formidable stock market portfolio of his own. Jonathan had assumed, with the innocence of youth, that Craxton was marrying his widow for her money. But now he began to wonder whether the relationship might not be more complicated. Perhaps Craxton was actually attracted by her display of American confidence, redolent of the power that only great wealth can buy, and her barely masked determination to get her own way in all essentials. There was an air of coiled energy about her. She must have some qualities to attract this well-known British politician who was not without distinction himself. Did she appeal to some curious, hidden streak in this vulnerable man? Jonathan had been beginning to think that he understood Craxton. Now he was not so sure.

It was hard to imagine Martha in bed. Perhaps she would have the usual accoutrements of high-level activity, the tapes, the cigarettes, the telephone. There would not be much room for anyone else. Taking a quick snoop around the bedroom floor, Jonathan had noticed with interest that she and George Craxton were occupying separate rooms. It would be that sort of marriage. In one small room, which Craxton seemed to use for his papers, Jonathan had come upon a photograph of a small, young woman with dark hair and slightly protruding teeth. He wondered whether this could be Sally Craxton, the ditched first wife. If so, it would be strange, and a bit touching and unwise, to keep the photo. Jonathan tried to envisage her. Whose fault was it that the marriage had gone wrong? Did it have to be anybody's fault? Perhaps she had just failed to make the grade when George had begun his dazzling ascent into the world of money and power. It was not at all unusual. Where was Sally living now? In the north, perhaps, where she had come from. It would be interesting to meet her, thought Jonathan. But he could hardly ask.

And now, on this sunny Sunday morning, Martha was picking her way down to join them on the terrace, dressed with a casual elegance in tweeds that were just a shade too good for this part of England. Jonathan wondered whether she ever really relaxed.

'What are we going to do to amuse ourselves today?' asked Martha in her rather firm voice. Perhaps she had been telephoning long-distance in the bath. Presumably she always had to be amused. It must be most exhausting.

'There's always the Sunday papers,' suggested her fiancé, a bit feebly.

'I've done them,' snapped Martha. 'Filleted the whole bunch before breakfast. Where's the action in this neck of the woods?'

'Action?' echoed Craxton in some bewilderment. 'I don't know about that. Suffolk is one of our quieter counties. People here just potter around at weekends.'

'I don't potter around, George. You must have noticed that.'

Jonathan had once watched a lioness prowl continuously from side to side of her cage at the London zoo, a pathetic exercise in frustrated energy. The animal needed scope for the release of its own internal momentum. Martha Freeport must be a bit like that. There was no peace in her at all. In the Karmic cycle, she would be a new, raw soul, avid for the experiences of the long pilgrimage.

'I noticed a quaint, scenic little church not far away,' continued Martha. 'Perhaps we could take in a service. The moral majority must be a useful voting block. We Republicans use it to balance the Democratic ethnics. I'd like to project a little personal charisma in that direction.'

'I'm sure people would be delighted to meet you, dear,' said George Craxton. 'They will be all agog to see my fiancée. But the congregation is somewhat sparse these days and Vernon Selwood is not exactly an inspiring preacher. I can't really recommend it. I fear you would soon be bored.'

Jonathan knew what he meant. Martha must have an unusually low boredom threshold. The sonorities of the English Church would not hold her capricious attention for long. It would not be pleasant to watch her nervous fingers drumming on the edge of the seventeenth-century pews, as she glanced pointedly at her tiny, bejewelled wrist-watch. Martha would never complain. She would not need to do so. People would sense her feelings by her manner. Thus were great empires ruled.

'It might be better,' continued Craxton hastily, 'for you to meet the neighbourhood at our wedding celebration. We'll make it a real shindig. There will be feasting in the park. Sweetladies is such a wonderful house for parties. As the very name suggests, it has always been noted as a place for pleasure.'

'Hank promised to jet over,' said Martha. 'He's giving up two days' shooting.'

'Shooting?' asked Jonathan, confused.

'His new movie, honey. Hank has left horror. He's now into space.'

'I thought of asking the Prime Minister,' said Craxton. 'But then I thought not.'

'That's all very well, George,' pointed out his future mate. 'But I need to do something here and now. Never waste a moment. That's our ethic in Texas. It's all right for you Europeans to sit lolling around in the sun. When there is any. I think I may make church all the same. This cute young man will escort me. An appearance by me will be good for your image.'

'I'd rather you made a big entrance, darling,' said Craxton. 'Some other day. When they all see you for the first time around here. At the wedding feast. You could appear at the head of the staircase and then walk slowly down. It could be a Hello, Dolly effect.'

'Very funny, George,' said Martha, not entirely put out. 'What do you think I am, a show business vulgarian? You forget that I'm Sweetbriar and Vassar.'

In spite of Martha's excessive gentility, Jonathan could see that the idea of making a big local splash at the wedding did rather appeal to her. Craxton could not have selected a tactic better suited to influence his bride. For the first time, Jonathan saw a glimpse of the political acumen which had got Craxton, in spite of marked limitations, into several Cabinets. And kept him there for years.

'Perhaps you're right though, honey,' continued the elegant fiancée. 'I don't want my charisma to ejaculate prematurely. But we've got to do something. My analyst says I am never to be left to brood.'

'What about croquet?' suggested George Craxton hastily. 'It combines mild exercise with a glimpse into the jungle.'

'OK,' agreed Martha. 'We tried that the other day. Hugo made the most divine partner. He pushed my ball through all the hoops and we won by miles. I like to win. It's an old American custom.'

'There are only three of us,' pointed out Craxton. 'So we shall each have to play on our own. Without partners.'

Martha did not seem to do so well on her own. She was too well bred to make a fuss but each failure on her part was greeted with low clucks of disapproval. The climax came when Martha was poised to go through a hoop and George managed to dislodge her ball and knock it to the other side of the lawn. The genteel Martha did not exactly scream in fury but she did look decidedly put out. As Jonathan had noticed before, there was something about the supposedly polite game of croquet which unleashed the killer instinct.

'That was unkind of you, George,' she said crisply.

'It's only a game,' replied Craxton, the colour flushing into his heavy face.

'Orson always let me win games,' commented Martha. 'He knew I'm not a good loser. Croquet was spoiled for me by playing with that divine Hugo. Every inch the English gentleman.'

'I don't think you've met Hugo,' Craxton explained to Jonathan. 'A very old friend of mine who was here the other day. Martha liked him a lot.'

'He's got a fine figure,' said Martha calmly. 'I do love a man of that age who keeps his weight down.'

Jonathan suddenly felt sorry for George Craxton, plump and rumpled, his heavy face telling of countless nightcaps in the smoking-room at the House.

'I thought it was just peachy,' continued Martha. 'His cute little moustache. And calling himself an old plum. You English will be the death of me.'

'He only meant,' said Craxton heavily, 'that he is a retired officer of the Royal Halberdiers. In fact he became a lieutenant-colonel and commanded the Regiment in Germany for a short time. Now he lives in the Lake District and paints.'

'Paints what or whom?'

'Landscapes,' replied Craxton. 'Hugo Wilderness was a great help to me, when I was on my own. Before I had the joy of meeting Martha. You changed my life, darling.'

'Big deal, honey.'

'Colonel Hugo might have met your father, Jonathan,' said Craxton, trying to be friendly. 'He was in the Plums too, I believe.'

'Oh . . . Yes.'

'That was what Glossop told me.'

Jonathan cursed the wretched Major, who had booted him into this web of deception. He was tired of evasions and feared that, some day, he would make some blunder which would blow the whole thing sky high. It had become intolerable to spy on a person like George Craxton. In spite of his defects, or perhaps because of them, Jonathan had almost grown to like him. The man was an ambitious careerist. But wasn't he himself too? And it was rather awful to see Craxton delivered to this tough cookie, who combined a softish exterior with an inner core of steel. They would make a strange, if distinguished, couple in the embassy in Washington.

'I think I'll go and tape a piece for my chat-show,' declared Martha. 'There's a new presenter in New York but they still ask me to do bits. You can come with me, Jonathan, and check my voice levels.'

'It will be lunch soon,' said George Craxton.

'Lunch may have to wait,' announced his light of love. 'Orson got used to that. I can't just be turned on and off.'

As she moved towards the house, displaying her well-tailored figure to advantage, Craxton's smile, thought Jonathan, appeared to be decidedly strained. Martha seemed outwardly a civilized and well-bred woman, a not entirely unfitting occupant of the marble halls of the British Embassy in Washington. But, with that formidable willpower, she might also be a pain to live with.

Jonathan eyed Maureen with mild distaste. As usual, they were installed in the Charge of the Light Brigade. For once, Rupert had gone to the bar to buy drinks.

'You confuse me,' said Jonathan. 'After that shock at Glyndebourne with your parents.'

'It was my evening with the wrinklies. Digging up my roots, to make sure they are still there.'

'All that stuff about Connemara. A tissue of lies.'

'That's a hard word, my darling boy,' said Maureen, relapsing into her irritating mock-brogue. 'We prefer to call it romancing. A touch of the blarney.'

'Nonsense,' countered Jonathan firmly. 'From now on, I shall call you Tess.'

'You can if you like,' said the false Hibernian. 'But it won't make one scrap of difference. I live in my own mind, not in yours.'

'Stop bullying her, Jonathan,' said Rupert, returning with the brimming beakers. 'She's a tender creature. In her cradle, she was danced round by the little people.'

'Stuff and nonsense,' said Jonathan. 'She's tough as old boots. That's why she sticks you.'

'You are so very prosaic,' complained Rupert. 'I shall make you a founder member of the Salieri Society.'

'What's that?' asked Jonathan.

'My new enthusiasm. A league for the second-rate, for the mildly talented. Salieri, as you will remember, was Mozart's venomous rival in musical Vienna. We ought to adopt him as our patron saint, we whose work will never prove immortal.'

'Better to be second-rate,' said Jonathan, nastily, 'than to achieve nothing at all.'

'You speak too soon,' replied Rupert. 'Maureen and I are in work. We've found an employer.'

'You astonish me,' said Jonathan.

'It's nice, flexible work,' explained Maureen. 'We do it in our own time. Mornings are still a no-go area.'

'I'll bet,' said Jonathan.

'We want to get you involved,' said Rupert. 'You may be able to help us, with all your posh friends. Don't you spend weekends at Sweetladies, mingling with the local gentry?'

'He's here now,' said Maureen with sudden excitement. 'Just come in. This is where we always meet him.'

'Who?'

'The boss, of course. Our revered employer.'

A rather seedy, elderly man was making his way towards them, no doubt in the hope of being offered a drink, thought Jonathan sourly. He did not care for the look of the newcomer, who seemed decidedly shifty. The Charge of the Light Brigade disported a somewhat bizarre bunch of regulars. They were odder still at the Lucifer in Starlight.

'This is our promising Foreign Office young friend, Jonathan Fieldhouse,' explained Rupert with mock gravity. 'Our eminent mentor, Professor Harold Montrose.'

'Professor Emeritus,' said the elderly man. 'I have been retired for some years. From my chair in architectural history. Now I just potter around, a sad decline. From Palladio to the Palladium. It's the story of my life.'

'Nonsense, Professor,' countered Maureen. 'You still have a role. You influence the young.'

'So did Socrates,' said Montrose. 'And look what happened to him. One day, it will be hemlock for Harold.'

'I don't understand,' said Jonathan. 'Are you the Salieri Society?'

'Certainly not,' snapped Rupert. 'There's nothing second-rate about Professor Montrose. He's a beacon-light to all of us who care about conservation. Isn't he, Maureen?'

'Begorra, he is.'

'You are too kind, dear children,' responded the Professor Emeritus with an amiable smile which Jonathan found unconvincing. 'Hardly a beacon-light. Just a tiny spark perhaps in a dark world. Thank you, as you press me, I will have just a drop.'

'You're in business together?' asked Jonathan, feeling decidedly surprised.

'That's the idea,' replied Montrose. 'It's gradually getting off the ground.'

'We had a fabulous notion,' explained Rupert, displaying unusual enthusiam. 'It's going to make us a mint of money.'

'I need money,' said Maureen. 'To buy blankets and soup for my poor old mother, over there in the West. She spends hours every evening, you know, watching for the lights of the fishing fleet to come in.'

'Oh, shut up,' said Jonathan, flashing her a look of reproof. 'We've had enough of your Celtic blathering.'

'We are forming a company,' explained Rupert. 'You can invest, if you like. It will be called Quaint Domiciles.'

'What's the point of that?'

'If you work in the Foreign Office,' said Montrose, 'that's one of the quaintest domiciles of all.'

'The Professor is a world expert,' continued Rupert, 'on the old buildings of London.'

'Sadly vandalized, alas,' said Montrose, shaking his straggly locks. 'It is a disgrace to the nation how much fine architecture has been destroyed to be replaced by grossly inferior modern buildings. I should like to send some of these so-called architects and property developers to the gallows.'

'A bit severe, perhaps?' murmured Jonathan.

'Not at all,' snapped the Professor. 'They are guilty of a crime against humanity.'

'Well, fortunately, there are still a good many funny old buildings left,' said Rupert. 'We are making lists of them. Then we shall advertise as agents for quaint domiciles. Lots of people want to live in gothic towers, mediaeval chapels, disused breweries, old shunting sheds, river banks. You apply, we find them, for a fee. The Victorian era alone left a wealth of curious property. We are combing Kilburn, Kentish Town, Camberwell, the Isle of Dogs. Let us know if you find anything weird.'

'It sounds relatively honest,' said Jonathan.

'Of course it's honest,' expostulated Professor Montrose. 'The kids here are harnessing my immense expertise. I'm taking Rupert tomorrow to visit an abandoned nunnery in Cricklewood. At least, I suppose it was a nunnery. It certainly seems to have housed a lot of single ladies.'

'I know some odd places in Maida Vale,' said Jonathan. 'One of my friends works in a Victorian mansion flat, monumentally contructed in red brick. The lavatory is a veritable temple of advanced plumbing.'

'Feel free to phone in,' said the Professor courteously. 'We plan to pay for useful leads.'

Jonathan liked the idea of letting the so-called Corcoran Research Library in Bangalore Mansions to a client of Quaint Domiciles. Perhaps they could get extra if Major Valentine Glossop, late of the Royal Halberdiers, went with the property.

'Our young friend here,' said Montrose, 'seems enthusiastic. Ought we to admit him more fully to our counsels?'

'No,' snapped Rupert. 'Jonathan is a civil servant.'

Jonathan wondered a little about this exchange. Perhaps they were up to something else? If so, it was better not to know. Some diddling of the tax authorities, perhaps? He did not really trust any of them. Rupert had been all right at college. But now he had too much time on his hands.

'Look after Rupert, will you,' said Maureen to Jonathan. 'Don't let him fall for some designing hussy. He's easily fooled, where women are concerned.'

'Aren't we all?' agreed Montrose sadly. 'I thought that Flavia had money.'

'Why?' Jonathan asked Maureen hopefully. 'Are you going away?'

'Only for a wee holiday,' said Maureen. 'To visit my poor old mother. The one in Connemara. She needs my help with cutting the peat.'

'Is this the right time of year for cutting peat, Tess?' Jonathan enquired nastily.

'You can do it whenever the ground's wet. And it always is, thanks to our misty Irish rain.'

'I'll concentrate on the Professor,' said Rupert. 'I have heard tell of a fabulous hermitage in Willesden.'

'I'm so glad you made it, Tess,' said Sir James Leyland. 'We see too little of you for most of the year. Your mother and I rather enjoy your company, believe it or not.'

The three of them were sitting on the little patio, overlooking the pool, in the house near Toledo. Other people bought houses in Spain on the polluted coast. But the Leylands had invested in Castile and had never regretted it. August was intensely hot but you had your own swimming facilities and no tourists in their slumbering village. They always went there in that month when Brussels closed down. It was wonderful, thought Charmian as she lazed over the *Times Literary Supplement*, getting away from the horrors of diplomatic drudgery, the placement and the protocol. She could feel the warmth seeping into her thin bones and tired skin. It was the only time in the year when Tess seemed willing to join them. And, for once, the girl was being quite nice.

'You could have brought your boy-friend,' said Charmian pacifically. She did not mean this at all, but it seemed a decent thing to say.

'Oh no,' said Tess hastily. 'The poor lad has had to go back to Ireland. His family have been let out and are on the road again. And they've summoned Rory there, to the Wicklow Hills. They have to do the rounds of the summer fairs. Poor Uncle Toby's still in the nick again for sheep-stealing. So Rory will have to play the violin.'

'What does he play?' asked Sir James.

'The Brandenburg Concertos.'

How odd, thought Charmian. Really, the young man, these days, had become excessively hard to understand.

If Lady Leyland had only known, it was not the episode of the picnic in the Andes which had turned her daughter against her so irrevocably. That had seeped into Tess's consciousness without specific recollection. What the girl could never forget was the sort of thing that had happened a few years later. Tess was acting in the school play, a grave and learned young Portia, too angular to be conventionally beautiful but with a certain adolescent fire as she stumbled out of childhood. James had been too busy to come, of course. But Charmian had gone out of a sense of duty. It embarrassed her to see Tess acting. At first she feared that her daughter would fail. Then, when it turned out the other way round and the applause was generous, Charmian had begun to feel strangely jealous. It was an emotion that made her ashamed, and that in turn caused her to become peevish. After the performance, while the girls were changing to be taken out to supper, an old friend had made a complimentary reference to her daughter's performance.

'It's nice of you to say so,' replied Charmian in her clear Oxford voice. 'But I'm afraid she's still a bit of an ugly duckling. I suppose the poor lambs have to go through this gauche period.'

Tess, returning suddenly, bubbling with excitement and relief, had heard.

At supper she had erupted. Flushed now with a glass of wine, allowed by Charmian as a special treat, Tess had burst out:

'You didn't think much of it, Mummy, did you?'

'I enjoyed it,' replied Charmian calmly.

'But you only came because you had to. Because Daddy couldn't manage it.'

'Don't be silly, dear.'

'Daddy did want to come. I know. He wrote to tell me. But then he really loves me.'

'We all love you, dear,' said Charmian in a decidedly cool voice. 'And now, won't you drink your soup?'

It had not really been a row. You couldn't have rows with Lady Leyland. It was not her way. Rows might have cleared the air. But incidents like this festered under the skin. And there had been many of them before Tess abandoned the struggle to obtain her mother's love.

It had been a strange day from the start, thought Jonathan. Usually his relationships with other people kept on an even keel. But sometimes there were these jagged, hectic movements which threw everything out of balance. Fiona had arrived at Bangalore Mansions in the morning in a subdued mood. After a bit, Jonathan realized with surprise that she had been crying. He thought it better to say nothing. The girl was supposed to be his superior. But, more than ever, he longed to put his arms round her, to comfort her with actions. She looked so extremely young. Yet usually she fiercely rejected sympathy as an affront to the feminist cause. Major Glossop did not take long to summon her to his lair. He had sensed that something was wrong. Jonathan was beginning to realize that the Major's powers of intuition should not be underrated.

'Are you all right?' barked Major Glossop, sitting at his desk in his usual ramrod posture.

'Quite all right,' replied Fiona stiffly.

'I only asked.'

'I only answered.'

'I have a right to ask, you know.'

'Because I'm a girl?'

'No, of course not. Because you are an operative of the moon-pool.'

'I hardly see,' said Fiona crossly, 'how my private life has anything to do with you.'

'Oh, but it does. Very much so. In this organization, as you know, we apply our laser-beam to investigate the life-styles of public servants. The object is to see whether these in any way render our clients subject to pressures which, in certain circumstances, might threaten their loyalty to the nation.'

'Oh, don't be so stuffy,' murmured Fiona.

'I am stuffy,' agreed Major Glossop. 'I admit the soft impeachment. Wasn't that Mrs Malaprop? We Plums, you know, can read. It comes from those long hours in the bivouacs. Where there is no box to watch.'

'I'm unhappy,' wailed Fiona. 'Isn't that obvious?'

'I think I ought to know why. Otherwise you're not fit to investigate others. Someone has to guard the guardians? I don't enjoy it. With me, snooping is an acquired art, rather than a natural taste.'

'I'm not having an affair with the East German Trade Counsellor. Or anything like that. I can give you an assurance.'

'I accept that, Fiona. But something must have happened to make you miserable.'

'Not necessarily. You can just be miserable without reason.'

'That's endogenous depression. A business for the psychiatric adviser. I have sent some of our most eminent public servants to Sir Reginald. His waiting-room carpet in Wimpole Street has been trodden by many a Permanent Secretary. From there the route leads in plain vans to the Treasury clinic in the Mendip Hills.'

'You can't frighten me, Major Val. This isn't a police state. It only happens to look like one.'

'In the old days long ago, my dear, one didn't inform on one's colleagues. Certain oddities were understood. One pretended not to notice. The Plums had a distinguished commanding officer in the thirties who believed himself to be entirely made of glass. That was why he kept pouring liquid in at the top. But then look what happened. The other side exploited our human weakness, our gentlemanly tolerance. A small minority was systematically got at. Some people gave away secrets, betrayed the nation. Now we have to be serious.'

'To hell with you, Major Val,' said Fiona. 'If it comes to that, you look pretty awful in the mornings yourself.'

'That is brandy,' snapped Glossop. 'An acceptable form of self-mutilation. Please don't worry about my private life.'

'Nor you about mine.'

Jonathan felt afraid. He was too fond of the girl, that was his trouble. It was always the one who loved the most who was thereby rendered the weaker. It was a thought that had begun to obsess him. He didn't want to spoil everything by a false move. She might never go out with him again. But all day, as they sat agonizingly in the same office, she felt his compassionate attention, his silent longing.

'OK,' snapped Fiona, at the end of the afternoon. 'Let's go.'

'Go where?' asked Jonathan.

'To your place, of course. We can't go to mine.'

On the tube to Brixton, Fiona never spoke. Jonathan longed to ask her what the matter was. Obviously something had happened. Was it connected with Aunt Mary, the mysterious personage whom he had never met? Perhaps it was better not to know. In the flat in Tulse Hill, Fiona astonished Jonathan by behaving in a totally uncharacteristic way. She undressed first herself and then him, and then bundled them both into bed. It was what Jonathan had been seeking for weeks. But it worried him, happening in this way. There was something hysterical about the girl's mood. He knew that she didn't feel passionately about him. It was just that, through his agency, she sought the oblivion of the senses. She was a strange person.

At first Fiona responded to his stimulus. He felt that at least he was giving her pleasure. But when at last he entered her, her excitement seemed rapidly to fall rather than to mount. By the end, it seemed that he alone was enjoying it, that she was simply tolerating him out of politeness. Climax came almost sadly. He remembered some depressing phrases out of the manuals. Was she just a clitoris girl, doomed to eternal frigidity of the vagina? Would it always be like that, with promising foreplay and disappointing performance? If so, whose fault was that? He had always suspected that it would be difficult to make love for the first time to a girl you were actually in love with. There was such an inevitable gap between the glorious ideal and the sweating, messy reality. The whole thing seemed so much neater in the mind. It was easier if you were less involved, if the outcome mattered less. But this particular occasion, he reckoned, was more of a disillusionment than most. He wondered whether it would always be like that.

'Thank you,' he said politely, reaching for the tissues.

Fiona did not speak. Jonathan put his arms round her. They lay still. He heard the ticking of his alarm clock. The street outside was very noisy with evening traffic on the hill. He felt grimy and wanted a shower. Had the physical contact really brought them closer together? Or would it have been better to remain disembodied to each other, as they were before? The yearning was for total union with the other person. But you didn't achieve that just by entering their body. Jonathan suddenly felt afraid. It wasn't going to be all right between him and Fiona. You always, somehow, knew.

Then she started to sob.

'Poor old Squiffy,' said Sir Marcus Stewart-Stibbs. 'He was my first ambassador, you know. In Buenos Aires. He used to spend most of the day in the Jockey Club. He had a special nook in the bar. It was a way of keeping ear to ground.'

'By the time I knew him,' said Bernard Gilbert, 'he was usually sunk in one of those deep armchairs in the smoking-room at the Voyagers. He often needed a younger arm to pull him to his feet.'

'It will be hard on Jessamy,' said Sir Marcus. 'Living in Cornwall. And with nobody left to boss around.'

They had been attending, as so often, diplomatic obsequies. As Permanent Under-Secretary and Chief Clerk in the Foreign Office, it fell to them officially to represent the Service at memorial services for retired officers. Usually these were held in the Chapel of St Michael and St George in St Paul's Cathedral, the associated Order being a special preserve of those who serve the Crown overseas. Sir Marcus had come to know the place only too well. He was noted for the neat and cautious, yet kindly, panegyrics which he preached on these occasions, to the satisfaction of the suffering family. They were usually too upset to miss the slight whiff of evasion, of tales untold, of promise not entirely fulfilled.

And now, as they stood on the steps of the cathedral, dive-bombed by pigeons in the early September sunshine, they saw friends. Squiffy had known a lot of people. His own memorial service, thought Sir Marcus with melancholy satisfaction, would be even more distinguished. It was quality that counted, rather than mere quantity. The Royal Family would surely be represented. He had reached the top. Squiffy, or Sir Lancelot as the world knew him, had stopped one rung down. He had attained a KCMG, not a GCMG like Sir Marcus. But it did not seem to matter much in the end.

'I thought Jessamy bore up well,' said Bernard.

'That's the shock,' replied Sir Marcus. 'It's actually worse after six months. When the numbness wears off.'

He wondered how Felicity would take it. His own death. Sir Marcus always assumed that he would be the first to go. Actuarial records suggested that the first year after retirement was the most dangerous time. Some of the colleagues failed to recover from the shock of rejoining the general public and getting cut off from the supply of diplomatic booze. If you survived that, you might live another twenty years, like old Squiffy. With any luck, thought Sir Marcus, he himself would be joining the House of Lords before long. You usually got it, as Head of the Service, unless the prime minister did you down. It would be a pleasant place to totter to after lunch, in those declining years. Felicity could do those damned embassy parties on her own. That would be one of the delights of retirement. He would no longer have to be polite to foreigners.

But Felicity actually enjoyed charming people. She swam through her natural element of social life, just as a fish moves through water. Even now, on this melancholy occasion, she was busy fixing up an impromptu lunch party.

'Let's all go to the Savoy,' she said cheerfully. 'Bernard and Amaryllis too, of course. It's nice and near. Memorial services make me hungry. I always think the Savoy goes so well with St Paul's.'

Sir Marcus wondered whether Felicity would adjourn to the Savoy after his own memorial service. It was a macabre thought. But then it was hard enough to imagine the world going on at all in one's own absence. We were such intensely egotistical little beings.

'I don't feel like a big lunch,' said Sir Marcus. It seemed an unnecessary extravagance. Besides, he had an early afternoon meeting with the Secretary of State. You had to keep a clear head for that. He didn't care for meals that left you still feeling sober.

'I know you're upset about poor old Sir Lancelot,' said Felicity. 'But he *was* nearly eighty. And I never even knew him. You were a gay bachelor in BA.'

'I assume,' said Sir Marcus, 'that you are using the phraseology of those distant, innocent years.'

'I'd love to lunch at the Savoy,' interposed Amaryllis Gilbert. 'Bernard and I are making the best of London. Before we embark on the horrors of the Antipodes.'

Bernard frowned. It was an open secret that his wife was unhappy about their posting to Australia. She had told her numerous diplomatic intimates, in strict secrecy, how miserable it would be to go so far from Timothy and Camilla, both of whom badly needed the parental hand on the tiller. But there was no need to make this so clear in front of the Head of the Service, who must be considered primarily responsible for the repellent posting. It would not do, thought Bernard, to alienate Sir Marcus. His own knighthood had not yet been mentioned, though it surely could not be too far away. Extreme egalitarians, like the Australians, would not think much of a plain Mister. But Marcus could never be taken for granted. He was quite capable of the odd nasty surprise.

'You see, Marcus dear?' said Lady Stewart-Stibbs, with a triumphant giggle, 'Amaryllis is hungry too. She has come in all the way from Lewisham.'

'Blackheath,' said Bernard hastily.

Felicity, a geographical snob of the first water, always affected ignorance of topography south of the river and north of the park. She had never quite recovered, thought Bernard sourly, from queening it over the embassy in Paris and sleeping in Princess Pauline's state bed. Not everyone knew that her father had been a dentist in Herne Bay. It was a mistake to get above oneself in the Foreign Service. You danced indeed at glittering balls, under the chandeliers. But, at the end of the day, you left by the stage door. You forgot that at your peril.

'What about a spot of lunch?' asked Sir James Leyland, joining them. 'Charmian knows a little Italian place near Covent Garden.'

Really, thought Sir Marcus, those people are always in London. Admittedly, James had his excuse for coming over from Brussels for consultations. But now he usually seemed to have Charmian in tow, looking more than ever like a maypole in her severe frocks. Even her new sun-tan seemed to have come out in all the wrong places. She might have been the wife of a singularly unworldly don from north Oxford, rather than of a very senior diplomat with a mission to represent Britain abroad. The Belgians tended to have rather strange shapes themselves. But American fashion-writers could be merciless. Perhaps it would be as well if the Leylands did not get Washington after all. No doubt they kept coming home to remind the powers that be of their existence. But they had both developed into slightly repellent eggheads, longer on intellect than on charisma. It was a pity, thought Sir Marcus, that the senior colleagues so seldom seemed to look into the mirror.

'I would settle for Italian food,' said Felicity.

'I expect it will be a lot cheaper,' volunteered Amaryllis, rather unnecessarily.

'Charmian is quite upset about poor Squiffy,' said Sir James Leyland.

'He was so awfully nice to us in Madrid,' agreed Charmian. 'I was gawky and shy. Well, I suppose I still am. He once showed us all the tombs in the Escorial. We shall have to go once and stay with Jessamy.'

'It's miles beyond Bodmin,' pointed out Sir James. 'And they say she's become odd. Drinks mead for breakfast.'

'We all become odd,' said Sir Marcus.

'Yes, dear,' agreed Felicity with one of her silvery laughs. 'But some get odder than others.'

'While we are together,' said Sir James, 'what's the latest about Washington? Do I still have any chance?'

Sir Marcus almost hissed with suppressed fury. It was typical of James to raise this awkward topic on the steps of St Paul's Cathedral, at the start of the lunch-hour, just when it looked like beginning to rain. The man might have a first-rate intellect. But he had absolutely no sense of occasion.

'Yes,' chimed in Charmian. 'We should like to know.'

'Nothing firm yet,' murmured Sir Marcus. 'You must leave these things to me. There's no special hurry.'

It's all right for you, thought James Leyland. You've already got to the top of the greasy pole. But spare a thought please for us poor fellows, still struggling on the way up. Marcus was not a bad chap but, like so many who had already made it, he was temperamentally not averse to kicking away the ladder by which he had made his own ascent. It was one of the less attractive aspects of human nature. If he did take Belial, thought James, he would at least be at the summit of the academic ladder himself. And there would be no need to worry about Charmian's clothes. Surely she was wearing quite the wrong things for a memorial service for a distinguished public servant?

'That fellow Craxton seems to be on the rampage,' said Charmian, her train of thought only too apparent. 'He's invited us to his new wedding. I can't think why.'

'He's invited absolutely everybody,' explained Felicity helpfully.

'I can't think why they didn't take the Albert Hall. It's to be in the country, I hear. But we shall have to go, Marcus.'

'We have to go to lots of things,' said Sir Marcus. 'But that doesn't mean we like them. Take the French National Day. I was never in favour myself of the storming of the Bastille.'

'You're an old relic of the past,' accused Felicity.

'So was Squiffy,' said Sir Marcus. 'A hangover from the pre-war era. When people had money. The ruling few and all that.'

'There are still a ruling few,' said James. 'But they are different nowadays.'

'It was better then,' said Amaryllis. 'There wasn't Australia.'

'Nor the bloody Common Market,' pointed out James, with even greater emphasis.

Sir Marcus eyed both ambitious couples with distaste, masked by a smile which a casual observer might have misunderstood as kindly. It was sad to see intelligent people who seemed to think only of themselves. He decided firmly against treating them at the Savoy.

'Hello,' said Sir Dominic Trowbridge.

Sir Marcus did not expect to see the small, bald Head of the Security Service on this occasion.

'What are you doing here?' he asked.

'I've known Squiffy and Jessamy for ages,' said Sir Dominic. 'I was at school with one of their boys. He used to come to us sometimes for holidays.'

'How's the moon-pool?' asked Sir Marcus, lowering his voice.

'A great success.'

'I haven't seen the product.'

'You will, Marcus. You will. What about you?'

'We're having an economy drive in the office. Cracking down on people who have used their official telephones for private purposes.'

'Are there so many of them?'

'You'd be surprised, Dominic. I'm beginning to think nobody is absolutely straight.'

Sir Dominic Trowbridge could not help remembering the call he had made that morning to Sylvia in Devon – one of many. This time she had gone on a bit about the children's gymkhana. It had been hard to cut her off. Might this show up on the computer?

Perhaps he should have offered to pay. But one could hardly be too nit-picking. There just wasn't the time.

'It will be fascinating,' continued Sir Marcus, with an edge of menace, 'to see what turns up in the moon-pool. It was all your idea, you know. You dreamed up those deep laser probes. My theory is that we all have secrets.'

'We may all have secrets,' agreed Sir Dominic heavily. 'But that doesn't mean we are unfit for public service. That's the real point, isn't it?'

'That depends,' retorted Sir Marcus. 'Some would say that our great public servants need to be without flaw. At least, that's what the taxpayer expects. It may all be a myth. But one shatters these kindly myths at one's peril. The whole moon-pool concept could prove a great disaster.'

'Excuse me,' said Sir Dominic, a shade abruptly. 'Unlike you, I haven't brought an umbrella.'

'Women,' said Rupert Mills, 'are perfectly bloody. And I'm too damned poor to be able to get away from them. It's almost enough to make one think of taking a job.'

He had raised his voice and it echoed round the comfortable saloon bar of the Charge of the Light Brigade. But, on this occasion, Jonathan was too immersed in his personal problems to feel the usual embarrassment provoked by Rupert's penetrating tenor and braying laugh.

'It was awful,' said Jonathan. 'Afterwards, I mean. Her poor little face. Of course, this is strictly between the two of us.'

'I'll bet Fiona is telling that Aunt Mary of hers,' said Rupert. 'She sounds a dark horse.'

'I felt so bad,' Jonathan almost wailed.

'The more fool you,' countered Rupert robustly. 'Can't you see? You were being used.'

'It was the other way round.'

'No, it wasn't. You're too simple, Jonathan. Something happened to Fiona. We don't know what. Then she badly needed a shoulder to cry on. Yours was handy.'

'We did more than that. It wasn't just a shoulder.'

'All right. Perhaps she needed to experiment. To try it out. To see if it would work.'

'Well, it didn't. At least, not for her.'

'Then she knows better now. You can't be blamed.'

'It's still awkward. Seeing her in the office all the time. I've got them to send me out of town for a day or two.'

'Lucky old you. But you'll be missing the Craxton wedding. I thought that was the event of the year.'

'I can bear that. I'm not sure that Mrs Freeport really likes me.'

'Perhaps she scents a rival. Where are you going?'

'State secret, Rupert.'

'Nonsense. I heard you buying a ticket for Windermere.'

'Well, you'll be all right while I'm away. You've got Maureen back.'

'I'll say. That girl never left me alone, all the time she was supposed to be out of town. She kept calling me from Galway.'

'Galway?'

'That's what she said. But you can't trust anyone these days. We need a return to Victorian values.'

'Isn't that Professor Montrose trying to reach us?' asked Jonathan, with a certain distaste. 'He looks well oiled.'

'We keep him that way, when he's on duty. Like the Channel swimmers.'

'I don't feel strong enough for him.'

'He's just been to Hornsey for the firm. To see an old brewery, with walls crenellated like a castle. We're hoping to add a drawbridge.'

'He keeps talking about the same thing.'

'You're a good one, said Rupert affectionately. 'One day you'll join the human race.'

'Colonel Hugo?' Major Glossop had said to Jonathan. 'Of course I know him. One of the ripest of the old Plums. This is a most interesting lead.'

'Hugo who?'

'Hugo Wilderness of Kirkland Hall in Cumbria. It's the quiet end of Windermere.'

'Well, he seems to be an old friend of Craxton.'

'That's rather odd, isn't it?' said the Major. 'Craxton never said anything about him to me, when we met at the Club. One usually mentions one old Plum to another.'

'You don't always put these things together.'

'People like Craxton do. It's the way they get on.'

'Come to think of it,' said Jonathan, 'he didn't mention him to me, either. It was Martha who volunteered him.'

'I should like you to meet Colonel Hugo.'

'What's he like?'

'Oozes charm. Like so many of us Plums. Perfect gent. He's become quite a good landscape painter. Lakes in the mist, mountains in the snow.'

'Has he got a family?'

'Not really. A bit of a loner at heart. But with masses of friends. He was well liked by his personal staff. I'll drop him a line. Say you're having a few days in the Lakes and have a connection with the Regiment. It would be worth investigating his set-up. I expect it's mildly mysterious.'

'What do you mean?'

'You'll see.'

'I haven't got any leave days left.'

'This isn't leave. You're on expenses.'

'Thank you. I'll be glad to get out of this office for a bit.'

'So I would imagine. You seem to have reduced your immediately superior officer to a state of dull misery.'

'That wasn't just me,' protested Jonathan.

'Of course it wasn't just you. Nothing ever is. But you've been a link in the chain of causality. Now please go up to Cumbria and be a link with Colonel Hugo.'

'I feel a brute. This horrible snooping.'

'Just think of it in military terms. Synchronize your watches, gentlemen, for Operation Iscariot.'

But Jonathan felt fewer misgivings when he arrived at Kirkland Hall. As a northerner himself, he felt more at home here than in London. It was a perfect day of early autumn. The house was grey and undistinguished. But the garden, with its small row of cypresses pointing towards the lake, might have been in Italy. The tall, erect figure which met him on the verandah clearly belonged to a retired officer of the Plums.

'I was warned to expect you,' said Colonel Wilderness affably. 'Val Glossop says he knew your father. You must tell me all about it. Some time.'

125

Jonathan felt an instinctive feeling of relief. He guessed that this man would not probe too deeply, that he had rather soared above regimental detail in his retirement.

'We'll have tea first,' continued Colonel Hugo. 'I've finished my sketching for the day. The light's gone wrong again. And I'm afraid it's not warm enough to sit out.'

They established themselves in a comfortable drawing-room, bright with fine water-colours and old porcelain. The young man took the opportunity to survey Colonel Hugo more closely. First impressions had been correct about his upright, soldierly bearing. But his face was more sensitive than Major Valentine's. He belonged presumably to the artistic wing of the Regiment. His new profession as a landscape painter now became understandable. They were gifted people, these Plums.

The door opened and the tea things were brought in by a young man. Jonathan noticed that he was slight, with dark hair.

'This is Vince,' said Colonel Hugo. 'He runs this place. They sent him to me, when he left the Regiment.'

Vince grinned. He looked like the sort of person who was incapable of merely smiling. Jonathan noticed that he had a gap in his white front teeth.

'Jonathan is staying for dinner,' said the Colonel. 'You are, aren't you? I'm sure your friends will lend you for the evening. We can ring them, if you're worried. And Miss Wetherby will be back, too. She was hiking up some fell.'

Vince retired with another grin, this time delivered over his shoulder as he shut the door.

'He's a great help to me,' said Colonel Hugo. 'I'm hopelessly undomesticated, you know. There's a certain type of soldier who makes an excellent servant. Vince is one of nature's batmen.'

Colonel Hugo, Jonathan suspected, would always find people to help him. His charm was self-conscious but effortless.

'Sally Wetherby is an old friend,' continued Colonel Hugo. 'She's been staying here for some time. I'm afraid she's been going through a rough passage. One tries to help.'

It was a peaceful spot, thought Jonathan, just the place to recruit your strength after some searing experience. This man would be a kind and attractive host. There would be painting on the lawn, sailing, long walks on the wild hills. And a certain undefinable gentleness.

'Poor Sally,' continued the Colonel. 'This weekend will be particularly tough for her.'

'Why is that?' asked Jonathan politely.

'Her husband is getting married.'

'Her husband?'

'After a divorce, of course. You'd think he'd have the decency to do it quietly. But he's not that type.'

Jonathan sucked in his breath. The penny had dropped. And when the penny dropped for him, he found it hard not to make a slight noise.

'I think I know him,' he said. 'It's George Craxton, isn't it?'

The Colonel looked at him in surprise. His temples, Jonathan noticed, were a distinguished shade of grey.

'Yes,' said Colonel Hugo. 'Sally was Mrs Craxton. Now she prefers to use her maiden name. His is rather too well known for her liking.'

Jonathan explained how he had been lent by the Foreign Office to provide unofficial briefings for the former Cabinet Minister, in preparation for a future appointment. But he played down the amount of time he had been spending privately with Craxton, at least before the reappearance of Martha.

'Oh yes,' said the Colonel, as if this explained everything. 'He's going to Washington.'

'It's supposed to be a secret.'

'That's why he's marrying this Martha lady. Quite a character, isn't she, behind that refined exterior? She tends to cheat at croquet.'

'So I discovered.'

'I was at Sweetladies not long ago,' continued Colonel Hugo. 'George has behaved badly to poor Sally. But I've become a friend to them both and I want to keep it up. Even Martha has a certain macabre fascination. George has, at last, met his match.'

'Aren't you going to the wedding?' asked Jonathan.

'I was warmly invited. Poor old George needs a bit of support, as you probably discovered. For all his worldly grandeur, he's terribly vulnerable at heart. But I couldn't leave here just now. Sally also needs help. The damned wedding will be on all the front pages.

'It was Sally I knew first,' continued Colonel Hugo. 'Long ago. It sounds awfully feudal to say so, but her aunt used to help out at my uncle's place near Hexham. We've always been from the north, too. Then she met this George who was a young MP at the time. I thought he was horribly pushy. But they got married, and he became more assured, and I came to realize that he does have a certain quality. He's a monster but a sad monster. I used to think of them as Beauty and the Beast. Then it all collapsed. George soared into the political stratosphere. Sally couldn't follow him, didn't want to. She's always been a country girl at heart. Why am I telling you all this?'

'I don't know.'

'I should be more discreet. But you have a face that can be trusted. It's the kind of thing you learn in the army.'

Jonathan felt a small stiletto twisting in his heart.

'It was awkward when they broke up,' said Colonel Hugo. 'At least they made it awkward. Each chose me to confide in. Sally was always wanting to come and stay here. So was George. I had to keep them apart. But I wanted to help and I did genuinely see both sides.'

'So George came here a lot? When he was in the Cabinet?'

'Oh yes. He always had the turret bedroom, with its view of the lake. It became quite a bore. We had detectives almost permanently camped in the boat-house. And young Vince was having to take him whiskies and soda at all hours of the day and night.'

Jonathan remembered that grin. He could imagine Vince's discreet tap on the door in the turret.

'I think we helped,' continued the Colonel. 'Poor George was so bloody lonely. And it didn't help to hold high office at the time. The work held his mind but he couldn't talk to many people. I was almost glad when Martha came along. She engulfed him, like a moderately strong tidal wave. One day, I'm afraid, he'll be thrown back on the shore. But meanwhile, she takes the strain.'

'It's sad for the first Mrs Craxton.'

'And a relief too, I suppose. Marriage must be a dreadful trap, when it doesn't work. Sometimes suicide could seem less painful than divorce. Quicker, at least.'

Jonathan felt himself warming towards this amiable soldier turned painter. This man had the knack of reaching towards the

128

heart of things. People would confide in him, and he would not be shocked. Jonathan wondered why the expansive Craxton had never mentioned him. Perhaps he had wanted to keep Kirkland Hall almost as a secret get-away, where at last he could be truly himself. Jonathan was glad he had come. It helped to explain something undefined. He did not quite know what.

Between tea and drinks, Jonathan was left, firmly but politely, to himself. He wandered out on to the lawn and down to the boat-house where once the Special Branch had held their vigil. Britain was no longer a safe country for its rulers. Suddenly Jonathan saw a dark head among the azalea bushes. Vince was idly skimming stones into the lake.

'You from the Foreign Office?' asked Vince.

'Yes.'

'George Craxton's going to work for you, isn't he?'

'Is he?'

'You needn't be careful with me. Everybody here knows. I know Craxton, too.'

'So I heard.'

Vince gave the grin.

'It's bloody boring here,' he said.

'It's beautiful,' remonstrated Jonathan.

'You can't live on beauty. At least, not alone. I have to come to London sometimes.'

'I suppose so.'

'I've got friends there,' said Vince darkly. 'You get to know all types, when you live in a barracks. I might look you up some time.'

'Oh yes, do,' replied Jonathan politely. He doubted whether Vince would be an asset to his circle. But he didn't want to deliver a snub. After all, he himself was only from Otley. The grass-roots extended a long way.

Back in the drawing-room, with shadows falling on the hills and the water eternally lapping, Vince served drinks demurely in a white coat. It was an old-fashioned style. The Colonel might still have been commanding on the Rhine.

'I'm Sally Wetherby,' said a slim woman, not young. 'I know who you are. I hear you know George.'

'Yes.'

'Well, now you know me. Does that seem odd?'

'Not really.'

'Does he ever talk about me?'

'Oh no. Not at all.'

'I'm glad to hear that. It's better that way.'

'I suppose so.'

'Breaking up a marriage can be rather like abandoning a faith. You can't just go quietly. You feel a silly urge to justify, to explain. Though no one else is all that interested.'

'I understand. At least, I hope so.'

'Do you understand? You haven't had time to go through much. I don't mean to be rude. But you see, I've had to learn to cope with a completely new situation. I feel like the monk who leaves his monastery. The place must, by definition, be no good. Otherwise I'd still be inside, with my vocation intact.'

'I can't think of George Craxton as a monastery.'

'He's a strange man. I don't know how well you know him. All that talent and effort, simply a huge attempt to be someone else.'

'Else than what?'

'What he was meant to be.'

Jonathan longed to ask this first Mrs Craxton about her marriage. But that would have been insufferable presumption. Although she was being remarkably frank, he had only just met the woman. Even the laser-beam operatives of the moon-pool, secure in their deep cover, could not go so far. In any case, he could see, without asking, some of the truth. There was a loneliness in those grey eyes, and it had been there for a long time. It must be hell to love a man like Craxton, who was an uncomfortable cross between a great booby and an empty shell. Love, in any case, was always hell, as Jonathan knew to his cost. You always loved too much or else not enough. You either bled silently or got nagged. There seemed to be no half way.

'What are we meant to be?' asked Jonathan vaguely. 'Often we don't know ourselves.'

'People like George have a very clear idea of what, at least, they intend to be. Rich and famous, powerful and happy. They're the trees who push themselves up to the top of the forest and take all the light and air. It's hard on the others.'

It was a subject on which Sally clearly had a lot to say. She might be discreet about her marriage but she wasn't going to pull her punches when it came to George. He was only half listening because by now he was aware that Hugo was telephoning in the next room. Jonathan had noticed him closing the door rather carefully and, self-conscious as ever, the wild notion had suddenly occurred to him that Hugo was discreetly talking to Craxton. Could it be that his own authenticity was being checked? Surely there was no need for that? Major Glossop had already provided an introduction. Was Colonel Hugo wanting to be sure how much, if anything, he, Jonathan, knew? If so, part of the truth might have been deliberately withheld from him. But why? More than ever, he felt he was on some trail.

'Oh, there you are,' said their host, entering cheerfully. 'I'm glad you two have got to know each other. Did you have a good walk, Sally?'

'Up Brown Scar. And then back by the farm.'

'That's miles. This is a real country lass, Jonathan.'

'George always hated walking,' said Sally. 'Except for golf. I don't know what it is about golf.'

'Young Vince is giving us Morecambe Bay sole this evening,' said Colonel Hugo, almost too promptly. 'And some of my better Chablis. I've sold another picture.'

'Dear Hugo,' said Sally. 'It's better than the parade ground.'

'I was never keen on the parade ground. Or the mechanical things. I just liked the people.'

After dinner, Vince was instructed to drive Jonathan back to Windermere.

'Thanks a lot,' said Jonathan, as he got out.

'A pleasure, I'm sure,' replied Vince with his wolfish grin. 'I might look you up, when I'm in London.'

'You haven't got my address.'

'I could find out. I'm good at finding things out. I expect you are, too.'

Was this some awful confession of complicity? Jonathan felt quite certain on one point. He hoped never to see Vince again.

'Who is that distinguished-looking woman over there?' asked Charmian Leyland. 'In that very expensive dress and impressive pearls.'

'That is the bride,' replied Sir James dryly. 'Martha Freeport.'

131

'The woman who wants to take my place in Washington,' commented Charmian waspishly. 'I can't see what she's got that I haven't.'

'A bigger ego,' said her husband. 'And a lot more money.'

'I think one needs a British wife,' said Charmian, 'to preside over the embassy in Washington, of all places. She doesn't look quite right to me.'

'Don't underrate Martha,' warned Sir James. 'She has some solid assets besides those oodles of loot. A shrewd political brain, beneath all that expensive hairdressing, and a lot of contacts. Craxton knows what he is doing.'

'I wonder if she will be a real companion to him,' mused Charmian. 'On the intellectual plane.'

'You don't need an intellectual companion, when you're ambassador to the United States,' said Sir James. 'At night you just flake out.'

'Isn't all this amazing?' said Tess, temporarily abandoning her role of Maureen. 'And such a shame when the house is so lovely. Pevsner raves about it, you know.'

They were standing, with a thousand other people, under a huge marquee on the lawn at Sweetladies. A fashionable decorator brought over from New York had transformed it into something that might have been the Desert Inn at Las Vegas. It would have been a surprise to Inigo Jones, who had created classical porticos, now concealed, on this very spot.

'Americans *are* peculiar, aren't they?' said Tess.

'Yes,' agreed Sir James. 'And getting steadily more so.'

It was, after all, a full generation span since he had first gone to Washington, as an eager young man who needed to learn about high-balls. That amounted to one-seventh of the total history of the Republic since independence. No wonder there had been changes. In his day, the American Government had been in the hands of East Coast lawyers and bankers mostly with old money from the Ivy League colleges. They had on the whole been, in old-fashioned terms, ladies and gentlemen. They tended to spend their holidays in England and to stay at the Cavendish before it was rebuilt. Now the whole balance of American power had shifted. California was at least as important as New England, perhaps more so; Texas easily eclipsed Virginia and Maryland. The new people were much brasher, more confident, more disposed to flaunt their money and their power. James Leyland did not much like the change. He had preferred the Washington of the fifties, with its simpler ways and perhaps more idealistic approach to world affairs. But you had to live with realities. In his day, a woman like Martha, reeking of Texan oil wealth, might not, for all her superfical sophistication, have seemed credible as British Ambassadress in Washington. Now, he was not at all sure. Many British politicians nowadays liked to ape American ways and would prefer Martha's extrovert and worldly manner to Charmian's academic reticence. James Leyland felt depressed by the thought. The occasion had hardly been worth making yet another trip from Brussels. People were beginning to complain now that he was never there.

'This is Professor Harold Montrose,' said Tess. 'I smuggled him in with me. He adores parties.'

Portly and flushed with one of the cheaper brands of champagne, one of the few male guests not wearing morning dress, the Professor extended a sweaty and inadequately washed palm.

'I've heard about you,' he said warmly. 'How nice you could get over.'

'Oh, I come quite a lot,' said Charmian.

'Glad to get away from the natives, I suppose?'

'They're nice but greedy,' said Charmian.

'Too many potatoes and too much illegal whisky, I suppose,' said Montrose. 'Famine diet.'

'Actually, they prefer steak and claret.'

'I imagine you came in the boat. For economy, I mean. But the Irish Sea can be rough.'

'Irish Sea?' ejaculated Charmian. 'It's the English Channel between here and Ostend. This man is drunk,' she whispered to her daughter. 'Drunker than the others, I mean.'

'I'd like to come and stay with you some time,' said the Professor. 'I've heard so much about your cottage in Connemara.'

'Actually we live in Brussels.'

'Maureen must have confused me. I do get confused these days. The wits are wandering. In strange seas of thought alone.'

'Our daughter,' countered Charmian coldly, 'is called Tess. Perhaps she might accompany you to the refreshment tent for a cooling glass of cold lemonade.'

She turned to Tess who seemed uncharacteristically occupied in taking photographs of them all.

'Are you, by any chance, *the* Professor Montrose?' asked Sir James. 'The one who wrote those fine articles about the proposal to pull down St Martin's in the Fields.'

'The same,' replied Montrose with a flamboyantly low bow. 'A poor thing, but mine own.'

'I do so agree with you,' said Sir James. 'It's monstrous what the developers have done to London. And to other British cities, too. It's people like you who have forced them to call a halt.'

'I'm glad you are on our side,' said the Professor. 'Perhaps I could interest you in buying a quaint property for your retirement years. Something with scenic charisma, as the new Mrs Craxton might say. A High Anglican Church perhaps, in Upper Norwood, complete with incense-dispensing equipment and baroque confessionals? It's a small gem of the late-Victorian renaissance.'

'No, thank you,' replied Sir James. 'We already have our little place at Iffley.'

'You look tired, Harold,' said Tess. 'I should like to lay you out quite quietly on the grass, somewhere well away from the others.'

'A splendid idea, my darling Maureen. It's so noisy here. Rather too Miltonic for me. What's his nice phrase? The sons of Belial, high-flown with insolence and wine.'

'My brother was at Belial,' interposed Sir James rather coldly. He would not be sorry to get Charmian installed in the Master's Lodge at Belial, the Oxford College which had sharpened many a fine intellect. She could reorganize those dowdy chintzes. It would give her something to do, if Washington really did fall through.

'Lead me away, Maureen,' said Montrose. 'Take my withered arms, guide my tottering feet. Methinks, I am a prophet, new inspired. Or old blind Oedipus. You're a dear girl.'

'A most peculiar friend for Tess,' said Charmian in one of her stage whispers.

'Tess is odd,' said Sir James. 'You've got to face facts. I can't think where she got it from.'

'You here again, James?' asked Sir Marcus Stewart-Stibbs, in a mildly disapproving tone.

'We couldn't resist it,' explained Charmian. 'A chance to see the opposition in full fig.'

134

'Isn't it all splendidly flamboyant?' said Felicity Stewart-Stibbs. 'I do so love people who go the whole hog.'

'Like the Gadarene swine,' said her husband. 'They went right over the cliff.'

'It's so brash, so confident,' enthused Felicity. 'So different from our poor, battered old England.'

'I'm a European,' said Sir James. 'Though that doesn't mean,' he added hastily, 'that I want to stay on in Brussels. I shall be the only diplomat to leave that city thinner than when I arrived.'

'That's all your nervous energy,' opined Charmian. 'It keeps you skinny.'

'Who are these extraordinary people?' asked Sir Marcus peevishly. 'I've never seen them before. That dark woman, over there, seems to be wearing some kind of nightie.'

'Conspicuous consumption,' murmured Sir James. 'Not at all good for the social fabric.'

'You've got to hand it to Martha,' said Felicity. 'She does know how to organize a wedding reception.'

'She's had practice,' said Charmian nastily. 'I believe she has had more than one husband already.'

'There's no point in just sneering at that type of American,' said Sir Marcus. 'They represent a Super-Power now. We have to find ways to influence them.'

'And people to do so,' said Charmian. 'My James would be wonderful. The embassy in Washington needs a typically English couple. The Craxtons are certainly not that.'

Nor, thought Sir Marcus, were the Leylands with their donnish ways. The Craxtons were all image, the Leylands all brains. Were there no straightforward candidates available? People at the top, unfortunately, were so often mildly weird. That was how they had come to stand out from the rest, to be heard above the crowd. It did not make personnel selection easy.

The bridegroom, looking rather pink and slightly flustered, rushed up to their group.

'Is my carnation all right?' he asked.

'Not so much a carnation,' said Charmian. 'More like a small shrubbery. Burnham Wood coming to Dunsinane.'

'Have any of you seen the Prime Minister?' continued George Craxton. 'They promised to try to look in.'

'Not around here,' replied Sir Marcus. 'I think we should have noticed. These days the Prime Minister hardly travels alone.'

'The security has to be tight,' agreed Craxton. 'And especially today. After what happened in London this morning. Perhaps that's why the Number Ten party hasn't arrived. I must tell Martha. She was beginning to wonder.'

'What did happen?' asked Felicity. 'Nobody tells me anything. It was just the same in Paris.'

'Part of that large government block in Knightsbridge was blown up in the small hours,' said Sir Marcus.

'Oh, good,' said Charmian. 'I hope the top has gone. It spoiled the view from all over the park. Modern architects have no manners.'

'That may be true,' said her husband cautiously. 'But it doesn't justify violence. People might have been killed.'

'Fortunately the caretakers got out,' said Sir Marcus. 'They were warned in time by telephone. There's some talk of an Irish accent.'

'Violence achieves nothing, I'm afraid,' said George Craxton sententiously.

'Oh yes, it does,' snapped Charmian. 'History suggests that it often works quite well. On people who won't listen to argument. We might still be ruling large tracts of our empire, if we hadn't got so scared of the subject races.'

'I shall be sorry if the PM doesn't make it,' said Craxton. 'This is such a lovely place to relax.'

As if in mockery of his words, the formidable and restless bride swung into sight. Her face was wreathed in a seraphic smile appropriate to the occasion but, as she caught sight of her groom, the corners of her mouth turned rather purposefully down.

'Where's that archbishop, honey?' she whispered. 'You said there would be an archbishop. I thought I caught a glimpse of a man in a robe.'

'That would be the Apostolic Pro-Nuncio,' said Craxton. 'Last seen in the refreshment tent.'

'Aren't you Sir Marcus Hewart-Hibbs?' asked Martha.

'Stewart-Stibbs,' said Marcus.

'George told me about you. You and I need a cosy word. I have to have the whole of the Washington Embassy re-done.'

'Do you?' asked Sir Marcus, blinking. 'That would cost a lot of money.'

'Then you'd better start saving,' said Martha calmly, with a disarming smile. 'I warn you, dear Sir Marcus, I'm not taking no for an answer. It's just not a word that figures in my vocabulary.'

'When I was last in Washington,' demurred Sir Marcus, 'the residence looked quite nice.'

'Nice,' echoed Martha, tight-lipped. 'Yes, that's just about the word. Those soft, pansy colours in the ballroom. But I don't have my houses nice. They hum and boil and fizz. Something for people to talk about. Orange walls with red tigers painted all over them. That's what we had in Dallas. Who is that unusual-looking woman over there?'

'That is my wife,' replied Sir Marcus coldly.

'No, I mean the one she's talking to. The tall, angular one. As thin as a beanpole.'

'That is Lady Leyland. A very old and dear friend of ours.'

'I hear she wants my job,' snapped Martha. 'Poor thing, she doesn't look up to it. More suitable for some hick college in the boondocks. Washington needs style these days. Brio, panache, charisma. Sex appeal, if you like.'

Sir Marcus sighed. He had hoped that the moon-pool operation would quietly sort things out in private. Now the rivalry seemed to be out in the open. It might be simplest just to let the awful Craxtons have their way. Then the file could be closed, and he himself might get a straight run before dignified and profitable retirement. But Bernard Gilbert would then tell the Service that he had ratted. Not for the first time, the Permanent Under-Secretary felt himself trapped between the upper and the nether millstone. It was not an entirely comfortable posture for a senior diplomatist.

'Charge your glasses,' said Craxton. 'I'm going to say a few words.'

'They can move on now to the Spanish champagne-type, Pepe,' Martha whispered to the Filipino butler temporarily imported from New York, an efficient person of diminutive stature with wary eyes. 'It doesn't cost such a bomb. This is the marriage feast at Cana in reverse. The booze keeps getting worse. But, by now, we're all sozzled.'

'Unaccustomed as I am to public speaking,' Craxton boomed

into the public address system. There was a roar of appreciative laughter at this traditional opening by a professional politician.

'I hope there are no bombs around here,' murmured Sir Marcus.

'It looks to me,' said Sir James Leyland, 'as if Craxton had plenty of strong-armed men about. He's just the type. Some of the American guests are dripping with jewellery.'

'I'm glad Myron came,' said Martha. 'He's a deep bore man.'

'I can well believe it,' said Sir Marcus.

'Oil, you know. The best part of Oklahoma.'

'I looked everywhere for the archbishop,' said Pepe. 'I think he may have sneaked away.'

'That's too bad,' said Martha. 'I was promised Royals, too. Where are all the Royals?'

'The Royals stood you up,' agreed Pepe.

'I don't see the point of having Royals at all,' wailed Martha, 'if they don't come to a big shindig like this. I thought my George was the tops over here. He kept telling me so.'

'So wonderful of you dear people all to come,' Craxton's unctuous voice was wafted, hideously amplified, through the large marquee.

'Who are all these dreadful, middle-class people?' asked Martha severely. 'I can't see many major political personalities. Except, of course, my husband and I.'

'A special programme of entertainments and diversions,' Craxton's voice came over, loud and clear. 'To mark the transatlantic nature of the occasion. English country dancing by the lake.'

'I don't even see Hank and his team from outer space.'

'Excuse me, madam,' said Pepe softly. 'I hear the telephone. It could be that call you expected from the Vice-President.'

'At first I thought it was funny here,' said Charmian. 'Now I don't.'

'We could all have dinner,' suggested Felicity, 'at that place near Chelmsford. It's in the *Good Food Guide*. I feel the need for something thoroughly English.'

'A West Virginian square dancing team will perform in the Long Gallery,' continued Craxton. 'And there's a country music disco in the Stables. Let joy be unconfined.'

'Pardon my intervention, sir,' said Pepe politely. 'But you're wanted on the telephone.'

138

'I'm too busy to take a call, Pepe. Unless it's Downing Street or the White House. Or someone big in the media.'

'It's a person called Vince.'

'Vince?'

'He said to say he just wants to congratulate you. He's calling long-distance from the north.'

'I don't know anyone named Vince,' said George Craxton.

'Dominic Trowbridge seems to have lost his cool,' said Major Glossop. 'He keeps sending me memos. Operation Calpurnia, he calls it.'

'What on earth for?' asked Fiona.

'Caesar's wife,' explained Jonathan. 'She had to be above suspicion.'

'I'm not educated,' snapped Fiona.

'Someone has given Trowbridge the fright of his life,' said the Major. 'I hope he's not going bonkers. It wouldn't do at all for the Head of the Security Service. He's got it into his head that there might be a scandal in the moon-pool itself. Then we should all look perfect fools. More than usual, I mean.'

'What's his special fear?' asked Jonathan.

'He keeps emphasizing that official telephones mustn't be used for private purposes. I don't know where he got that one from.'

'Fiona keeps dialling Tasmania,' said Jonathan.

'Well, please stop, darling. I read your report, Jonathan. On your visit to Colonel Hugo. Very interesting. I've passed some of it on. When are you seeing Craxton next?'

'I don't know. He's down at Sweetladies on honeymoon.'

'They could have gone anywhere in the world,' pointed out Fiona. 'But they stayed at home. Isn't that cosy?'

'It's an alarming idea,' said Jonathan. 'Connubial bliss with Martha. That could be tiring. I hope he takes care.'

'Well, take care of yourself,' said the Major. 'Bangalore Mansions could be the next target. So could almost anywhere.'

'Yes, there was another bombing last night,' said Fiona. 'They got that big government building at the Elephant and Castle.'

'It looks as if they're going for government offices,' said the Major. 'At least both have been so far.'

'It would be a pity to blow up Bangalore Mansions,' said Fiona.

'Even if we weren't inside. It's quite pretty, in a weird, Edwardian way. A sort of rose-red city, half as old as time.'

'That's not very relevant from the standpoint of security,' said the Major.

'It could be,' said Jonathan. 'This is much more important for the Security Service than checking abuses in the use of official telephones. What you have to do is to work out the common denominator between the two buildings already bombed. That will indicate where the next attack might occur. It may have nothing at all to do with their being government property.'

'An interesting theory,' commented Major Glossop. 'Jonathan has raised our intellectual standards here.'

'Oh yes,' agreed Fiona sarcastically. 'We were little nobodies until he arrived.'

After that, Jonathan felt he simply had to have it out with her. He closed the door carefully, when they returned to their own office.

'I'm sorry,' he said.

'About what?'

'The other night.'

'You have nothing to apologize for, Jonathan.'

'I'm sorry that it didn't work out right for you.'

'That was my bad luck, not your fault.'

'I felt I had been selfish.'

'Aren't we all? But it was I who used you in the first place. I was upset. Don't bother about the reason. I turned to you, hoping it would help to anaesthetize the pain. Well, it didn't. I shouldn't have treated you like a pad of chloroform. You deserve better than that.'

'I still love you, Fiona.'

'I'm sorry about that. It's hard on you. Would you like to move out of here? Or I could?'

'No. Please. I'd rather spend the working days together.'

'I'm glad. I want that too. You make a good friend. But you mustn't think too much about me, Jonathan dear. I'm not worth it.'

'Yes, you are.'

'I'll never be any good to you. And I don't want to hurt you any more. We'll have to cool it somehow. Tune our friendship down a few notches. It can be done, you know. With affection on both sides.'

'You sound awfully wise,' said Jonathan. 'And rather sad.'

'I'm not good for you,' said Fiona. 'I'm not good for anyone.'

'You be careful of that young woman,' said Rupert, when Jonathan reported to him later in the Charge of the Light Brigade. 'She sounds like *La Belle Dame Sans Merci*, as I have warned you before. You'll end up all alone, on the bare hillside.'

'And you,' snapped Jonathan, 'had better be careful too.'

'Careful of whom?'

'That old Professor Montrose.'

'What's wrong with him?'

'I'm not sure that he's as permanently pickled in alcohol as he would like us to believe.'

'Professor Montrose,' said Rupert, 'has been mixing in the highest society, while you were away climbing fells. My lovely friend escorted him to the fashionable Craxton wedding.'

'What on earth for?'

'She had a motive. I don't know what. That girl has a motive for everything.'

'She seems so fey, so out of this world.'

'That's her camouflage. It's the opposite of yours.'

'What's mine?' asked Jonathan.

'To pretend that you're a worldling. When actually you're as innocent as a lamb. That's why everyone tells you so much. I expect it makes you a good diplomat.'

'I'm sorry to have to call you in,' said Bernard Gilbert to Jonathan. 'I'm not keen on rubbing it in to the Security Service that you and I have this direct link.'

'I understand.'

'But we have to make absolutely sure that nothing is being concealed from the Foreign Office. It's too important this time.'

'Why should that happen?' asked Jonathan.

'You never know. The security boys have a long-standing reputation for playing the cards close to their chest. Given half a chance, they like to go straight to Number Ten. We don't want that.'

'I haven't any evidence of that.'

'Not yet. But I don't trust anyone, Jonathan. Never have. Believe me, it's the safest way.'

Jonathan guessed that the older man was telling the truth. For all his friendly twinkle, the eyes, deep down, were disconcertingly cold. This would never be a person to confide in.

'The stakes are high,' continued the Chief Clerk. 'I'm under pressure. An announcement has to be made. We've got to wrap up this moon-pool investigation quickly.'

'I only wish we could. I've never liked it. It goes against the grain. The trouble is I haven't found out anything at all. Or, at least, not relevant.'

'Oh yes, you have, Jonathan. I've been reading all your reports. You have unearthed some fascinating material.'

'It's not fascinating to me.'

'That's because you're not reading the signs aright. It takes a trained eye. And a highly suspicious mind.'

'I feel I'm still fooling around, waiting for the hounds to pick up the scent.'

'That's not true,' said Bernard softly, playing with his expensive watch. 'Not true at all. Do you know what you are actually doing?'

'No?'

'Closing in for the kill.'

'Yes, sir,' said Pepe. 'Can I do something for you?'

Vince had decided to approach Sweetladies by the huge Jacobean front portal. It was an act of nerve. But he felt good in his best clothes: blue blazer, dark flannels, white shirt. Obviously not a layabout.

'I've come to see George.'

'George?' Pepe's voice rose to a slight squeak.

'George Craxton.'

'I don't think Mr Craxton can see you. He rests in the afternoon these days.'

'I'll bet.'

'Are you that Mr Vince, sir? The one who rang during the wedding?'

'Yes, I'm Vince. The only one I know.'

'He won't have anything to do with you. He says he doesn't know you.'

'Tell him I'm here, please. In the flesh.'

'If you insist,' said Pepe dubiously. 'Just wait there, please.'

Vince heard him using an internal telephone. Then the small major-domo returned.

'Mr Craxton doesn't know you,' he said. 'He won't see you.'

Vince shrugged and turned away, with what dignity he could muster. He was shaking with suppressed rage. In the train to London, he kept muttering to himself. People watched in surprise but they were careful not to catch his glance. They had read of such things.

In London, Vince took the Underground to Brixton. From there, he made his way to Jonathan's flat in Tulse Hill and rang the bell.

'You?' said Jonathan.

'Yes, it's me,' said Vince, giving his usual grin which completely concealed his true feelings. 'I said I'd come and see you. I always keep my word.'

'How did you find the address?'

'Easy. Rang the Foreign Office. Asked for Enquiries. Very helpful little lady there. May I come in?'

'Of course.'

'You're making some kind of an investigation, aren't you? Undercover.'

'What makes you think that?'

'I'm sharp. You have to be, in the life I've led. I notice the little things.'

'And what did you notice about me?'

'You gave yourself away, Jonathan.'

'How?'

'About the old Plums.'

'We didn't talk about the old Plums.'

'That was the point. It wasn't natural. Here were you, whooping it up with a former commanding officer and your father only a corporal. Colonel Hugo's bored stiff with the whole thing, but you weren't to know that. You should have produced some spicy regimental anecdotes. Damn it, your father must have told you something. If you was on the level. So I know you're not.'

143

I must remain calm, thought Jonathan. I can't afford to alienate this dangerous person.

'Have a beer.'

'Thanks. I don't expect you've got whisky?'

'And what do you think I'm investigating?'

'Not what. Who. I figured it out. It couldn't be dishy old Colonel Hugo. He wouldn't hurt a fly. Retired a bit early because he didn't like the noise. And Sally Craxton's dead dreary. Nobody's interested in her. Never were.'

'So you think I came to find out about George Craxton?'

'You sure did. That's what makes you so interesting. At least to me.'

'You want to tell me something about Craxton.'

'I certainly do.'

'Is this some malicious gossip? Do you dislike the man?'

'Oh no,' said Vince, assuming a pious expression. 'It's nothing personal. Just that I feel I have this duty to the nation. I'm patriotic, see. The public has a right to know.'

'You know Craxton well?'

'I did. He doesn't come to us any more. Not now that this American cow has taken him over. I've seen her picture. But we saw a lot of him at Kirkland Hall when he was so lonely. After Sally broke it up.'

'*She* broke it up?' Jonathan had always assumed that it must have been the other way round.

'Oh yes. She knew it was all no good. So we had to look after him. Between the women.'

'I understand.'

'Do you? Look, would you like me to stop.'

'Oh no,' said Jonathan. 'I'd like you to go on.'

'But this is delightful,' said Charmian Leyland. 'So extremely ethnic.'

She must not be patronizing. It would be a mistake to enthuse too much. But the Charge of the Light Brigade *was* rather a quaint old place, with its engravings of military scenes and its antique helmets. Lady Leyland had been glad to be invited there by Tess. It was a nice way of winding up one of her shopping days in London. And it was unusual for the girl to make overtures of this sort, except when she had some specific object in mind. Charmian was pleased. Tess was a troublesome daughter but she was the only one they had.

'You remember Harold?' said the girl. 'You met him at that ridiculous wedding.'

'Yes, of course,' agreed Charmian. 'How do you do, Professor Montrose?'

It was disappointing that they had to bother with this rather bibulous old man. Charmian had hoped for a nice little chat with her daughter, mother and repentant child pouring out their hearts. She had half made up her mind to tell Tess how disappointed her father was about the Washington appointment. It made children more compassionate if they realized, before it was too late, that their parents had their own cause for suffering. It was a mistake to remain too uniformly stoical. People took your pose at its face value and denied you sympathy. Children had to realize some time that you were not just a figure of confident authority, that at heart you were weak and vulnerable like them.

'Enchanted to see you again, dear lady,' said the Professor with a courtly bow, which Charmian considered a bit exaggerated. Politeness was one thing, burlesque another.

'You wouldn't be after a quaint property by any chance?' continued Montrose. 'A disused pumping-station on the Hackney Marshes, perhaps? No troublesome neighbours.'

'You have asked us that before,' replied Charmian rather coldly. 'My husband and I are not interested in owning anything more. Possessions can be such a tie. And you can't take them on with you.'

'On?'

'Into the unknown,' replied Charmian bleakly.

'This is Jonathan Fieldhouse,' said Tess.

'We too have met before,' said Charmian. 'At Glyndebourne. 'You're the boy who kept addressing Tess as Maureen. I thought it so strange.'

At least this young man was properly dressed. He looked as if he did a serious job in the Foreign Office. The same could hardly be said of the shambling person with unkempt hair and ragged jeans who now approached them.

'This is Rupert,' said Tess. 'My boy-friend.'

'How do you do, Lady Leyland?' said Rupert politely.

'Rupert?' exclaimed Charmian. 'I thought you were called Rory.'

'I don't think that names matter much,' said Rupert. 'Or clothes. It's the person underneath.'

'You'll be telling me next,' said Charmian severely, 'that you don't come from Ireland and your parents aren't tinkers.'

'It's you that comes from Ireland,' said the Professor. 'You have a horrible little hovel on the Connemara coast.'

'What nonsense,' commented Charmian severely. 'Tess has been fooling us all.'

'It's the creative imagination, Mother,' explained Tess. 'A great gift and a great snare.'

'You're a little liar,' snapped Charmian.

'A romancer, dear lady,' pleaded Montrose. 'So were the poets. Bards of passion and of mirth.'

'Well, young man,' enquired Charmian firmly. 'What is your name and where do you really come from?'

'I'm Rupert Mills. We live near Lechlade.'

'I know,' said Charmian triumphantly. 'Your mother is called Molly and she was a Fairfax-Thompson.'

'So she says.'

'We were at St Paul's together,' said Charmian. 'In the early years of the century. Really, Tess, this is too bad of you. You've been causing your father and me a lot of quite unnecessary worry. You led us to believe that you were going around with some Irish layabout. Whereas he comes from a perfectly respectable family and his mother is even an old schoolfriend. She was rather good at the cello, I seem to remember.'

'Life is full of surprises,' murmured Tess defensively.

'I'm still a layabout,' said Rupert.

'Yes, well you are rather oddly got up,' said Charmian. 'What makes you appear like that?'

'It comes naturally,' explained Rupert. 'It's the way I have developed.'

'Someone ought to spruce you up,' said Charmian. 'I don't know what your mother must think. You don't look at all like the son of Molly Fairfax-Thompson.'

'That is my aim,' said Rupert.

'You'll never get a job,' said Charmian. 'Not dressed like that.'

'I don't want a job,' replied Rupert. 'I'm in the quaint property business. It's going to go like a bomb. People are longing for a return to the picturesque. Harold and I are scouting all over London.'

'What on earth are you doing, Tess?' asked her mother.

'Just taking a few flash shots,' explained Tess. 'You make such a charming group. A sort of conversazione.'

'It's not like you,' grumbled Charmian. 'You never bothered about photography before. We gave you a camera once for your birthday, and you never used it.'

'Children are perverse,' said Tess.

'I'll say,' her mother agreed. 'Talking about property. It seems to be being destroyed in London at quite a rate. There was another bomb early this morning. That large block overlooking St Paul's Cathedral.'

'Again a warning,' said Jonathan, 'and no one hurt.'

'That makes three, I think,' said Montrose. 'This was the first to be a commercial property.'

'So they are not all government buildings,' commented Jonathan. 'I thought there might be some other criterion. It's not a random selection.'

'All the buildings destroyed,' said Charmian, 'were extremely ugly. Horrible, arrogant examples of modern architecture. I'm glad they are gone. Whoever blew them up has done the nation a good turn. I take my hat off to them.'

'Be careful, Mother. That's seditious talk. You're supposed to be a pillar of the Establishment.'

'Not when I'm off duty, dear. What's that you are fumbling with, Tess?'

'Just my holdall. I have to fumble with something. It's because I was taken off thumb-sucking too young.'

'Nonsense, dear. You were sensibly brought up.'

'That was the trouble.'

Charmian sighed. The girl didn't entirely mean it as a joke. Perhaps she really had missed out a bit, in the things that mattered. James had loved her, but then men were usually funny about daughters. Charmian had found it more difficult. It was not her fault. Not everyone could be warmly maternal. Especially when

147

you lived mainly in the world of books. Books were safe, they didn't make messes or let you down.

'Will you take me to the tube, dear?' Charmian asked. 'I *have* enjoyed it here. A glimpse into Hogarth's London.'

When mother and daughter had gone, Professor Montrose also melted away. Jonathan refilled Rupert's glass.

'Well, young Jonathan,' said Rupert. 'You're in a bad way, aren't you?'

'I suppose so.'

'Not your usual sparkling self.'

It was strange, thought Jonathan, how hard it was to discuss his real misery even with his best friend. We humans have these in-built barriers, these sad little walls round our personalities. The truth was that he didn't know how he could go on, now that he believed he had lost his incomparable Fiona. Of course they were still working in the same office. But that almost made it worse. He was sure now that she didn't love him and never would. You couldn't make people love you, it wasn't susceptible to the exercise of willpower. It was the luck of the dice. He had been given his chance, and he had muffed it. Oh, the little further and what worlds away.

He could pretend that she didn't matter, that she was just an ordinary, limited girl. But she wasn't. Love's alchemy had turned her into the centre of his world. Rupert would tell him to get another girl. But that was a bad joke, there wasn't another Fiona. Yet he had to live, he had to be somewhere, the brain and heart wouldn't stop just because you screamed for them to do so. He thought he might go back to his mother in Otley. She at least would give him love. She showed it through the bread and scones she baked so specially, when he was at home. He had to have love. He could only reach God through love for another human being. Otherwise the world became a hideous, flaming limbo, even a hell.

'What is more important?' Jonathan found himself saying. 'Loyalty to institutions, or loyalty to a friend?'

It wasn't what he had meant to say at all. He hoped to talk to Rupert about Fiona. But now the moment had arrived, he found himself dreading his friend's flip words of conventional counsel. How could anyone understand what he felt about Fiona? It was deep within the soul.

148

'You are a strange boy,' said Rupert. 'Is this an argument in academic philosophy? Or do you really need to know?'

'I need to know.'

'You've discovered something bad about someone you care for?'

'More or less.'

'I should say, to hell with the institutions. It's the friend that counts. Isn't that the E. M. Forster line?'

'It's all right for you, Rupert. You're not a government official.'

'Happily not. And I don't intend to be. I have resisted the pressure. Dad wanted me to go into the Bank of England.'

'Poor old Dad. He must be leading a sheltered life.'

'Well, that's my advice, Jonathan. Stick to your friends. Loyalty is to individual people first.'

'I wish it were as simple as that,' replied Jonathan sadly. He felt he was being engulfed in the moon-pool.

'Marriage is wonderful, Jonathan,' said George Craxton. 'You ought to try it some time.'

It was the first time Jonathan had been down to Sweetladies since the wedding. Craxton did indeed look more relaxed, while Martha had the air of a basking shark.

'George has no defects,' said Martha. 'That's what worries me. He's too good to be true.'

'Oh, we all have defects,' said George. 'I start from the assumption that everyone is weak and foolish. I don't expect too much. That makes me a happy pessimist.'

'That's not the kind of thing you say in American politics,' warned his bride. 'Never apologize, never explain. Orson the Second would have done better, if he hadn't tried to explain.'

'You've been unlucky with your first husband,' said George. 'But this time you've struck gold, though I say it myself. And so have I. You like to present yourself as a toughie, Martha. But underneath you're soft and loving.'

Jonathan privately thought that it was the other way round. Martha, who looked at first so gently groomed, was inwardly as hard as nails. Now she rang the bell imperiously.

'Another vodka-tonic, Pepe,' she demanded.

Marriage had improved them both, thought Jonathan. Strange though it might seem, this ambitious and unscrupulous politician and female careerist seemed to have embarked on a period of happiness together. There was a glow of fulfilment about them both. Jonathan could not help wondering how long it would last. But at least it was genuine for the time being. They were right to make the most of it, the last of the summer wine.

'We're out of vodka,' said Pepe. 'It will have to be gin, madam.'

'Hell's bells,' bemoaned Martha. 'You know I always drink vodka.'

'We ordered it, madam. But it has not been delivered.'

'The usual British slackness. They wouldn't get away with it in the States. It's so damned primitive down here. No access even to the basic necessities of civilization.'

'Never mind, darling,' said George, in a gently crooning tone of voice which Jonathan had not heard before. 'It won't be long before we're living in the States.'

'I sure hope you're right,' said Martha, slightly mollified by this pleasing thought. 'That wretched little neighbourhood store here does not even stock Smirnoff. It's about time our appointment to Washington was announced. We should have had a better turn-out at the wedding, if all my people had known. They'd sell their grandmother for an invitation to the British Embassy.'

'It's the classiest joint in town,' agreed Craxton, aping the American intonation. 'Or at least it will be, when we get going on the razzle.'

'I need to start on the refurbishment,' said Martha. 'It's a full programme but our first shindig has to be the tops. We've got to be bigger and better than those lousy French.'

'It's the Foreign Office, I'm afraid,' said George apologetically. 'Jonathan will know. Old-fashioned sticklers for the conventions.'

'Well, don't stand for it, George,' Martha said in exasperation. 'Orson never stood for things like that. Wherever we were, he used to call the White House long-distance.'

'I believe they usually transferred him to the Revenue,' retorted Craxton with a flash of spirit. 'They were the ones who wanted to talk to him.'

'Ring up that funny old buzzard,' suggested Martha. 'The one that looks like something out of a Game Park. Lord Magnus Fluffington-Duck.'

'Sir Marcus Stewart-Stibbs? Oh, all right. I'll have another try.'

'Say I'm getting impatient,' said Martha. 'I could take my broker out of sterling. And I won't leave my Grecos to the National Gallery.'

'First thing Monday morning,' promised George.

It was amusing and a bit sad, thought Jonathan, to see how easily this confident man was mastered by an overwhelming woman. He was warming to George Craxton now that he saw so clearly his underlying weakness and vulnerability. It made him seem so much nicer. Even Martha possessed a certain earthy warmth which was not without its appeal. Jonathan hoped he was not going to start liking them both. This would make everything so much more difficult.

'Tell that Marcus he wrecked my wedding,' said Martha. 'They thought I was marrying a has-been. It's too bad. I may not be having another for some time.'

'It was a lovely wedding,' said George. 'And most distinctive. I'm sorry you missed it, Jonathan. By the way, I hear you met Colonel Hugo in the Lakes. Hasn't he got a wonderful place to live?'

'Oh yes.'

'Hugo's divine,' said Martha. 'I don't know why you've never taken me to see him.'

I do, thought Jonathan. I know now. Vince had made it all clear. That was the real reason why Jonathan was beginning to feel compassion for the former Cabinet Minister. He had come to realize that George was skating on some very thin ice.

After that talk with Vince, Jonathan had made an attempt to clear the matter up with Major Glossop. He had tried to do so in a casual manner, so as not to give too much away.

'What exactly are we looking for?' he had asked one morning over coffee in Bangalore Mansions.

'How do you mean, Jonathan?'

'Well, we're supposed to identify character defects which might impair a person's fitness to be entrusted with state secrets. What kind of defects, then? Presumably we don't mind vanity, cruelty, hypocrisy, arrogance and overwhelming ambition.'

'Of course not,' said the Major. 'Those are the basic qualifications for high office. We're thinking of things which might cause a person to be liable to manipulation. Drink. Drugs. Secret perversions.'

'What do you mean by perversions?' pursued Jonathan.

'Oh really, Jonathan. You don't need me to give you a lecture on that.'

'The love of one man for another?'

'Certainly.'

'That's not illegal among adults. I don't see why it has to be a bar to security clearance for the Foreign Office.'

'They are vulnerable to blackmail.'

'Not necessarily. Not if it's open.'

'Those are the rules,' said the Major. 'I didn't make them.'

'It seems illogical and unfair. They can't be open because they wouldn't get clearance. Therefore they are vulnerable to blackmail. And that makes them a risk. The whole thing is going round in circles.'

'Maybe it is,' agreed the Major. 'But life is not fair. And public service is a privilege, not a right. The whole point of the moon-pool is to see through people. And that means everything.'

'Everything? I wonder if that is a feasible aim.'

'Have you got some special reason for raising this subject?' asked Major Glossop, with a long stare. 'Are you asking for yourself or for a friend?'

'I'm not asking for anyone.'

'Pure zeal for knowledge?'

'I suppose so.'

'Are you quite sure, Jonathan, that you have told me everything?'

'Yes.'

'There is not some special piece of information which it is your duty to reveal? Please think very carefully about your reply. Is there?'

'No.'

Jonathan had relived this conversation several times in the last week. It still made him break out in a cold sweat. He had taken a risk which could wreck his career. But he had simply felt unable to betray George Craxton. He had grown fond of the man and had received his friendship and his confidences. It had not really been a conscious decision. He had felt obliged to follow his deepest feelings.

And now at Sweetladies, watching George and Martha in their intimacy of shared physical delight, Jonathan dared to hope that it might all come right. Vince had shot his bolt. Craxton's relationship with him had been temporary, the isolated action of a lonely man. His real bent was elsewhere. He would stick loyally to Martha, there would be no more trouble. It would have been foolish to ruin him for so small a cause. You had to keep a sense of proportion in these things. George would make sure that his new wife did not penetrate further into Colonel Hugo's circle. It would be an elementary precaution. Cabinet Ministers knew how to defend themselves. That was how they got on.

'To hell with Hugo,' said George facetiously. 'From now on, my darling, you have to live for me alone.'

'You're quite cuddly, George,' said Martha, with controlled dignity. 'I might have done worse.'

George turned towards Martha and ran his fingers lightly up her soft white arm. Jonathan felt a little embarrassed to see these two mature and worldly people begin a caress which was obviously going to end up in bed. But it made him feel a bit better, all the same.

'Oh, I do love women,' said George enthusiastically.

It hit Jonathan in the face. There was something too self-conscious about the assertion. Some things you didn't have to say. He had been hoping that all would be well. Now, he was not so sure.

'How's life?' asked Bernard Gilbert casually.

'All right,' replied Jonathan cautiously.

'Craxton's married bliss proceeding according to plan?'

'So far as I can judge.'

'Are you sure you are telling me everything?'

Jonathan gulped. This was dreadful, a nightmare coming true.

'Oh yes,' he replied.

'Who is Vince?' asked Bernard urbanely.

'Vince?'

'Yes. You know who I am talking about?'

'I suppose so,' agreed Jonathan miserably.

'He rang the Resident Clerk last night. Said it was urgent, a threat to national security. They put him through to me.'

'I see.'

'We didn't talk for long,' said Bernard. 'There wasn't any need to. He said he'd given you all the details. He just wanted to make sure that the necessary action would be taken on his information. He was frightened it might be pigeon-holed or otherwise suppressed.'

'Oh, was he? I suppose I'd better tell you about Vince.'

'I think you'd better,' agreed Bernard grimly. 'And, if you don't mind, I'll turn on the tape recorder.'

Later that night, George Craxton telephoned Jonathan Fieldhouse.

'Martha and I are having a frolic in the Forbidden City tomorrow,' said George.

'Where's that?'

'Lisson Grove. It's a splendidly succulent Chinese restaurant. Specializes in bamboo cuisine. We'd so like you to join us. Warm-up drinks first at South Eaton Place. Pepe will be at hand to minister. Such a useful little chap.'

'I'm afraid I'm not free,' replied Jonathan sadly.

He never would be free. Not now. Not to meet the man he had betrayed.

'You summoned me across London for lunch,' said Rupert, after Jonathan had filled his glass in the Rialto Bridge. 'We unwaged people don't find it easy to keep these rendez-vous so early in the day. But I've managed to combine it with an official visit to Cricklewood this afternoon. We located an old vicarage there with a fine view of the gasworks. How come that you happen to be here?'

'I'm up here on a course,' said Jonathan. 'Man management for the young executive.'

'OK baby,' said Rupert. 'What's the matter now?'

As before with Rupert, Jonathan found himself coming out with an anxiety quite removed from the one nearest his heart.

'I'm beginning to come to a conclusion about that Professor Montrose of yours,' he said. 'I think he may be a nut.'

'Of course he's a nut,' agreed Rupert cheerfully. 'Nutty as a fruitcake.'

'He may do you harm.'

'I can take care of myself, thank you.'

'It's his eyes,' said Jonathan. 'There's a sort of manic light in them.'

'I'll talk to Maureen,' conceded Rupert. 'They're thick as thieves.'

'Can you trust Maureen?' asked Jonathan. 'That isn't even her real name. She lives in a world of fantasy.'

'You're becoming paranoid.'

'I don't trust people with creative imaginations,' said Jonathan.

'It would be a boring world without them.'

'Perhaps a safer one. Some people can't live without excitement. It's some glandular deficiency. They feel a bit ill until danger turns them on. They have to turn to heroic virtue. Or to crime.'

'Dear old Jonathan,' said Rupert. 'I really do need you.'

'I can't think why.'

'I find you so deliciously predictable.'

Jonathan walked slowly back to Bangalore Mansions in the mellow sunshine of early October. Major Glossop, who was waiting around, whisked him into his office.

'I was down at headquarters this morning,' said the Major. 'Saw the great Sir Dominic himself. Another injunction about all employees being as pure as the driven snow.'

'Is that his only anxiety?'

'It certainly isn't. A fourth London building has gone up, you know. One common factor is clear now. They were all modern and ugly. We're looking for a bunch of protest maniacs with an unwholesome devotion to good architecture. And a pretext for snooping round London.'

'I see.'

'You know something, Jonathan. About these bombers, I mean.'

'What makes you think that?'

'A flicker in your eyes.'

'I've never pretended to be a good liar.'

'Is there anything you ought to tell me? I seem to have asked you this before. It's getting pretty muddy, here at the bottom of the moon-pool.'

Jonathan wasn't going to be caught out a second time. He had not forgotten that moment of pure horror, when Bernard Gilbert had first so unexpectedly mentioned the name of Vince. That had been between him and the Foreign Office. It might not yet have been passed on to the Security Service. But then there was this other horrible thing, about the destroyed buildings. Jonathan was even more closely affected by that.

'Don't be afraid of getting things wrong,' said the Major charitably. 'We shall take time to check the details.'

'I imagine you would.'

'Well, Jonathan, what about it? *Have* you got something to tell me?'

'I suppose I have,' replied the young man.

It had been a pleasant walk across the park. The October sunshine continued to bathe monumental London in its mellow glow. Sir Marcus Stewart-Stibbs felt a mild urge to gambol like a young lamb. At breakfast Felicity had imparted the news that she was going down to Bournemouth again to see her mother. Sir Marcus looked forward to a nice, lonely dinner at the Voyagers. It would be good to eat a meal, for once, without conversation. Felicity was just wonderful but it was becoming increasingly difficult to turn her off. Sir Marcus sometimes wondered whether she might have taken a lover. He concluded that this was unlikely. Felicity would not wish to go to bed with anyone who wanted to go to bed with her.

Still brooding on this subject, Sir Marcus gave a cheerful smile to the new girl who had entered briskly with morning tea. Except that she wasn't a new girl any more. He remembered her name quite clearly now, it was Lucinda. On days like these, his memory felt as sharp as ever.

'Mr Gilbert wants to see you urgently,' said Lucinda. She really was a very pretty child. 'He says there's a new development.'

Bernard bounced in, positively smirking. Sir Marcus knew at once that whatever had happened was highly favourable.

'Good news?' he asked.

Bernard composed his plump, mobile features into an expression of compassion and concern. It looked highly artificial, like the attempt of a naturally jolly man to look sad at the funeral of a remote, moneyed relation. But in the Foreign Service it was considered inelegant to display what the Germans called *schadenfreude*, that terribly human instinct to derive delight from the misfortunes of others. It was the kind of emotion in which foreigners seemed to specialize. The English indulged it only in private.

'Rather sad, I'm afraid,' said Bernard with becoming gravity. 'About poor old George Craxton.'

'What has he done?'

'We've had a reaction from the moon-pool. They were doing his positive vetting.'

'I thought that was, more or less, a formality.'

'So did we all,' agreed the Chief Clerk, a shade unctuously. 'But something rather surprising has come up.'

'You mean, a shadow on his record?'

'I'm afraid so,' replied Bernard dolefully. It was apparent that he could hardly contain his glee. 'Craxton has had a compromising relationship with a young man.'

'Good heavens!' said Sir Marcus. 'I thought he was robustly normal.'

'That's the impression which most politicians seek to convey.'

'No, but he has women.'

'This was between the wives. A person called Vince.'

'Vince!' echoed the Permanent Under-Secretary, almost with a shudder. 'Does that make it any worse?'

'It doesn't make it any better.'

'Is this absolutely certain, Bernard?'

'Yes.'

'He can't seek to deny it?'

'Oh no. Vince has provided a very full account.'

'So this means that Craxton can't go to Washington?'

'I'm afraid it does,' replied Bernard primly.

'Suppose Craxton says it doesn't affect his second marriage, or his loyalty to the nation, or anything else?'

'That could all be true. But the rules are clear. We don't employ known homosexuals in positions which require a high degree of security clearance.'

'Craxton could still say that this was something casual, and in the past.'

'I don't think the point would be clear to the great British public. Can you imagine our distinguished press? They'd give the man a most terrible time.'

'I suppose you're right,' agreed Sir Marcus. 'He'd never risk it.'

Bernard permitted his air of solemn gravity to slip a little. With some effort, he suppressed a small smirk of triumph. It was about time, he thought, that he had a success. Amaryllis had been quite upset by that postcard they had received before breakfast that morning from Timothy. It seemed that he needed money yet again.

'Then we are back to square one,' continued Sir Marcus. 'The professional candidate will have to go forward. James Leyland, I mean.'

'There can't be any doubt about it,' agreed Bernard.

'I suppose there is nothing against him?' asked the Permanent Under-Secretary. 'Or Charmian? She has always seemed very odd to me.'

'Odd but incorrupt.'

'They don't have any funny habits, I hope?' asked Sir Marcus. 'Flagellation? Bestiality?'

'You are quite safe with them. Their idea of a night out is reading Sophocles in Greek.'

'Well, that's our man, then. And now we can go ahead with all the moves we had planned for the top of the Service, before this little difficulty. What a relief.'

'Yes,' agreed Bernard heartily.

'Including your own posting to Canberra.'

'Thank you.'

'You will be splendid there,' said Sir Marcus. 'The Australians will clasp Amaryllis to their bosoms.'

'They don't have much in the way of bosoms. It's all that surfing.'

'This little episode,' said Sir Marcus thoughtfully, 'will be rather instructive for ministers. It may encourage them in future to leave diplomatic appointments to the professionals.'

'That is certainly my hope,' agreed Bernard.

'I always thought Craxton seemed a bit shifty,' continued Sir Marcus. 'But then most politicians are. In retirement, I shall mingle more with the city gents.'

'You're not retired yet, Marcus. You've still got to tell the Foreign Secretary why he has to veto the Prime Minister's candidate for Washington.'

'You think that's my job?'

'Oh yes. You could go direct to Craxton. But I think it would be best to have ministerial backing first.'

'Wouldn't it all come more elegantly from Dominic Trowbridge?'

This time, Bernard really did grin.

'Dominic Trowbridge and his staff know nothing about this,' he replied with quiet satisfaction.

'Dominic? But he's Head of the Security Service.'

'It came through my special hot line.'

'Your hot line, Bernard?'

'Security is too important to leave to the experts. Those majors in mackintoshes. I thought it wise to establish my own personal probe, deep into the moon-pool. This is the result. It bypassed the proper channels.'

'You astonish us, Bernard. The Service owes you a deep debt of gratitude.'

'Thank you,' said Bernard simply. He knew what this meant, though Marcus had been too refined to spell it out. He would go to his next post as Sir Bernard. And Amaryllis would be a Lady at last.

'This leaves me clear to approach the Foreign Secretary direct,' said Sir Marcus. 'But Dominic will have to be informed at some point.'

'I am looking forward to doing so,' said Bernard with satisfaction.

'This has all worked out very well. Even for poor old Craxton. At least, he has been spared a public scandal. People can be so cruel. And James will offer a more intellectual approach to Washington.'

'I'll say,' agreed Bernard.

'And we have kept Washington for the Service,' continued Sir Marcus with a touch of euphoria. 'It means such a lot to me, you know, preserving the Service with its wonderful tradition of *esprit de corps*.'

'Me too,' echoed Bernard. 'Besides, we have to find places for the boys.'

'You have displayed quite unusual qualities of pertinacity, my dear Bernard. Fighting off the enemy.'

'Frustrating the decision of the Prime Minister?'

'That would be another way of putting it,' agreed Sir Marcus with a dry smile.

Lucinda had entered to clear away the teacups. The view of her retreating figure, full but neat, filled Sir Marcus with elation. He felt just a little drunk with the joy of it all.

'I say,' he said impulsively, 'what about a little binge?'

'A little binge,' echoed the Deputy Under-Secretary of State, in mild astonishment.

'Felicity is away. I do hate eating alone. If you and Amaryllis are free, why don't you join me tonight for a bite at the Voyagers?'

'We should love to, Marcus.'

'I shall try to see the Secretary of State earlier in the evening,' said Sir Marcus. 'It will give him something to think about.'

He did not say it maliciously. But he did just permit himself the ghost of a grin.

'Clever old Jonathan,' said Rupert, a touch patronizingly. 'How on earth did you locate us?'

'You did mention this refurbishment site when we met yesterday. There aren't all that many mock-Byzantine chapels around Primrose Hill.'

'Can we interest you, young man?' asked Professor Montrose. 'This choice property is just ripe for development. The Tabernacle of the Holy Spirit would make a quaint penthouse, with unrivalled views over the King's Cross gentrification zone.'

'It's a monstrosity,' gasped Jonathan.

'The archimandrite had big ideas,' agreed Montrose. 'His mother was a Vanderbilt. Aren't people gorgeous?'

'People are horrible,' said Maureen. 'In Ireland we prefer donkeys.'

'But you don't come from Ireland,' pointed out Jonathan.

'You can come from anywhere you like,' riposted Maureen, rather coldly. 'It just takes a leap of the mind.'

'Jonathan doesn't go in for leaps of the mind,' explained Rupert, quite kindly.

'I like the pulpit,' said Harold Montrose. 'That stuff is lapis lazuli. Sort of.'

'Do you buy these extraordinary places?' asked Jonathan. 'How on earth do you get the money?'

'Of course we don't buy them,' replied Rupert. 'We just find locations and recommend them to clients. All we get is a small commission. But it's fun.'

'And splendid exercise,' added the Professor. 'I've been round London in all weathers. Our ancestors left us with a marvellously eclectic and eccentric heritage. If we can interest the moneyed private buyer, that represents something saved from the rapacity of the developers.'

'The climate has turned against them,' said Jonathan.

'Not a moment too soon,' opined Montrose. 'Their work won't last, mark my words.'

'Someone is helping it not to last,' said Rupert. 'Wasn't there another bombing the other day? A tower block, I think, down by the docks.'

'Good for them,' commented Maureen.

'What is your attitude, Professor?' asked Jonathan, very directly. 'Towards these – manifestations?'

'The direct action, you mean,' replied Montrose cautiously. 'Well, I can't say I am sorry.'

'Some people,' said Jonathan, 'would describe them as outrages.'

'It's only a question of point of view,' said Montrose. 'One man's terrorist is another's freedom fighter.'

'But you can't justify these violent attacks on property,' expostulated Jonathan. 'It's just lucky that no one has been killed so far.'

'It might be worth dying,' said Montrose, 'for our London. The flower of cities all. Action is the only thing the brutes understand.'

'We found that in Ireland, too,' added Maureen.

'Jonathan, you didn't come to argue,' said Rupert. 'Or to admire the mosaic of Christ in Majesty, a work contemporaneous with Bernard Shaw. You're all of a tizzy.'

'I imagine the archimandrite must have had unusual tastes,' opined the Professor. 'There are some distinctively curious frescoes in the private robing room.'

Suddenly something snapped inside Jonathan.

'Get out,' he said in panic.

'Get out?' echoed Rupert. 'The walls look quite safe.'

'Get out of the country,' explained Jonathan. 'Before they come for you.'

161

'Poor old Jonathan,' said Rupert softly. 'It has all been too much for him. That damned Foreign Office is a modern Minotaur. Devouring the flower of our young men and maidens.'

'Harold looks quite porphyrogenitos in that pulpit,' said Maureen. 'Born in the purple, you know.'

'I should have made a good emperor,' agreed Montrose. 'At least on the Golden Horn. You couldn't be too squeamish there about removing eyes and balls.'

'You admit you're not too squeamish?' Jonathan asked him sharply.

'Nor are the greatest surgeons. But people are grateful, all the same.'

'I wouldn't bank,' said Jonathan, 'on gratitude.'

'Jonathan may be right about that,' said Rupert. 'He has access to the top. Where they take a chill, clinical view of the world.'

'I never liked him,' said Maureen, as if Jonathan were not present. 'A little nark and goody-goody. One of daddy's bright young men.'

'But I came to help you,' expostulated Jonathan, almost bursting into tears. He hated to be hated. 'It was a long, tiring walk from the bus-stop at the Zoo.'

'It's all a zoo,' commented Montrose. 'The great reptile house of the world.'

'I don't understand you!' Jonathan shouted. 'I never have.'

'Oh yes, you do,' said Rupert, almost grimly. 'We are what you have abandoned. You have created your own personality by reacting against mine.'

'And vice versa.'

'That may also be true,' agreed Rupert. 'It takes all sorts to make a world.'

'Thought for the day,' snapped Maureen sarcastically. 'My parents go for luminous ideas like that.'

'Don't try to be clever,' said Jonathan. 'Just get the hell out of here.' After what he had been obliged to tell the Major, they might be picked up at any time.

'I always wanted to see the South Pacific,' ruminated the Professor.

'Get out!' Jonathan yelled again, running out of the chapel and all the way down to Swiss Cottage. Now he hated them all. And feared them, too.

George Craxton had driven much of the night. Now, in the wet, soft morning, he had reached the shores of Lake Windermere. There was no need to travel in such an uncomfortable manner. But he knew that he would not have been able to sleep. Not after that poisonous interview at the Foreign Office with Sir Marcus Stewart-Stibbs in that large, uncurtained room surrounded by the autumn gleaming in the park. As soon as he had entered, Craxton had sensed danger. It was something you got used to in politics. Sir Marcus had motioned him to a sofa, just a shade too politely. Craxton guessed at once that something had gone wrong.

'It was kind of you to call at such short notice,' said Sir Marcus. 'The Secretary of State asked me to talk to you as soon as possible.'

'Is the announcement ready at last?' bluffed Craxton. 'I'd like to start briefing the press. And Martha will do a photo-call.'

'I'm afraid I have some rather bad news for you,' Sir Marcus said.

'You mean, to do with Washington?'

'Yes.'

'The Prime Minister promised me,' said George Craxton, with an angry flash. 'It was a firm understanding.'

'We had to do a security check. I did warn you of that.'

'So what?'

'A snag has been revealed.'

'I don't know what you are talking about,' said the former Cabinet Minister. He was getting rather tired of this snide diplomat who pretended to be on his side but wasn't really.

'Are you sure you don't?' asked Sir Marcus softly. 'Is there nothing in your private life which might make it impossible for you to receive a top-security clearance?'

'Nothing at all.' Craxton had gone red. But Sir Marcus had noticed that senior politicians often did go like that, especially after a long, late lunch.

'We have a statement here,' said Sir Marcus. 'By a man named Vincent Smith. Do you know him?'

'Smith? It's a common name.'

'He claims to have known you very well.'

'Vincent, you say? Perhaps that does ring a bell. It could be a boy called Vince,' said Craxton thoughtfully. 'A sort of soldier servant. Worked in the house of an old friend of mine.'

'That's the one,' agreed Sir Marcus. 'I think you'd better read what he says. If you'll excuse me, I'll just be glancing through the telegrams. Tell me when you have finished.'

As Craxton read, his heart plunged. He thought all this had been decently buried. The damned, malicious little fool. Craxton's large, bold face started to crumble, his self-confidence oozed out like air from a burst balloon. It was tactful of Sir Marcus to bend over his own desk. That gave Craxton time to regain at least the semblance of composure.

'Well?' said Craxton at last.

'I'm sorry,' said Sir Marcus. 'These things have to be done.'

'It's hardly your fault.'

'You have to admit, it seems pretty conclusive.'

'If it's genuine.'

Go on the attack, an inner voice whispered to Craxton. Unleash the killer instinct. A protected bureaucrat like Marcus Stewart-Stibbs would have nothing to match it. Take the muzzles off the Alsatians. But keep smiling all the time.

'I presume,' said Craxton with an urbane smile that Sir Marcus found rather alarming, 'that you took the most careful steps to check that this statement *is* genuine. Before going to the Foreign Secretary, one of my oldest friends and political allies.'

'It certainly comes from this Vince person,' said Sir Marcus, with some distaste. 'I don't know whether he is telling the truth or not. These things rather lie outside my experience.'

'Then might it not have been better to tackle me first?' asked Craxton with a steely glare. 'Before bothering your Secretary of State?'

Sir Marcus remembered, with a distinct feeling of unease, that Craxton as a Cabinet Minister had enjoyed in Whitehall the reputation of being difficult to deal with. There had been a heavy turnover in his Private Office. Now Sir Marcus was learning why.

'I thought it best to keep the Secretary of State informed,' retorted Sir Marcus in his best dead-pan voice. 'I am acting now with his full authority. This is a highly political area.'

'I'll say it is,' growled Craxton.

'The Foreign Secretary is quite clear on the point,' said the Permanent Under-Secretary. 'If there is any truth at all in these allegations, it will be quite impossible to make you ambassador in Washington.'

'What makes you so sure of that?'

'The rules are positive. The Americans wouldn't work with you. Besides, the press would crucify you and your wife. On both sides of the Atlantic.'

'I see all that. But what evidence have you got, to support the accusations of this Vince person?'

'None at all,' conceded Sir Marcus. 'So far as I know.'

'Then it all stands or falls,' pressed Craxton, 'on whether or not Vince is telling the truth?'

'I suppose so.'

'His word or mine. What happens if I ask you to prefer mine? If I just deny it all?'

Sir Marcus had been dreading this question, from the beginning. But he was not unprepared.

'We should naturally be disposed,' he replied courteously, 'to take your word against his. After all, you are a Privy Councillor. A Right Honourable.'

He spoke without irony, using an almost dead idiom without literal meaning.

'Nice of you to remember that,' snapped Craxton. The irony now was on his side.

'That would be all right,' continued Sir Marcus, 'if Vince is really lying. But suppose he isn't? Then you would be infinitely wiser to admit the truth in strict confidence. Your Washington appointment could be quietly cancelled. No harm would have been done. An announcement has never been made. So none would be needed. You would be spared all humiliation. The alternative is almost too awful to think of. Do you really think that Vince would keep quiet, if you have something to hide and we still go ahead with announcing your appointment?'

'There have been cover-ups before.'

'This is the age of the investigative journalist. The Sunday papers would set whole teams on to you. Failed dons and rejected diplomats, with bitter little minds. They'd turn you inside out. It wouldn't do the Foreign Office any good at all.'

'I could live with that. The Foreign Office has no political clout.'

'Or the government,' added Sir Marcus. 'Or the Party.'

That was the point, thought Craxton. Stewart-Stibbs had struck a raw nerve. If he caused them public embarrassment, the Party would be merciless as ever. After all, his Parliamentary colleagues wanted to be re-elected themselves. They would not forgive a former minister who let the side down. He would have to resign from his clubs and take up social work among people who drank water for lunch.

'So you see,' added Sir Marcus more gently, sensing that he had achieved a palpable hit. 'There's only one thing for it. Complete confidence between the two of us. I'm on your side, you know.'

No, you're not, you smug bastard, thought Craxton. You dislike me on principle because I'm a political appointee to one of your top embassies, a job I shall fill with the greatest distinction. It will be like the Duff Cooper days in Paris again. With me and Martha, the Washington Embassy will dance and throb and hum. But you want to replace me by one of your grey, faceless civil servants. All you care about is jobs for the boys. So you're delighted to sabotage me. And I'm beginning to hate the Foreign Office. Because your opposition isn't open. It's conducted on the back stairs. And you cloak the pleasure you feel at the mess I'm in with that upper-class veneer of good breeding. I'd like to smash your jaw, to get you on the floor and put the boot in.

'Are you all right?' asked Sir Marcus doubtfully.

Control yourself, thought George Craxton. This aggression was a form of hysteria. It could lead him to do something terribly stupid. He had found that, just occasionally, in the House. He must treat this like a big Debate. By sheer force of his willpower, he must calm himself down, slow his pulse. Above all, he must choose his words with great precision. This bloody man would forget nothing.

'I understand the position clearly,' said Craxton at length, fighting down the incipient mania. 'Everything depends on whether this Vince is prepared to back his statement.'

'I suppose so.'

'And if he isn't?'

There was a short pause. Craxton heard a great clock tick.

'That would be a new situation,' conceded Sir Marcus slowly.

'We'd better leave it at that,' said Craxton.

'I think we'd better. Come and see me again. Soon, please.'

'Yes, please.'

Right up to the end, Craxton noted, Sir Marcus had refrained from asking him outright whether Vince's statement was true. That had been clever. It was the way these English mandarins operated. No time was to be lost on temper and emotion. You simply got together to try to cope with these little problems. Except that it wasn't a little problem. It was his whole future life. That depended on getting the Washington Embassy, the foundation for all the cloud-palaces which Martha had constructed so lovingly. It would be terrible to have to face her with the news. Craxton was far from certain that it would bring out her more attractive side.

Sir Marcus stood at his large window overlooking the park, as Jasper Tenby escorted Craxton down to the park door. Sir Marcus needed a short breather before the Swedish Ambassador arrived to complain about acid rain. It had been a trying interview with Craxton. The man had a lot of violence in him, simmering away just beneath the surface.

One nasty thought shot across the mobile mind of Sir Marcus. By evading the central issue, he had left it open to Craxton to return and claim that Vince had withdrawn his charges. What would they do then? Would it really be safe to proceed with the Washington appointment, with the shadow of blackmail always looming in the background? It would be an awful risk for ministers, who weren't really all that fond of Craxton in the first place. With an uncomfortable jolt, Sir Marcus remembered that they had bypassed the Head of the Security Service himself. Perhaps they had rather jumped the gun. But the lead from the moon-pool had been impeccable. Suppose now that Vince disappeared, or was found dead? Sir Marcus would have some moral responsibility, through pinning so much on his accusation. Sir Marcus hadn't at all cared for that violent red spot in Craxton's left eye. The man might be capable of anything. Sir Marcus did not trust politicians on the make. Or on the run. He had known Privy Councillors to do some quite peculiar things.

But Craxton had decided to fall back on a non-violent weapon in the political armoury: unbounded confidence in one's own power to charm. Vince was a poor thing, vulnerable and easily led. It had been a mistake to cut him off so totally and let him go sour. Vince would have to be magicked. It shouldn't be difficult. The boy, as he remembered, had been avid for presents and for love. But there was no time to lose. Stopping only to tell Martha that he was called north, for he never told unnecessary lies, he got the Daimler out of the House of Commons garage and made for Finchley Road, honking his horn to encourage others to clear the route.

And now, in Colonel Hugo's garden, everything looked morning-fresh. Craxton had almost forgotten how beautiful it was at Kirkland Hall, at the lush, quieter end of Windermere. Living soberly here, thought Craxton, one could lead a life of celibate innocence. Well, he had missed the chance for that. The main need now was to get hold of Vince quickly and alone. If it had been raining, he would have rung Vince and invited him for a drink in some local pub. But as it was a fine day he decided to bank on Hugo and Sally being out on the hills. In the rainy Lake District you had to take advantage of fine weather.

He noticed that the garage doors were open and the garage empty. Perhaps he was in luck. Summoning up his courage, he rang the front doorbell. To his relief, when Vince opened the door there seemed to be no one else around.

'Vince!'

'Good grief, Mr Craxton.'

'You look well.'

'I haven't had anything to make me ill.'

'How lucky for you, Vince. I wish I could say the same. The Colonel is out, is he?'

'Yes, sir. He and Miss Wetherby have gone off to climb Helvellyn.'

'Well, frankly, Vince, it was you I came to see. Can I come in? Or perhaps you'd rather stroll down to the lake?'

'Right, sir,' said Vince, with one of his grins. 'A spot of fresh air would be good for me.'

They moved off together into the garden.

'You don't come to see us much any more,' said Vince. 'You used to be such a regular visitor.'

'I'm married now, Vince.'

'Well, the best of British luck to you, George.'

'You know why I've come?'

'Oh yes. It sticks out a mile. As the actress said to the bishop. I was expecting you.'

'Because of what you did?'

'I don't know that I quite follow.'

'What you told them about us.'

'It's no use being cross with me, George. I've been a serving soldier. I just did my duty.'

'I'm not cross with you, Vince.'

'Yes, you are. You're furious. It's the way you screw up one eye. I know you very well.'

'You betrayed me.'

'It wasn't my fault. They asked questions and I gave them truthful replies.'

'Nonsense! You volunteered the whole thing. To harm me.'

'Don't lay hands on me, George. I shall scream. There are people passing in the lane.'

'Don't be stupid. I've no intention of touching you. But I am certainly hurt. I thought I'd been kind to you.'

'You were until the end. Then you let me down. When you were getting married at Sweetladies, I tried to telephone and you wouldn't take the call. Then you had me turned away from the big front door. I was awfully hurt, too. It made me see red.'

'It was a misunderstanding, Vince. I was tremendously busy and tense.'

'I thought you thought I wasn't good enough for you. You liked me well enough up here. But you didn't want to introduce me to your posh friends in the south.'

'That's not true, Vince.' The thought of the boy walking onto the beautifully manicured lawn at Sweetladies, to the astonishment of the elegant Martha, was indeed rather awful. Vince had been acceptable at Kirkland Hall. But only because Hugo Wilderness seemed to live in a world of his own.

'I suppose I knew it all along,' continued Vince. 'Even when you gave me a good time. When I tried to come closer to you, you simply weren't there.'

The visit was turning out to be disturbingly confessional. An encounter with Sally would probably have been even worse. Dear me, this place was indeed a Heartbreak House.

'I was always very fond of you,' said George.

'Well, perhaps that was all you could manage. Some people are like that. I'm sorry I got so cross. I didn't mean to do you harm.'

'Never mind.'

'Have I hurt you a lot?'

'That depends, Vince.'

'What do you mean?'

'You could help to undo the damage.'

'Now you're talking. I thought you didn't come all this way just for the pleasure of my company. What can I do?'

'You can promise to say nothing else to anyone in future.'

'Sure, no problem. Mum's the word. I feel better already.'

'So do I, Vince. And very grateful.'

'I'm very glad to oblige. No use crying over spilt milk. Is that all, George?'

'Well, not quite. You see, they have that long statement.'

'The one I made to Jonathan Fieldhouse?'

'Yes. Why did you choose him to confide in?'

'I was mad with you at the time, as you know. And he had so obviously come up here specially to check up on you.'

'All the way here?'

'Oh yes. It was clear to me. Though not to Hugo.'

George felt a chill at the heart. Jonathan's betrayal hurt him more than Vince's. It was the cold act of an educated person who knew exactly what he was doing, not the capricious gesture of someone warm and young who felt himself spurned.

'Well, it's that statement which is doing me harm now,' said George.

'I wish I hadn't made it. What can I do about it?'

George Craxton paused. This was the moment he had come for, all the way up that long motorway.

'You could withdraw the statement,' he said.

'Say it was all a lie?'

'Yes.'

Vince looked out across the lake, showing his weak profile. How on earth could I have ever cared for the wretched chap? thought George. I must have been quite desperate.

'I don't think I could do that,' said Vince miserably.

'Why on earth not?'

'Because it *is* true. I know it is. And so do you, George.'

'Then it can stay between us.'

'That would have been all right, if I had never made the statement. I do regret that now. But I can't lie about the past. It meant a lot to me that someone in your position should take an interest in me. It's been a big thing in my life. Something to be proud of, even if I could only be proud in private. You've never really understood that. I couldn't deny our friendship now, as if it had never happened, as if it were something to be ashamed of.'

'You could do it to help me.'

'Not even to help you, George. You can't unlive the past. It did really happen. I won't be branded as a liar.'

'Can we go somewhere else, Vince? Where we can talk more quietly.'

'We certainly cannot. I know your tricks, George.'

Suddenly Craxton realized that it was all quite hopeless. After a great deal of bullying, he might just be able to force Vince to sign a recantation of his statement. That might satisfy the authorities for the moment. They would feel obliged to believe him. But, in the long run, it would be useless. Vince was not at all ashamed of their relationship. On the contrary, he gloried in it. It was the greatest thing that had happened in his young life so far. He would find it extremely hard to keep quiet about it for ever. With George installed in the grandeur of the Washington Embassy, Vince would feel sorely tempted to blab about this friendship in the neighbouring pub to visiting Americans. And one, some day, would be an investigative journalist. Vince would mean no harm. On the contrary, he was basically fond of George. But the bonds of love could be as constricting as the bonds of hate. It would be a mad act, George now realized, to subject Martha and himself to such a risk of public hounding. It had been less dangerous before Vince made the statement. But now more people knew. And it was apparent that Vince could never be relied upon to deny their past.

It would be a blunder, Craxton felt instinctively, to offer the boy money. His love, once turned to hate, would be even more difficult to manage. For one wild moment, Craxton thought of murder. It would be easy to get Vince into the lake, off the deep-water jetty. And the slum-bred boy, he knew, could not swim and would panic quite quickly. His own subconscious, well under control, would imbibe the incident as an accident. But it would be too terrible a risk. Besides, in real life you did not actually do things like that.

'I'm sorry,' said Vince. 'You've meant something big to me. I'll never forget you, George.'

'I'll never forget you, Vince.' That was certainly true, thought the statesman ruefully as he climbed back into his big Daimler. He should be able to make the Sharrow Bay for lunch. It would be good to eat a substantial meal alone. He had, that morning, had enough of the human race for the time being.

'I do like cemeteries,' said Charmian. 'Especially these great Victorian graveyards. And I enjoy funerals too. It's only weddings and baptisms that depress me.'

'You were always cussed,' commented her husband.

'Not cussed but contrapuntal, dear. Who wants the main tune? I have always preferred the secondary theme.'

'No wonder you produced Tess.'

'She's your daughter, too. Unfortunately gifted with my temperament and your figure.'

'Tess has gone to ground,' said James Leyland. 'She doesn't seem to phone any more.'

'She was unexpectedly sweet the last time we met,' said Charmian. 'Actually took a photograph of me. I can't think why.'

'Black magic, perhaps,' suggested Sir James. 'They stick pins into your private parts. It's quite in the mode again.'

'As a matter of fact, she was with that rather interesting Professor, Harold Montrose. An expert on the architecture of London, it would seem. But not notably sober.'

'Your friend Montrose would be in his element around here,' said James. 'It's a paradise for lovers of the mausoleum and the sarcophagus.'

They were enjoying one of their habitual walks round the Brompton Cemetery, one of the least appreciated green lungs of West London. It was handy for the basement flat, just off the Boltons, which they kept for their visits to London. And it reeked of history.

'There's Richard Tauber,' said Charmian. 'Doesn't that tell a sad story? Born Linz 1891, died London 1948.'

'The greatest Mozart tenor of the age,' extemporized James. 'Victim of Gentile rage.'

'They didn't last long in Penang,' said Charmian. 'Or in West Africa either. Poor things, just look at the youthful ages.'

'"The bight of Benin, the bight of Benin,"' quoted James. '"Where few come out, though many go in."'

'Thank God we aren't going there,' said Charmian. 'I couldn't stand any more of that prickly heat.'

'It's pretty hot in Washington in summer,' said James dryly. 'That's where you are going, my dear.'

'Oh, James, it *is* definite this time?'

'Yes, it's definite. Marcus rang me this afternoon. An announcement will be made very soon.'

'That's marvellous, James. I ought to congratulate you.'

'I owe a lot of it to you, dear.'

'What on earth happened to George Craxton?'

'Craxton faded out rather suddenly. Some security foul-up.'

'Poor old Craxton. Lucky old us.'

'I suppose we *are* lucky,' said James. 'Though Belial would have been quite a creditable alternative.'

'You can hob-nob now with the finest minds in the States. That's the real job of an ambassador. Not to give all those silly parties for the social circuit.'

'We shall have to give a few parties,' protested James. 'That's what we get the allowances for.'

'All right, dear,' said Charmian, very much the professor's daughter. 'But I'm not going to try to compete with women like that Martha person. I'm not going to spend a fortune in dolling myself up.'

'Glad to hear that, my dear.'

'The great thing at a social gathering, James, is to organize stimulating talk. Not drunken chit-chat.'

'It will be a new approach, dear,' said Sir James. 'I feel somehow that you're going to make your mark.'

'I'm going to try to go on being a real person.'

'You are, Charmian. There's no need to try.'

'What a beautiful monument. I do enjoy those weeping angels and those forlorn cherubs.'

To love another person might be to see the face of God, thought Jonathan Fieldhouse. It was certainly the only way he knew to approach God. But there was a lot of pain in it too, when the only love you got back was the reflection of your own.

The Rialto, their usual Maida Vale pub, was crowded. Fiona and he had been squashed on a bench with two elderly women. Against the buzz of conversation, it was necessary to talk too loudly.

'You look bad, Jonathan,' shrieked Fiona.

'I feel bad.'

'I think you did the right thing.'

'What?'

'Telling Major Val about Rupert's weirdies. It's too much of a coincidence, isn't it? Those bombings of modern buildings and, at the same time, Professor Montrose going round London saying how much he hates them all.'

'I didn't enjoy informing on them,' said Jonathan. 'Rupert's my friend. I don't want to make trouble for him.'

'It was your duty.'

'Lucky old you. To see things so simply.'

Privately, Jonathan suspected that the indomitable Rupert could well take care of himself. What really worried him more were the revelations about George Craxton which Bernard Gilbert had dragged out of him. It was bloody of that Vince boy to speak directly to the Foreign Office. He must have suspected, rightly, that Jonathan would try to stifle his malice. Jonathan feared now for George Craxton. He knew there was a very vulnerable interior beneath that arrogant bluster. Now that he knew about Vince, he realized that George had been fond of him too. It seemed to be an awful world in which infinite loves moved in parallel without ever meeting, begotten by despair upon impossibility.

But he must be careful. There was an important distinction. The lead he had given to Major Glossop about Professor Harold Montrose and his architectural cavortings had been processed through official channels. It had entered the archives of the moon-pool and was known to all in Bangalore Mansions. On the other hand, he had resolutely refused to betray Craxton to Major Glossop. The damaging information supplied by Vince had been forced out of him only by Bernard Gilbert, thus bypassing the usual hierarchy of the Security Service. It was therefore unknown both to the Major and to Fiona. He must watch his tongue.

'I says to her,' screamed a voice in his ear, 'don't be so bloody cheeky.'

'Serves her right, the bold thing.' It might have been the screeching of two unusually articulate parrots.

How lovely Fiona was. That soft face, that fair skin. And unattainable now, he realized that. It had only been a little spark between them and it had not lasted long. In fact, it seemed in retrospect that Fiona had only warmed towards him on the day she had had some row with that tiresome older woman whom she insisted on calling Aunty Mary. It would be best to avoid her now. Perhaps he could get transferred to something else. He had not greatly enjoyed the seamy side of the moon-pool. Unreachable beauty was torture.

'Mind you, she has quite a temper, does our Bess. Shut your trap, love, I says. You're waking the street.'

'She wouldn't mind that. Voice like a factory hooter.'

'I know you think I am simple,' said Fiona aggressively. 'That's what you mean, isn't it?'

'Not simple – deficient. Simple – pleasantly uncomplicated.'

'That's because I don't have your powerful mind. I didn't go to university.'

'Oh, shut up about that, Fiona. University is where most people have their few original ideas pounded out of them.'

'Don't be rude about education. It's Aunty Mary's great thing.'

'Sometimes I feel I loathe that woman.'

'That's because you've never met her.'

'Perhaps. It's easier to hate people in the abstract.'

'She's not big and butch, you know. Actually, she's quite gentle. If I left her, she'd go quietly desperate.'

'Has she told you that?'

'She doesn't need to. I should have broken it off, months ago.'

'It?'

'Our relationship. Must I be specific?'

Was this a surprise to him? wondered Jonathan. He concluded that it was not. He had felt all along with Fiona that she was an unapproachable being on another cloud. Now it was spelled out. The girl's love had been bespoken, and by another type of human creature. But possibly not for ever. That damned spark of hope refused to die down.

'I suppose I ought to feel sorry for Aunty Mary,' he said.

'I suppose you should. Her future could be quite grim. She relies too much on me and it sometimes gets my wick.'

'How did you meet her?'

'Adult education classes. Italian lessons for Florence. She was the teacher.'

'And what about your security clearance? They don't like it for women, either. In the Security Service, of all places.'

'It didn't come up at first,' replied Fiona. 'My emotional preferences were quite standard when I joined the Service. How was I to know that Mary and I were going to fall for each other, a lot later?'

'You must always have known something,' said Jonathan.

'What do you mean?'

'About being that way inclined.'

'Do you really think it is so cut and dried? Just because I'm living with an older woman now, does that mean I shall always do so. It's not so hard for me to love a nice person who happens to love me.'

'Except when it's me.'

'Oh, poor Jonathan. You came along too late. I'm just a girl, behaving in the way that comes naturally to me. And trying to do a good job.'

'But the job itself is to spy into the private lives of other government officials. After all, we are at the centre of the moon-pool.'

'Damn the moon-pool,' said Fiona. 'It's a nasty idea, anyway. I think I'll get out.'

'That might be wise. And I'll pack up too. Go back to the Foreign Office, where I belong. Most people's lives don't really stand up to investigation. It's a sad, undignified business.'

'If we both left the office,' said Fiona plaintively, 'I shouldn't see so much of you.'

'True. But that might be easier for me.'

'Not necessarily for me though, Jonathan. You've made me fond of you.'

'Fond is not enough. I don't see that you can have it both ways.'

'So she picks up everything, does our Bess,' said a shrill voice beside them, 'and moves out, bag and baggage. Leaving nothing but the empty gin bottles.'

'She was always a one for gin. She swore it preserved you. Used to put her teeth in it at nights.'

'I think you should sit it out,' proclaimed Martha Craxton.

They were relaxing before Sunday lunch in the conservatory at Sweetladies. It was the best place in the huge house for enjoying the October sun. George usually enjoyed this time of the week, the hour of the Bloody Mary.

'They don't like it here,' explained George miserably. 'At least, not in government.'

'They don't all like it in the States,' said Martha. 'But I see no need to get uptight. Just because you had a bit of a fling. After that foul woman left you high and dry.'

'I was neither high nor dry,' countered Craxton with dignity. 'And she wasn't a foul woman. She was human.'

'We're all human, honey,' said Martha. 'That's the bull point. I reckon we just go ahead and hit Washington.'

'Go ahead?' gulped George.

'Why ever not? There's no real reason to think that this will ever come out. And, if it does, you'll just have to step out of the closet.'

'I don't think the Foreign Office would like that,' protested George miserably.

'These people give me the heeby-jeebies,' said Martha. 'Leave it to me, George love. I'll fix it direct with the President and the Prime Minister.'

'It wouldn't work,' warned George. 'You don't understand our Security procedures at all. And, even if it did, I couldn't stand the publicity. All that horrible hounding by the gutter press.'

'Get along with you, George. Politically it could be a good broad platform in Washington. My folks were all Baptist preachers and robustly normal. Orson and I were always in with the fine, upstanding, red-blooded American boy types, the salt of the Republican party in the West. Riding into the sunset and all that. I could manage those big hairy fellows. And you could appeal to the Gay Liberation people. They're always big in the media. That way, we'd cover the waterfront. That's the secret of American politics. Maximum spread, maximum coverage.'

George gave a little shudder.

'So that's fixed,' continued Martha. 'If you don't want me to fix it with your Prime Minister, you can call at Number Ten yourself and have it all out.'

'I would rather not,' replied George. 'We've just got to accept the facts.'

'Do you mean to sit there,' asked Martha, 'staring at my empty vodka glass and telling me, bold as brass, that we're never now going to become ambassador in Washington?'

'I do,' said George.

'Well then,' asked Martha coldly, 'what the hell am I doing here? In this awful, dull old place with worm in the woodwork. I've been turning myself from an American lady into an English woman. I put up with the cold bedrooms, the warm beer, the grotty little lavatories. I did it all for you.'

'No, you didn't,' snapped George. 'You did it in order to become ambassadress in Washington. To preside over that great ballroom.'

'Well, why not? Orson's share portfolio gave me the high-voltage charisma in the States. But I wanted the special prestige accessible only over here to old money. Those top diplomats on Massachusetts Avenue are big bananas socially. That's what I expected to become.'

'Life is full of disappointments,' said George.

'Not my life,' countered Martha crisply. 'I don't allow it to be. In America, we play to win. I warn you, George. I shan't take this lying down. What kind of life are you planning for us now?'

'I haven't really thought.'

'Well, you'd better start thinking, pretty damned quick. Could we be Governor of Bermuda or something?'

'I rather doubt it.'

'I'll not stay here and rust away in this horrible climate. That's for sure. I shall have to take steps.'

'What steps?'

'You'll see,' replied his wife, with an edge of menace. The sun, George noticed, had gone behind a cloud.

'The yen is up today,' said Major Glossop. 'I hope your brokers are well advised on the Tokyo market.'

'Very funny,' snapped Tess. 'I thought you invited me here for a spot of torture.'

'My dear girl. We gave up torture ages ago. Nowadays, it's the psychological probe.'

'I don't want your Freudian cattle prod,' said the young woman sourly, 'up my mental orifices.'

'You'll get it where we want it.'

'I know your type. Petty fascist.'

'I'm not petty,' replied the Major loftily. 'In fact I am rather grand.'

'Your premises are grand,' admitted Tess. 'I refer to the building, not your terms of reference. Bangalore Mansions has a certain faded cachet. I can't think what a seedy little outfit like yours is doing here.'

'We are saving the nation. From the eccentricities of some of its most gifted children.'

'My friend Harold Montrose would approve. Of the Mansions, I mean. Just look at those mouldings over the door.'

'It is about Montrose that I wanted to speak.'

'I don't have to answer any questions, Major. You're not even the police.'

'You know who we are. I explained over the phone when I invited you to call. We are making certain enquiries, to do with the security vetting of senior civil servants.'

'Why me, then? I'm only a poor Irish girl.'

'That is just a fantasy, Miss Leyland. I fear you have been retarded at the tiresome stage of girlish whimsy. Your distinguished family is of considerable interest to us. And we need to know more about your connection with this Professor Montrose.'

'I am in partnership with Harold. We act as specialist advisers for discriminating people who wish to occupy unusual residences. Like, for example, the old woman who lived in a shoe.'

'We know all that.'

'Would you care to rent a gazebo in the Caledonian Road?'

'Don't waste my time, Tess. I may seem light-hearted. That's the way I have been brought up. But, deep down, I am solid granite.'

'I can easily believe it.' Tess lit a cigarette and puffed smoke towards him. She was rather enjoying her confrontation with the Major. It reminded her of some of those tiffs with Mother.

'You would be well advised,' continued Glossop in a tone of

menacing urbanity, 'to be completely frank with me. Then you might get away with quite a light sentence.'

Tess responded with what she hoped was an irritating little smile. It never failed to send Charmian into a tizzy.

'A light sentence, Major?' she asked sweetly. 'Now you have become the fantasy merchant. You will be telling me next that Harold and I have been bombing all those nasty modern buildings.'

'We know perfectly well that you have. And perhaps your boy-friend, too. It's only a question of proof. So the question is simply this, Tess. Do you intend to go down with the ship?'

'Are you offering me a lifebelt?'

'Lifebelts are my business.'

'When you talk so lightly about sentences,' said Tess, 'you would do well to understand the implications. Harold has some notable associations.'

'No doubt you intend to trot them out.'

'I have a photograph for you here, Major.'

She passed it across to him. Glossop gulped. It was one of the flash shots that Tess had so unexpectedly taken in the Charge of the Light Brigade on the evening that Charmian had been so touched to be invited there by her wayward daughter. Lady Leyland's beaky, intellectual features were clearly visible, as were those of Professor Montrose, Rupert, Jonathan and Tess herself, all in various stages of alcoholic stimulation.

'That will be your mother,' said the Major. 'I know the face. Lady Leyland has been around for some time. And that will be your paramour, I suppose? The one with the vacuous grin.'

'He uses it for cover.'

'And who is this other young man?' asked Glossop innocently.

'Jonathan Fieldhouse. An earnest person, anxious to succeed.'

'All right, you had a drink together. Perhaps you invited your mother. Then she could hardly avoid meeting Montrose. What does that prove?'

'I have a tape here too,' said Tess with an ugly little smirk. 'I'd like to play a bit.'

The Major nodded assent. Tess started the tape. Scratchy pub noises came through, followed by Jonathan's eager voice.

'So they are not all government buildings,' said Jonathan on the tape. 'I thought there might be some other criterion. It's not a random selection.'

'All the buildings destroyed,' Charmian Leyland was heard to say, 'were extremely ugly. Horrible, arrogant examples of modern architecture. I'm glad they are gone. Whoever blew them up has done the nation a good turn. I take my hat off to them.'

'Be careful, Mother,' said Tess's voice. 'That's seditious talk. You're supposed to be a pillar of the Establishment.'

'Not when I'm off duty, dear,' came the voice of Charmian. 'What's that you are fumbling with, Tess?'

'Just my holdall. I have to fumble with something.'

Tess snapped off the tape machine. She smirked again.

'You're pleased with yourself?' Glossop asked heavily.

'It was neatly done.'

'It proves nothing. Your mother was just talking a bit wildly. It doesn't follow that she was involved.'

'No. But, according to you, she was talking to the very people who *were*. Doesn't that imply she was giving tacit encouragement?'

'It wouldn't convince a jury.'

'But it might interest the press.'

'I see,' said the Major. 'You're saying that if you and Montrose are prosecuted, you'll drag your mother in.'

'Why not? She's dragged me into plenty of her things. It wouldn't be too good for the great Leyland career, would it? There could be quite a stink in Washington.'

'You thought all this out, didn't you? You implicated your parents on purpose. It's the motivation that I find so chilling.'

'Perhaps I did it for self-protection. Not that I'm admitting anything.'

'No, it wasn't that. You don't care about Montrose. You don't care about old buildings. You just set out to ruin your parents. To deprive them of the coping-stone for your father's distinguished career.'

'How can you be so sure of that, Major?'

'I can tell hatred when I see it. It's a very naked emotion.'

'And who am I supposed to hate?'

'Your mother. I spotted it when you were listening to her voice on the tape. It was just something in your face, a sort of flicker around the eyes.'

Suddenly Tess's face began to crumple. She looked unexpectedly young and vulnerable.

'Mother always thinks that it is some special thing she has done wrong,' she said. 'One particular episode. But of course it isn't like that at all. For all her brains, she can't begin to respond to real people. It was her whole attitude that was unacceptable. She can't get that into her head at all. Do you understand that?'

'I think I do.'

'I used to love her once. Not as much as Daddy. But she was always cool and distant to me. And then my aunt let it out. It seems that Mother suffered some sort of trauma soon after I was born. She had to go away for a bit, on a holiday by herself in a convent with nuns. It happens to women more often than you might think. She couldn't take to the idea of having me around. She rejected me. That was how the psychiatrist put it. She wanted to be the professor's little learned daughter for ever and couldn't take the idea of becoming a mother herself. Apparently Daddy was very worried. I had to be looked after by the Italian maids. We were in Rome at the time.'

'But she came round in the end?'

'On the surface. She resumed her usual highly successful life.'

'You can't remember any of this, surely?'

'Not consciously. But it all made sense when I found out, years later.'

'Did you have it out with your mother?'

'Oh no,' replied Tess. 'That would not have been possible. Mother does not encourage the discussion of her little moments of weakness. But I did have a shot. On my eighteenth birthday, of all corny times. I got Mother alone, in one of her better moods. I asked her to tell me that she loved me.'

'And she said yes?' suggested the Major.

'Of course she said yes. Who wouldn't? But there was a tiny pause first, just the fraction of a second. I knew she was nerving herself to tell the necessary lie. She's rather too honest, you see.'

'Poor you.'

'That was when I began really hating the bitch. I knew that, at heart, she still rejected me. I had been denied the right to be her child. You don't like me much, do you?'

'I pity you. And I pity your parents, too.'

'They can't go to Washington now, can they? Not with this hanging over them.'

'I don't know. I don't decide these things.'

'No. But you'll report, won't you?'

'Oh yes. I'll report.'

Glossop suddenly felt weary. The girl was vile. And yet pathetic. It was probably something to do with her upbringing. It would be terrible for a child to have its love rejected, especially by a mother whom the world approved. He was not sure now that he cared much for Lady Leyland either. One thing was certain. Any prosecution case against Montrose would have to be handled with great circumspection. And so indeed must be the whole question of the Leyland appointment to the United States. This disgruntled young woman was potential dynamite. She would be party to none of those discreet cover-ups beloved of the official mind.

It was disturbing too that Jonathan could somehow appear to be implicated, however unfairly. Since he had squeezed the original information out of Jonathan, subsequent enquiries had revealed how close the boy had become to both Tess and Rupert. Major Glossop had always slightly distrusted him as too clever by half. Now, thought Glossop grimly, for a little personal confrontation.

'Well, thank you, Miss Leyland,' he continued with spurious affability. 'We mustn't take up more of your valuable time.'

'It was worth coming,' said Tess.

'If you ever need a good broker, feel free to call. On the way out, perhaps you'd like to see a little more of our fine old show-case. This way, please.'

Next door, Jonathan Fieldhouse was sitting cleaning his nails with an ivory-style paper-knife. He started up like a guilty thing surprised.

'Good God,' he almost shouted. 'What are you doing here, Maureen?'

'I was going to ask you that, Jonathan,' she said. 'But now I know.'

'So you two know each other,' commented the Major, with affected surprise. 'It's a small world.'

He returned to his own room, shut the door and started a small mechanism. It was distasteful to have to spy on his own staff. But these things had to be done. It had been a bold departure from standard procedure to bring a girl like that into the premises of the moon-pool itself. But it had been worth the break with established practice to obtain a tape of the conversation between Tess and Jonathan when both were under the influence of extreme surprise. He just had to know how deeply that young man was involved in the Montrose imbroglio. The Foreign Office had sent him to spy on the moon-pool. Now the compliment was being returned. That was life for you in the rough world outside the Royal Halberdiers, beyond the charmed Orchard of the Plums.

'I have a bone to pick with you, Marcus,' said Sir Dominic Trowbridge.

'Have a cup of tea,' suggested the Permanent Under-Secretary. 'And what about a piece of cake?'

'That would be nice,' said Bernard Gilbert. The lights had been turned on and the park outside had grown dusky. The days were short now that November had begun.

The Head of the Security Service favoured his host with a steely glare.

'I was quite astonished,' he snapped, 'about George Craxton.'

'So were we all,' said Sir Marcus Stewart-Stibbs, a little sanctimoniously. 'But I'm afraid people do have these moral lapses.' He favoured Lucinda's departing rear with an approving smile. That hardly qualified, he thought, as a moral lapse.

'I don't mean the boy-friend,' said Sir Dominic. 'Lots of people have them.'

'It's a mistake to get found out though,' said Sir Marcus. 'That's one thing they taught us at Harrow.'

'That's what I am talking about,' explained Trowbridge. 'The way he was found out. It should all have come through me.'

'It should indeed,' agreed Sir Marcus provocatively. 'You're supposed to be in charge of national security.'

'I was informed by the Prime Minister, of all people,' snapped Sir Dominic. 'Quite the wrong way round.'

'How very awkward for you.'

'You let me down, Marcus. I don't see why you didn't tell me.'

'I had to go straight to ministers. The odious Craxton was breathing down our necks. It was very delicate. Wasn't it, Bernard?'

Bernard nodded cautiously. It was all very well for the Permanent

Under-Secretary, shortly to retire, to make an enemy of the Head of the Security Service. But Bernard was not at all sure that he could afford to do so. He had not yet received his knighthood.

'I still don't understand how the Foreign Office came into it at all,' said Sir Dominic peevishly. 'All this unsavoury stuff about a person called Vince.'

'We owe that to Bernard,' explained Sir Marcus. 'He saved the government from a dreadful blunder.'

Usually Bernard was only too pleased to be given credit for his achievements. But, on this occasion, he felt uncharacteristically averse to taking a bow. He suspected that the wily Marcus, not unmindful perhaps of his own possible peerage, was deliberately deflecting Sir Dominic's anger in his own direction.

'So Bernard is running his own private security service these days, is he?' asked Sir Dominic nastily.

'I fished it out of the moon-pool,' explained Bernard. 'There's a lot of sludge lying down there at the bottom.'

'Like Narcissus,' quipped Trowbridge waspishly. 'He peeked into a pool, you remember, and saw his own reflection. Anyhow, what's the moon-pool got to do with you?'

'I have certain links,' replied Bernard evasively. 'As you will remember.'

'I'm in charge of the moon-pool,' snapped Sir Dominic. 'I invented the whole idea.'

'I thought of the title,' countered Sir Marcus, rather childishly. 'Anyhow, undercover surveillance of the private life of the citizens is not exactly a novel action. It's been practised for centuries. Caligula, Nero, Stalin.'

'That kind of jibe,' said Sir Dominic, 'does not sit well with my majors in mackintoshes. They are only trying to do their job.'

'So are we all, Dominic. So let's just accept the situation as it is. Craxton has been told, with full ministerial authority, that he can't go to Washington after all. He accepts the situation.'

'What will he do now, then?' asked Sir Dominic.

'Go on being a nuisance, I suppose. But only to ministers, not to us. Meanwhile, the Washington appointment has become urgent. Robin Compton is leaving later this month, on his sixtieth birthday. We'll get the announcement out this week about James Leyland.'

'You are proposing to send Leyland?' asked Trowbridge.

'Certainly. Ministers have agreed. He's the only other candidate. Presumably you have no objection, Dominic. Leyland has always sported the white flower of a blameless life. Hasn't he, Bernard?'

'He and Charmian,' said the Chief Clerk, 'are people of the highest principles. Their idea of an orgy is a small sherry and some dry biscuits.'

'I'm afraid there will be difficulties,' said Sir Dominic. He paused, to enjoy their consternation. He liked to think of himself as a good man. But he was human and to upstage the Foreign Office was one of life's rarest joys.

'Difficulties?' almost shrieked Sir Marcus Stewart-Stibbs. 'Leyland is the son of a bishop. He reads Aristotle in the bath. And Charmian visits the incurable. It must add a new terror to death.'

'They are people,' agreed Bernard Gilbert, 'of almost aggressive intellectual integrity.'

'Maybe they are,' said Sir Dominic. 'But they are poised on the edge of a volcano.'

He paused again for effect. It was a sweet moment and worth savouring.

'Just what is this nonsense?' asked Sir Marcus.

'Another whiff from the moon-pool,' replied Trowbridge. 'This time it came up through the proper channels. The Leylands are blessed with a daughter.'

'I know her,' said Sir Marcus. 'A funny little thing. What's wrong with her?'

'Quite a lot.' In measured tones, which he tried hard to divest of unctuous satisfaction, Sir Dominic embarked on the painful story of Tess's relationship with Professor Montrose. He described how both were wanted by the police for the architectural outrages in London and how, if found and brought to justice, Tess was determined to try to inculpate her own distinguished parents, or at least damage them deliberately by the association.

'She must be a monster,' commented Sir Marcus.

'Children can be,' said Bernard with feeling. 'Especially the children of the Establishment.'

'There's one point I don't quite understand,' said Sir Marcus with deceptive mildness. 'You say that this girl Tess was actually induced to visit one of your unobtrusive organizations, where she made clear her intention.'

186

'That is the case.'

'How is it then that your minions allowed her to slip through their fingers?'

'We don't have any fingers, Marcus. Our men in mackintoshes have empty sleeves. We are merely an advisory service. It seems that, when the girl came to us, the police didn't have enough evidence for an arrest. Now they think they have.'

'This would be terrible for the Leylands,' said Sir Marcus. 'They are so excessively upright.'

'It would be even worse,' said Sir Dominic, 'if his appointment to Washington had been announced. That would really excite the press.'

'I suppose you're right,' agreed Bernard. 'They don't care so much about the Community work in Brussels. It's too complicated for them to follow. Anyhow, poor James may have to leave Brussels too, if the storm breaks.'

'Just a moment,' said Sir Marcus. 'I'm not starting a witch-hunt. Whatever there may be on tape or film about Charmian Leyland, the idea of her getting involved in anything illegal is grotesque. At the worst, she may have been mildly indiscreet. I can't see how any of this need affect their security clearance for Washington.'

'That may be technically correct,' agreed Sir Dominic. 'But the family association is highly unfortunate. What about the political implications? Will ministers really want to run such a risk? In my experience, they usually prefer the soft option.'

'I'm afraid there *is* something in that,' agreed Bernard.

'It's kind of you to alert us, Dominic,' said Sir Marcus, with a trace of sarcasm.

'I'm glad to repay your help,' said Sir Dominic with the vestige of a grin. 'You were good enough to point out the security objections to Craxton. Now I'm pleased to co-operate with political advice over your man Leyland.'

The fellow was a bastard, thought Sir Marcus. He had always suspected it.

'Thank you,' he said with massive dignity. He wasn't going to give Dominic the satisfaction of witnessing a panicky reaction. 'All this has been most interesting. I shall discuss it with the Secretary of State. It is he who takes the decisions in this Office.'

This seemed a novel concept to Bernard. But he realized that this was the Permanent Under-Secretary's way of playing for time. It was good to watch an old master at work.

'I expect you'll find someone else,' said Sir Dominic kindly. 'Leyland's not the only onion in the stew.'

'Don't be too sure,' snapped Sir Marcus.

'And thanks for the tea,' said Trowbridge. 'I always enjoy our little chats. The moon-pool, I think, is beginning to prove its worth.'

After the Private Secretary, Jasper Tenby, had departed with the Head of the Security Service, Sir Marcus and Bernard Gilbert stared at each other.

'This is a hell of a mess,' said Sir Marcus.

'It is,' agreed Bernard. 'And I think the wretched man's right. Ministers simply wouldn't risk it.'

'But we've got to get the announcement out soon. Robin's aching to get home to Sussex. And the new ambassador will have to arrive after Christmas. If we're not careful, the whole damned business will go public.'

'I suppose there *are* other candidates,' said Bernard.

'There's nobody of the calibre of James Leyland,' retorted Sir Marcus. 'I'm jolly well going to try to keep him in the field. And I have just the glimmering of an idea.'

'What have you in mind, Marcus?'

'Leave it to me, Bernard. It's unorthodox but it might possibly work.'

Jasper Tenby had returned.

'The Spanish Ambassador is waiting,' he said.

And that evening, thought Sir Marcus, Felicity had committed them to a silly bridge party at the wrong end of Regent's Park. It was a miserable world.

'This is awful,' said Sir James Leyland. 'Total disaster. I'll have the Stilton, please.'

He and Sir Marcus Stewart-Stibbs were lunching in the long dining-room at the Voyagers. Normally James, on his weekly safari from Brussels, would have relished the familiar view of the handsome room in its blue and silver. But the news just broken to him by the Permanent Under-Secretary had quite spoiled his meal.

'I wanted you to know,' said Sir Marcus miserably. 'It seemed best to be totally frank.'

'Well, of course.'

'I know it's upsetting. About the Washington job.'

'To hell with Washington. Coriolanus got it right. There is a world elsewhere.'

It was bravely spoken. But James still felt a pang around the heart. The strain had been too much, even for a man trained to take the long view. At first his appointment had seemed certain, the climax of a well-planned career. Then the odious Craxton had interposed. His removal had seemed a godsend. Now there had come, out of the blue, this further crashing blow. In his mind's eye, James had a quick vision of the cloud-capped palaces disappearing – the lawns at Dumbarton Oaks, the warm red brick of George-town, the apple blossoms of the Shenandoah, the places he had known when young. Perhaps, in this gruesome pilgrimage called the human condition, you always deeply longed to return to where you had started, where you had first felt the joy of the heart. That didn't last all that long. Most of all James felt crushed by the implication of what Tess had done. He had always known that she disliked her mother, but had not realized to what extent, and that this hatred extended to him also. What a disaster it all was. Sophocles had got it right. Never to have been born was best.

'I am so sorry for Charmian,' said Sir Marcus.

'She will care more about the girl. To be hated so.'

'The young are difficult,' agreed Sir Marcus.

'It's much more than that. Tess felt rejected from the start. The thwarted, childish love turned first to indifference, then to hate.'

Charmian should never have had children, thought James. Some women were simply not maternal. It was absurd to make them undertake these roles, just for the sake of convention. Charmian was not incapable of love. But it had to be impersonal love for a deprived group, a vulnerable category, for the idea of people rather than their noisy, sweaty reality. She was not so good with individuals. And Tess had suffered, God how she had suffered. Now she would make them suffer in return.

'Have some more Stilton,' suggested Sir Marcus. 'It goes so well with the club claret.' Long years of man management had taught him the value of food and drink at these fraught moments.

'I'm afraid there is no doubt about it,' continued Sir Marcus. 'If your appointment to Washington went ahead and Tess were to be arrested, you would be gravely damaged by the family association. And so would the government. The Prime Minister is anxious to avoid controversy before the election.'

'I'll bet.'

'Of course, I don't know when the police will move. This Professor Montrose has apparently disappeared. And where is Tess?'

'I don't really know,' replied Sir James miserably.

'There is just one possibility,' said Sir Marcus. 'Could we perhaps discuss it over coffee?'

In the smoking-room downstairs, the Permanent Under-Secretary selected a remote divan, well out of earshot of the other members.

'I've had a little notion,' he said. 'I wonder if you would be prepared to consider it.'

'Tell me.'

'You and Charmian are not of course responsible for the antics of your grown-up daughter. They do not affect your own status as a highly trusted civil servant. The problem for ministers would be the possible association in the public mind. You know how simple people can be. Well, there is a way out. You and Charmian might sign a statement now to the effect that you have no authority over Tess, that in effect you spiritually disown her. I should be prepared to try that on the Secretary of State. It would only be used, of course, if the situation later went public. Ministers would then feel they had some protection. I could try to get the appointment through on that basis.'

Sir James Leyland took a moment to frame his reply. How severe his face is, thought Marcus, how fine-drawn the veins and bones. James was far removed from being the traditional laughing diplomat. In many ways, he was a tiresome and cussed old colleague. And yet, all the same, it would be good for the nation to get him to Washington. The Leylands would hardly entertain at all, the party-circuit would complain. But his fine mind would be at work, his incomparable powers of argument and analysis. There were many ways of being a good ambassador. One of the best in Washington after the Second World War had been a cool don who gave few parties but whose brain had been highly respected. It was time to produce another in that austere mould. The Americans were too important, perhaps too dangerous, to be dealt with now just on the basis of back-slapping amiability.

'Ingenious, Marcus,' said James at last.

'Thank you.'

'But damned insulting.'

'Oh, do you think so?'

'If you had children yourself, Marcus, you'd understand that it wouldn't work. Neither Charmian nor I can disown Tess. We helped to make her. If she's sad and pathetic, it's our fault. We can't renounce her. It would be against our principles.'

Damn the man, thought Sir Marcus, he's like a great oak whose branches break because they cannot bend. But one couldn't help admiring this craggy individualist. In his way, he was lovable precisely because he made no effort to be loved. That was the paradox of the special enchantment deployed by those who didn't set out to charm.

'You'd be paying a great price,' pointed out Sir Marcus.

'One has to accept,' retorted Sir James. 'There is no denying it. Our poor Tess is a quark. We are gluons.'

'I beg your pardon?' asked Sir Marcus politely.

'As you are aware,' replied Sir James, 'atoms are made up of electrons, protons and neutrons. Protons and neutrons, in their turn, are composed of quarks and gluons. It's a fundamental distinction like being Gladstone or Disraeli, Romeo or Juliet. Pity us poor gluons to have produced a quark.'

What a mind, thought Sir Marcus, how richly stocked. It was sad to think that it would now presumably have to be wasted on some backwater like Oxford or Cambridge.

'You tried to give me the slip,' said Jonathan reproachfully.

'Yes,' admitted Fiona. 'It seemed the best way.'

'I love you, Fiona.'

'You love your image of me. I'm not sure it's the real me at all.'

'I was staggered when Major Val gave me the news this morning. About your resignation from the Service.'

'I warned you I was planning it.'

'Yes, but I didn't know it would be so sudden.'

191

Distraught, he had rushed after work to the house at Wimbledon. He had been politely welcomed by Fiona's older friend. Jonathan did not quite know what his unruly imagination had led him to expect. Some moustached harridan perhaps, decked in mannish tweeds. Instead Mary was quiet and nice to look at. She had allowed him to join Fiona in a chintzy room overlooking the Common.

'I couldn't stand it any longer,' said Fiona. 'Some day they were bound to find out about Mary.'

'What reason did you give?'

'There didn't seem any need to offer any. Major Val just turned and stared at me. You know how straight and still he stands, like an angel of doom. He nodded, when he heard I was leaving. As if he had expected it all along.'

'I expect he had. You're far too pretty to be a security nark.'

'Sexist pig!'

'I'm going to miss you terribly, Fiona.'

'Sometimes the best thing you can give a friend is your absence, your silence.'

'That's rather a stark thought.'

'Well, I'm not quitting the planet.'

'Where *are* you going?'

'Mary is taking me to Italy. It will be an education.'

'Who for?'

'For me, of course. Mary is bilingual in Italian.'

'So this is goodbye.'

'Oh, I don't know,' said Fiona doubtfully. 'We don't leave for a few days. Mary has to arrange about her classes.'

'Sometimes I think you're a bitch. You don't want me and yet you won't let me go.'

'I know. I'm sorry. I'm still awfully muddled.'

'Rejected love festers,' said Jonathan.

'In the one who gives?'

'No. In the one who refuses to accept.'

'That's a strange notion.'

'Not really. You didn't want my love. So, deep down in your mind, you have to prove to yourself that it wasn't worth having It's emotional, not intellectual, like giving up the priesthood. That will make you implacable.'

'I might just be – indifferent.'

'You might be, Fiona. But you're not. You resent me, for breaking your cosy pattern.'

'We could still be friends.'

'I'm not sure I want that. I've always wanted to possess you.'

'That was the whole trouble,' Fiona sighed. 'The old must be happier,' she added. 'When the physical thing dies away.'

'I doubt if it *does* die away. Sex-maniacs, so called, are often old. As you age, you grow less confident, lonelier, more frightened of death. The need for physical comfort and reassurance actually increases.'

'Talk about an old head on young shoulders. Are you trying to scare me, Jonathan?'

'The line between happiness and misery is fine, isn't it? So much a matter of sheer luck. It just depends on one other human being, when you come to think of it. Their voice on the stair and the light snaps on inside you. And when they leave, they take it all with them.'

'You'll find someone else.'

'How do you know?' Jonathan almost shouted. 'You may be the only person I can love in my whole life.'

'Most unlikely. You're as loving as a puppy.'

'Puppy-love! Is that what you mean?'

'This conversation,' said Fiona dismissively, 'is beginning to hurt.'

They were both relieved when Mary knocked and sailed into the room, hands full of books. Jonathan knew it was time to go. The two women showed him out. Mary wore a look of unshakeable courtesy. But then she was the winner.

'I have come,' said Sir Marcus Stewart-Stibbs, 'to a decision which may well surprise you.'

Bernard Gilbert gulped. Normally the Permanent Under-Secretary spoke in a deceptively mild and diffident manner. But those, like Bernard, who worked most closely with Sir Marcus knew that he was ice-cold beneath the gentle manner, rock-hard below the charm. It came out just occasionally. Bernard suspected now that this was to be one of those occasions.

'About Washington?' asked Bernard.

'Yes. An urgent decision is needed,' said Sir Marcus. 'The

Secretary of State was saying that last night at the Palace. One of those ghastly State Dinners. I can't think why they always have soup. So a decision there shall be. As you know, there are two strong candidates.'

'Both blown.'

'Don't be too sure of that,' opined Sir Marcus, looking bleakly out over the park in winter. 'Admittedly each has a certain encumbrance. But one has to live in the real world.'

'I thought we had agreed, Marcus. Craxton has that awful boyfriend, James that appalling daughter. Those are insuperable obstacles.'

'They seemed insuperable,' said his superior pointedly. 'But only when there was another candidate in the field. We simply cannot afford to lose both our men. I admit there is a certain risk in both cases. But there are strong mitigating circumstances. Craxton is now respectably married again. And Tess Leyland has not, so far, been convicted of any offence.'

'Do you really think,' asked Bernard, 'that ministers will see it in that way?'

'I have decided, after prolonged thought, to let ministers decide. After all, what do we have ministers *for*? I shall now advise them officially, in my capacity as Head of the Service, that in my opinion neither objection is overriding. So they had better assess the risks for themselves and decide which one scares them least.'

'But these are dreadful risks, Marcus. I shudder to think of what the Sunday newpapers might make of it. Especially the heavies. Those creepy investigative journalists with good seconds in history, the type who live in Kentish Town and have wives who write about Provençal cooking. The up-market muck-rakers.'

'I got a good second in history,' said Sir Marcus ruminatively.

'Well, you know what I mean,' Bernard countered lamely.

'There are ways of arranging these matters, you know. The young man Vince could be paid off. That's the kind of thing we have secret funds for. As for little Miss Leyland, she's presumably fled abroad. Interpol have been known to lose files before now.'

'Good Heavens,' said Bernard, feeling genuinely shocked. 'That's the kind of way they behave in other countries.'

'We, too,' countered Sir Marcus, 'are another country.'

'Well, in that case, if both candidates are still viable, why not persuade ministers to plump for James? We always wanted the job for the Service.'

'Oh no, my dear Bernard, I'm not falling for that one. The position has entirely changed. As you point out, there *are* certain risks of public exposure. If this goes wrong, I'm not taking the rap. Ministers can decide for themselves.'

He's thinking of his own peerage, thought Bernard with inner rage. A mere GCMG wouldn't be enough for him. It was one of the wisest of British prime ministers who remarked that every man has his price.

'So we keep both men in the race,' continued Sir Marcus. 'No official preference. You understand?'

'And Dominic Trowbridge?'

'This will be a political decision.'

In the Permanent Under-Secretary, thought Bernard, the wisdom of the serpent met the obstinacy of the mule.

'Cheer up, Bernard,' continued Sir Marcus. 'I feel sure it will all come right. Then we can proceed with your whole lovely chain of promotions. Including, of course, your own appointment to Canberra.'

Bernard and Amaryllis, with their confident English tones so redolent of the upper-middle class, so imbued with an unshakeable sense of superiority, would become mild jokes down-under. Well, that would not greatly matter. There were worse things in life than becoming a mild joke. It only happened to those, like Bernard, who might be superficially amusing but had no real sense of the ridiculous. For that you had to feel the futility of things.

Sir Marcus suddenly felt tired and old. It had been quite a strain, deciding to leave the decision to ministers.

'I'd like to talk,' said Amaryllis Gilbert, as they put the dirty dishes into the machine.

'Feel free, darling,' riposted Bernard. 'My ears are always open.'

'That's just what they are not. You spend the day listening to other people's problems. At night you haven't got much time for mine.'

'Is that altogether surprising?' He carried the coffee into the early-Victorian drawing-room.

'I have come to a decision. You may find it a bit of a shock.'

195

Bernard was reminded of Sir Marcus. It seemed to be a day for other people to reveal their capacity for independent action.

'I know,' he said jovially. 'You've decided to take up tapestry.'

Amaryllis eyed him almost malevolently. It was not easy being married to Bernard, whose *bonhomie* was largely on the surface.

'I have come to the conclusion,' she said slowly, 'that the children need me more than you do.'

'We all need you.'

'That may be true. But Mr Watts-Dunton thinks that Timothy may be suffering from pyromania. Apparently it's not uncommon among disturbed adolescents.'

'Why should Timothy be disturbed?'

'An over-dominant father perhaps, combined with an unduly submissive mother. Timothy set fire to Mr Watts-Dunton's diary of his rambling holiday in Tuscany.'

'Perhaps he just doesn't like Mr Watts-Dunton.'

'Then there's Camilla. She's having a ghastly time with Tuomo. He's homesick for pine trees.'

'She's beyond our reach now.'

'Nonsense, Bernard. A girl is never beyond her mother's reach.'

'All this is very interesting, my dear. But are there any practical consequences?'

'Yes,' said Amaryllis. 'There are.'

'What on earth do you mean?'

'If you go to Australia, Bernard, you go alone.'

'Alone?'

'That's what I said.'

Bernard goggled. 'What on earth will you do, then?' he asked.

'I shall stay here. So as to be near the children. Mr Watts-Dunton likes to phone frequently. He says he finds it comforting.'

'And what about me? Who is going to organize the entertaining in Canberra?'

'That's your problem, dear.'

'Who is going to make sure my collar is turned down at the back? Boost my ego?'

'I expect you'll find someone. You've never had to do very much for yourself, have you?'

'Have you been talking to some stupid woman?'

'No, dear. I thought it up for myself.'

'I suppose you have a lover, then? Someone you met watching football on the heath?'

'Oh, don't be so silly. You've got to understand me. I've never really cared for this diplomatic business.'

'It's the way we earn our living.'

'Well, I've got to be within reach of the children. At least on the telephone. Australia is just too damn far away.'

Bernard sighed. All right, Amaryllis had fallen out of love with him long ago. But it was still a working partnership. He needed it.

'You were willing to go to Europe,' he pointed out.

'That's near. You can just pop on a plane.'

'What about the States?'

'That would have been OK. There are lots of cheap Atlantic flights. Timothy could go to college in America. And the hateful Finn is longing to emigrate to the States. He has relations deep in the forests of Minnesota. But we're not going to the States, are we?'

'No,' replied Bernard softly. 'I don't expect we are.'

'I'm sorry, dear.'

'No, you're not. You're not sorry at all. You're glad you plucked up the courage to tell me.'

'I could come out for visits,' said Amaryllis more gently. 'Christmas and things. I wouldn't want us to be separated then.'

'That's big of you.' Bernard, crossed, was not a pretty sight.

Next morning he found Miss Johnson-Boswell all of a flutter.

'Oh dear,' she said. 'The telephone has never stopped ringing. News Department want to know when there's going to be a decision about the Washington appointment.'

'Tell them to stonewall.'

'Mr George Craxton wants to talk to you urgently. He's down at his house in Suffolk. And Sir James Leyland has called from Brussels.'

'I'll take Craxton first, then Leyland.'

The imp of mischief lurked in Bernard's face that mid-November morning. Or was it more of a gambler's desperation?

'Sorry to bother you, Bernard,' came Craxton's rasping baritone. 'But I couldn't get Marcus.'

'He went to Bonn for the day, I think.'

'I need to know for certain. Key decisions depend on it and have to be made at once. I want you to be completely straight with me.'

'I'll do my best.'

'I know you will.' It was rather awful to hear the professional flattery in the anxious voice of the former Cabinet Minister. 'What I must be sure about is this. Is it absolutely certain now that I shan't get the embassy in Washington?'

Bernard drew a deep breath.

'Yes,' he said.

'It was good of you to tell me straight, Bernard. I appreciate your being so frank. Oh well, I'll just have to bite the bullet.'

'I'm afraid so.'

Sir James Leyland had a similar question. Compared with his political rival, his voice sounded bloodless and academic.

'Charmian and I can't go on much longer like this,' he complained. 'We've got to make plans.'

'I do understand, James.'

'Marcus kept me frigging around with his compromise idea. But it won't work, Bernard. Now please tell me, once and for all. Is it quite definite that we are not to go to Washington?'

'Yes,' answered Bernard.

'Craxton will be appointed?'

'Maybe.'

'Thank you for letting me know,' answered James faintly. 'At least we have some certainty now.' In his mind's eye, the cherry trees were falling on the Potomac, the riotous October colours of Vermont had grown tarnished in their scarlet and gold, the old houses were crumbling in the mellow squares of Boston. His beloved America had always been visual.

Bernard put down the telephone. He sat appalled. What on earth had he done? The grotesque lie was bound to be found out. Ministers would decide in favour of one of the two tarnished candidates. Then the fat would be in the fire. What could have possessed him to act so foolishly? Now he risked having to retire without the accolade, to drag out life in some country village as a plain Mister like everyone else.

Unless? There was just one possibility, thought Bernard. It would be a matter of luck. He did not like to count on that.

'Just to remind you of your lunch,' said Miss Johnson-Boswell. 'At the Reform Club. With the Chairman of the Civil Service Commission.'

Most unusually, Bernard did not look forward to his lunch that day. In a notably greedy man, it was a sign of marked trepidation.

'I have known for some time,' remarked George Craxton affably, 'that you betrayed me.'

Jonathan Fieldhouse shifted uneasily in his Chippendale chair. This invitation to Sunday lunch at Sweetladies seemed to be turning out even worse than he had feared. Renewed social contact with Craxton was the last thing he wanted. But the former Cabinet Minister had been persistent. On arrival at the Suffolk seat, Jonathan was disturbed to discover that Martha had disappeared. Now came the accusation of treachery.

'They got it out of me,' said Jonathan. 'It was part of my job.'

'I know,' said Craxton. 'I don't blame you.'

'I still feel bad about it.'

'Please don't. You were a cog in the machine.'

He looked defeated, thought Jonathan, and a good deal older. With the aggression forced out of him, there was not a lot left. Jonathan supposed that many worldly and ambitious men must be like that. In the still centre of their personality there was simply a vacuum.

'I'm not going to Washington after all,' said Craxton. 'Bernard Gilbert has told me that for certain.'

'I'm sorry.'

'The worst thing was about Martha.'

'What has happened to her?'

'She left. She called a taxi and drove to the airport. When she knew the decision was final.'

'Surely that's not possible?'

'She had set her heart on the Washington Embassy. She had hoped to queen it there in long, shimmery gowns. To welcome the rich and famous. To be written about by those hugely malevolent gossip columnists. To have all eyes swivel towards her, with the attached necks uncomfortably craning, as she swept down staircases into ballrooms. A woman's simplicity, you know.'

'She didn't seem at all simple to me.'

'You couldn't know her as I did, Jonathan. Beneath that veneer of sophistication, Martha was at heart a little, frightened child. It was her upbringing, you see. She often used to tell me about her

199

awful father, an old-fashioned Biblical Fundamentalist with a weakness for the bottle. Her heart belonged to Daddy. But Daddy was too drunk to care.'

'It must have been a disappointment for her,' said Jonathan. 'About Washington, I mean.'

'That is something of an understatement,' countered the politician dryly. 'As Martha made abundantly clear. An American female in a temper tantrum is a truly awesome sight!'

Although Craxton spoke calmly and even with apparent urbanity, Jonathan could not help noticing the malevolence underlying his words.

'So she left. For the United States. For good?' asked Jonathan.

'Certainly.'

'But she's your wife.'

'Not for much longer, Jonathan. It now seems that she married me less for my personal charm than for my new position in Washington. It was apparently conceived of as a dynastic union. Her money, my everything else.'

'That's tough on you, George.'

'I hope you never encounter a Martha Freeport.'

'I never did care for her,' admitted Jonathan.

'She detested you, too.'

Jonathan felt sorry for the older man, deflated, sagged, suffused with bitterness.

'You're well rid of her,' he said.

'I have come to the same conclusion, my dear boy. It's damn humiliating, all the same. And I don't want it to get out. As a public figure, I have to watch my place in history. I shall need your help in concocting a cover story.'

'Seeing that we are speaking frankly,' said Jonathan, 'I think that Martha would not have been quite right as British Ambassadress.'

'How right you are,' replied George Craxton. 'I have only recently discovered that Martha's past associations alone would probably have disqualified us for Washington. So the thing was hopeless from the first. Rather a joke, when you come to think of it. The FBI have been in touch. Her previous husband, Orson Freeport the Second, died in decidedly fishy circumstances. He was being pressed for back taxes and may well have committed suicide. Martha faces some quite unpleasant publicity.'

'I can't say I'm surprised,' commented Jonathan.

'As a matter of fact, my poor Sally has come out of this better,' said George. 'She wrote me a very decent letter on my re-marriage, wishing me happiness. I almost feel tempted to get in touch with her again. What do you advise?'

'Caution,' said Jonathan.

'Perhaps you are right. Women are distinctly tiresome,' commented George. 'At least, that has been my experience. Don't you sometimes think that affection between men might be simpler, more clinical?'

'No,' said Jonathan hastily, 'I do not.'

After his telephone talk with Bernard, Sir James Leyland in Brussels took Charmian out for a winter walk in the Bois.

'This is not like you,' she said, almost playfully. 'Taking time off from the office during the week.'

'It's a special day,' her husband explained. 'I'm leaving the Service.'

'Washington is off, then?'

'Definitely. Bernard told me this morning.'

'I'm not all that sorry, dear. Except for you. At least we know where we are now.'

'We certainly do. Out in the cold. You can thank Tess for that.'

'Such a strange girl,' mused Charmian.

'And vanished apparently,' said James, 'into thin air.' He was worried about the girl. He remembered the thin, anxious child who had once sobbed in his arms, avid for comfort, gulping out that Mummy didn't love her, would never love her.

'She'll be back,' riposted Charmian a trifle tartly. 'With her dirty washing.'

'I had to press Bernard for something definite. I didn't disclose my whole hand.'

'You never do.'

'The truth is that the Belial election committee meets tomorrow. I've just told them that, if they want me, I'm willing to accept the Mastership.'

'And you'll get it?'

'Oh yes. I am incomparably the best candidate.'

He reminded her in these things, thought Charmian, of her

father, the Professor. There was the same Oxford intellectual clarity, which those outside might mistake for arrogance. If you happened to be the best, you made no attempt to deny it.

'So you've burned your bridges,' was all she said.

'I suppose so. And yours too.'

'I don't mind,' she said loyally. 'I've grown tired of diplomatic life. All that superficial talk.'

'You will rule the Master's Lodge,' said James, 'with great grace. I have always loved you very much.'

'Don't be silly, dear,' replied Charmian, secretly enchanted. 'We're a bit old for that now.'

'It's funny name, isn't it? Belial College.'

'No odder than calling a college Jesus or Brasenose. A hint of mediaeval devilry, perhaps.'

'They hope I will add a new dimension,' said James. 'They want me to obtain more foreign benefactions. Development money from the European Community.'

'I hope you'll be happy in Oxford,' said Charmian doubtfully. 'These colleges can be petty places. It won't exactly be the land of heart's desire.'

'Few men,' replied Sir James, 'achieve their heart's desire. Why should I be different from the rest?'

The thin tenor voice of Sir Marcus Stewart-Stibbs tended to rise when he was feeling peeved. His last remark had almost ended on a whinny, thought Bernard Gilbert unsympathetically.

'I don't understand it at all,' Marcus moaned.

'What don't you understand, Marcus?'

'The way they have both faded out. Most awkward, to say the least. The Foreign Secretary was meeting the Prime Minister tomorrow to select the man for Washington. He had agreed that the choice lay firmly between Craxton and James, whatever the hazards. The Secretary of State was particularly keen to pin the choice on the Prime Minister personally. Just in case something blew up afterwards. You know what these politicians are like.'

'Well?'

'Now that idiot James has gone and accepted the Mastership of Balliol.'

'Belial. It's a little college in the Turl, founded in the fourteenth century by a reformed satanist.'

'We didn't have silly names like that at Cambridge,' snapped Sir Marcus. 'I expect he'll find it very small beer.'

'Charmian will be happier. She's north Oxford to the core.'

'Then the wretched Craxton rings me to say that his marriage has collapsed in flames and he can't, on any account, be considered for a post abroad. I tried to persuade him but he says that Martha is sitting on top of a smouldering volcano.'

'That must be most uncomfortable,' said Bernard.

'Meanwhile, Robin Compton has told the National Press Club in Washington that he's leaving in a fortnight. News Deparment say that the press have a story about a row between ministers here over the question of a successor. Can you imagine the implications? A leak about Craxton's private life and the awful Leyland girl. I shall be made to look like a knave and a fool.'

'You're not a knave, Marcus.'

'It's worse being thought a fool. Much worse.' Sir Marcus had a mental vision of his peerage rapidly disappearing. 'What the hell are we to do, Bernard?'

'Appoint someone else.'

'There isn't anyone else,' moaned Sir Marcus.

'Oh nonsense. The Foreign Service is full of competent senior officers with energetic wives.'

'But none of them is of the same calibre.'

'I shouldn't worry too much about that,' said Bernard. 'As you have said yourself, just nominate a reliable man who wants to be posted abroad.'

'What sort of person do you have in mind?'

'Someone with plenty of confidence. An expansive and urbane manner. Ability to crack a joke. Jolly wife, under control. The kind of Englishman that Americans admire.'

'I don't know anyone like that.'

'Well, just start looking around.'

'I can't start scraping the bottom of the barrel,' said Sir Marcus. 'My credibility is at stake. I'm supposed to be a fine judge of horse-flesh.'

'Then judge.'

'Unless,' began Sir Marcus doubtfully.

'Unless what?'

'Ministers will have to accept that this is an emergency. Needs must where the devil drives. Isn't there some proverb along those lines?'

'I believe there is.'

'I suppose,' said Sir Marcus without much enthusiasm, 'we could nominate you.'

'Me?'

'Well, why not? You are all those things you were describing. At least, I hope you are.'

'Me? Ambassador in Washington?' Bernard, for once, seemed to be momentarily stunned.

'You and Amaryllis would look quite stately, receiving guests on the Lutyens terrace. Much better in fact than that scrawny old James and dowdy Charmian. And you're not an opinionated fool like George Craxton.'

'I'm terribly flattered, Marcus. I never knew that you valued my contribution so highly.'

Sir Marcus was on the point of replying that he was desperate. But he realized that this wouldn't sound too polite. Like most people, Bernard was a mass of self-doubt beneath that robust exterior.

'I think you'll be splendid,' said Sir Marcus dubiously.

'It's a wonderful post. I shall do my best to run it as a team. I'm an ensemble leader, not a virtuoso. At least I know where my forte lies.'

'And there won't be any problem, will there, over security vetting?' asked Sir Marcus plaintively. 'I couldn't bear that.'

'I'm pure,' said Bernard, 'as driven snow.'

'Excuse me for asking. But are you quite sure? No private kinks?'

'Certainly not.'

'And the children? Not doing anything odd?'

'Oh no. Dear young things.'

'Thank God for that,' said Sir Marcus. 'I'll tell the Secretary of State at once. He's become very restive about the whole thing. He lives in dread of a ministerial reshuffle. The Prime Minister wasn't too pleased about the way the Trade Mission to Japan worked out. Number Ten are trying to find somewhere to place the blame.'

'So we are let off Australia?'

'It will do for Toby. He's bursting to get away from Lagos.'

'Then everyone is going to be happy.'

'Not everyone, Bernard. Everyone never is. There has to be pain and grief. But I agree that this has all worked out rather nicely. Almost as if it had been planned.'

He darted Bernard a shrewd look. The ambassador designate to the United States returned an unwavering stare of fathomless innocence. But then they were both professionals, each in his way an old master.

In the outer office of the Permanent Under-Secretary, Jasper Tenby and Lucinda were astonished to receive smiles of seraphic beauty from the plump features of the departing Chief Clerk. A passer-by in the park, five minutes later, would have been even more amazed to see a stout, well-dressed official who seemed to be dancing a jig. Or was it a tango he was trying to execute with one of the weeping willows? This was ecstasy, thought Bernard. You had to express it physically. Like the whirling dervishes. The moment must be captured for eternity.

'I'm only a simple soldier,' said Major Valentine Glossop. How stiffly he sat, thought Sir Dominic Trowbridge, how superbly straight and erect. The man was a sort of grotesque but he had his uses. Sir Dominic did not much care for that affectation of soldierly simplicity. It was usually the prelude to some unusually dastardly act.

'But you feel I ought to know something,' said Sir Dominic, 'about Bangalore Mansions.'

'Yes. Of course at school we were taught not to sneak.'

'Oh were you? The Jesuits rather encouraged it.'

'Well, times have changed. It's too dangerous to sit on things. Especially in the moon-pool, of all places.'

'I quite agree. You'd get a damp seat.'

'It's about this boy, Jonathan Fieldhouse. The young Foreign Office man you landed me with.'

'Clever and keen, I thought.'

'Possibly. But I'm not happy about him. I think we should withdraw his security clearance for papers classified as secret and above.'

'That would ruin his career in the Foreign Office.'

'I can't help that. As you keep reminding us, public service is a privilege, not a right.'

'Is he misbehaving?'

'It's the company he keeps. He was very close to that girl Fiona Hopkins. The one I told you about, who turned out to be associated with a sexual deviate.'

'She worked for you, Major Val. Are you suspect too?'

'Certainly not. My case is quite different. Jonathan unfortunately fell in love with the girl.'

Sir Dominic wondered whether Major Val had ever been in love with anyone. His horses perhaps. It would be worth looking into his private life. He seemed to remember talk about a wife in the country. That left four nights a week for vice in London. You could never be too careful.

'You must have more on him than that,' said Sir Dominic.

'I do indeed. Through his idle friend, one Rupert Mills, young Jonathan has had a close association with Tess Leyland. You know all about her. Interpol are on her track.'

'I thought it was Fieldhouse who alerted you to Miss Leyland's suspicious activities.'

'He did. But only after I started to probe.'

'So you don't give him any good marks for that?'

'Not really.'

Come to think of it, Sir Dominic mentally continued, it was probably Fieldhouse who had spilled the beans to Bernard Gilbert about Craxton's relationship with Vince. This information had bypassed Sir Dominic himself, thus causing him to look a fool in ministerial eyes. He would not forget that painful incident in a hurry.

'And you want me to tell the Foreign Office?' asked Sir Dominic.

'Well, it's your side of the house.'

He would enjoy informing that self-satisfied Bernard that one of his young swans wore the darker feathers of a goose. The Chief Clerk was intolerably smug these days, now that he had been appointed to Washington. Sir Dominic had been put in charge of his security clearance on a basis of urgency. It had been a disappointment to find his record so clean. And there was no time now to put him through the deep trawl of the moon-pool. The Prime Minister had been adamant about that. Sir Dominic had sensed that

206

ministers were turning against the whole concept of the moon-pool.

'All right,' said Sir Dominic. 'We put the skids under young Fieldhouse. But I shall need something in writing from you. Oh dear, it's a wretched thing, isn't it? What will the boy do?'

'They'll find him something else. We can't take a chance.'

'Anything else, Major?'

'They're pestering us, over in Bangalore, about telephone calls. Unauthorized private use. Apparently you can trace them nowadays through the computer.'

'Soon everything will be on the computer,' said Sir Dominic grimly, worrying privately again about his phone calls to Devon. 'Then we shan't need the moon-pool.'

'I think we shall always need the moon-pool now,' replied Major Glossop. 'So long as human nature tries to conceal its darker side.'

Jonathan's sessions with Rupert in the Charge of the Light Brigade were usually pleasant occasions. But not tonight. Gloom filled Jonathan's young heart as he glanced round at the brass taps, the engraved glass, the stuffed pike.

'It's so unfair,' he wailed.

'Of course it's unfair,' agreed Rupert. 'I warned you not to try to get on in the world.'

Even now, Jonathan couldn't tell Rupert the whole story. That was part of the frustration, when he badly needed sympathy. He had entered Bernard Gilbert's imposing office so happily, confident that he would now obtain some reward after his good work in the moon-pool.

'You have done well in Bangalore Mansions,' began Bernard warmly.

'Thank you.'

'It was a decidedly curious assignment. Now you need a change of scene.'

'I should welcome that.'

Bernard cleared his throat nervously.

'There is just one small snag,' he added. If Jonathan had known the Chief Clerk better, he would have realized from the first that he never seemed so diffident, so inappropriately mild, as when he was about to do something rather awful. Bernard was a good butcher but his butchery had a touch of the amateur about it. When he swung the axe, you could understand why Doctor Guillotine had been inspired to invent his own more effective method of despatch.

'What's the trouble?' asked Jonathan, not yet fully alerted to his doom.

'A little matter of your security clearance. It seems kinder to be frank.'

'I don't understand.'

'You have had strange associates. These things have attracted notice. In the moon-pool, there is a terrible clarity.'

Bernard did not mention Fiona. Some rudimentary sense of fair play made him feel that it was not right to blame the young man for the private life of the Security Service officer under whom he had been instructed to work. But he did harp at length on Jonathan's unsavoury connections with the dubious circle surrounding Tess Leyland, Rupert Mills and Harold Montrose.

'In this world,' he added sententiously, 'a man is known by the company he keeps.'

Jonathan sat stunned, his hopes tumbling.

'What does this mean in practice?' he asked faintly.

'We retain full confidence in you, Jonathan. Of course. But it does mean a note on your file. We can't afford to take chances. Just for the time being, we'd rather not have you back in the Foreign Office itself.'

'Where on earth am I to go then?'

'I can arrange a secondment for you to the Home Civil Service.'

'You have something in mind?'

'Oh yes. It's all fixed. You will realize that it can't be a sensitive Department. The Treasury and the Ministry of Defence have the same high security requirements as the Foreign Office itself. But we can't all serve in the teeth arms, can we? We also need dedicated workers in the vast infra-structure, so vital to the well-being of the nation.'

'What on earth can this be leading up to?'

'I'm only trying to explain, Jonathan. It hasn't been easy to place you. Not with that note on the file and Miss Leyland and Professor Montrose still dangerously at liberty. But Tiverton-Clark in the

Department of the Environment has very kindly agreed to take you on.'

'What does he do?'

'I don't know that he does much himself. He is in charge of the Ancient Monuments and Historic Buildings Inspectorate. I believe it's a thoroughly gentlemanly outfit.'

'And it doesn't require much in the way of a security clearance?'

'That's the beauty of it. We have used Tiverton-Clark before. He took on Canterville after we had to pull him out of NATO. Now he's quite an authority on the Late Decorated.'

'But will I still have a career?'

'Of course you will still have a career, my dear boy. It's just a question of "*reculer pour mieux sauter*". A temporary withdrawal from the hurly-burly to recharge your batteries.'

'I don't know anything about Historic Buildings.'

'The Civil Service is not expected to know things. You will bring a talent for public administration.'

'It sounds a bit dull.'

'Dull? The beauty and majesty of ancient Rome? The heavenward yearning of the English Gothic? The playful fantasies of Jacobean baroque? You will be a guardian of the heritage.'

'It's not what I joined for.'

'We join to serve, Jonathan. Others decide where we should give our services.'

'Where do I work then?' asked poor Jonathan, somewhat desperately.

'The vacancy is for an energetic official to look after the ancient monuments in Northumberland and Cumbria. The Roman Wall and all that. It should be quite fascinating. Housesteads in the mist.'

'It's what I joined the Foreign Office to get away from.'

'How ironic. Well, life is full of surprises, isn't it?'

Bernard seemed quite unperturbed by the small tragedy, the blighting of young hopes. But then he had always been good at bearing the suffering of other people.

'They are brutes,' complained Jonathan to Rupert that evening.

'You were wrong to join the pack. It never was your scene.'

'I wanted to get up towards the light and air. To end up as one of the taller trees in the forest.'

'And all you did was to lose the mysterious domain.'

'You can afford to knock the system. It was different for you, Rupert. I was born in Otley.'

'You seem to conceive of that as a state of mind. Almost a profession in itself.'

'You never had to fight.'

'I never wanted to.'

'I don't think I want to fight any more.'

'But you'll go, Jonathan? To where they send you?'

'I suppose so. I have to be alive somewhere. And I can't let Mum down. She's got to have something to tell the folks back home. The truth is that I'm a flop. I lost Fiona, and now I've lost the job.'

'I don't really know what it's all about. But I somehow feel you must have got on to the wrong track.'

'I thought it would gently waft me upwards. On a sort of moving staircase.'

'I don't think the ruthless ambition line is really yours at all.'

'We have to be more ruthless, Rupert. That's the trouble with the country today. Too much feather-bedding of the unfortunates.'

'You think that but you don't really feel it. Your inner instinct is for compassion. That's your core.'

Rupert was waving his arms around now, in a manner that Jonathan remembered from college. People were starting to stare. For once, Jonathan didn't seem to mind. He felt that Rupert represented the voice of his conscience, his own true self. But he wasn't going to concede too easily.

'Don't imagine I don't envy you,' he almost shouted. 'Being a free spirit. But people like you need people like me. Someone has to drag the blocks for the pyramids.'

Rupert realized now how greatly Jonathan had changed, as a result of his experiences over the last few weeks. Once he would have gloried in his membership of the Establishment. Now he saw it as a kind of servitude.

'To hell with the pyramids,' remarked Rupert.

'What are you planning to do?' asked Jonathan.

'I have found a cosy little niche. Now that Tess has done a bunk with that awful Montrose, I've got to know her funny old mum and dad quite well. There were practical things to sort out. Tess left some kit behind. And Lady Leyland, as you may remember, is a childhood chum of my mother.'

'The old-girl network.'

'I managed to convince them that I didn't know what Tess was really up to. They accepted that all I'd done wrong was decline to be adored. In the end we got on quite well, and the upshot is that Sir James has given me a job. At Oxford, of all places.'

'Not a Fellowship?'

'Of course not, silly. But I'm going to be Head Wine Steward at Belial.'

'You don't drink wine.'

'I do, when older people pay. And I know quite a lot about it. It's a kind of hereditary flair.'

'Lucky old you. But your class always tends to fall on its feet.'

'The law of the jungle. I'm a believer in that.'

They had spoken in mock philosophical terms the whole evening, to avoid going deeper. But they had more in common than they cared to put into words. The truth was that they had both lost their girls.

Although it was now early December, the evening air was balmy in Lanzarote. Down there in the Canary Islands, thought the young German, the wind blew warm and arid from the deserts of nearby Africa. It was here that Europe got nearest to the beloved south. He pushed aside the jangling bead curtain and entered the small, crowded bar. Yes, they were here again this evening, the young English girl with long dark hair and the old man who seemed to be always with her. Tonight he would be brave and try to get them talking. It was lonely, being on holiday alone, and he regretted now that foolish row with Gisela in Munich.

'May I sit here?' asked the German boy. 'I am Manfred.'

'Please do,' said the girl quite politely. The boy noticed now that there was something curious about the colour of her eyes. They were a kind of violet, rarely seen.

'I went to see the caves today,' said Manfred. 'Wonderful rocks and coral.'

'It is an extraordinary island altogether,' said the older man. 'And not yet totally spoilt.'

'May I ask? Are you on holiday here?'

'That would be one way of putting it,' replied the girl.

There was something sarcastic about her manner, thought

Manfred. He was not sure that he liked that. But then he had heard that the English had an unusual sense of humour.

'May I offer you some more wine?' he suggested.

'That would be very kind of you,' replied the old man rather quickly.

'Could I enquire your name?' asked the German.

'I am Christina Rossetti,' said the girl. 'And this is my uncle, David Garrick. He used to be with the Royal Shakespeare Company.'

'An actor,' exclaimed Manfred. 'How wonderful! I myself work in a filling station. I only arrived on Saturday. How long will you stay?'

'That depends,' replied Christina Rossetti. 'Doesn't it, Uncle?'

'It depends,' agreed the old actor, 'on many things. From here the road winds downhill all the way.'

Manfred found this a mystifying remark. That part of the island seemed remarkably flat, a sort of lunar landscape washed by a green subtropical sea. There were no hills to be seen. Manfred was a practical young man and he liked things which he could see and understand.

'I shall be here,' he said, 'for eleven more nights. Twelve more breakfasts. Then I go home on my package.'

'I'm on a package too,' said Mr Garrick. 'But it doesn't include home.'

Manfred noticed that they were both rather pale. Everyone else was bronzed with the sun. He began to wonder what they could find to do on Lanzarote.

'On holiday,' said Manfred, 'I develop my body. I swim. I jog. I tan.'

'So we notice,' riposted the girl.

'I have almost abandoned the body,' said the old man. 'I'm just soaking up the peace.'

'Even here,' continued Manfred, 'there is danger.'

'Oh yes?' asked Miss Rossetti, though without much interest.

'Last night,' replied the German, 'there was a small explosion in the big hotel. In the manager's quarters. They are trying to keep it quiet, for fear of driving the tourists away.'

'It's a very ugly hotel,' said Mr Garrick.

'It has a beautiful Olympic pool,' said Manfred.

'Big hotels are out of place on Lanzarote,' commented the old man. 'Let's hope the next explosion is a big one.'

'Shut up, Harold,' said the girl quickly.

Why was she calling him Harold? Manfred found it most confusing. He wondered whether this might be some humorous allusion. The British were so odd. Sometimes they drove through Bavaria in their Japanese cars. Perhaps the old man could be persuaded to go off to bed and leave him alone with the girl. There was a kind of invitation in her face, almost a hunger. Her voice sounded old but her body was young and fresh.

'What do you do?' he asked her.

'Do?' She made it sound almost obscene.

'For a living?'

'I'm a merchant banker,' she replied promptly. 'I've been working in the city since the Big Bang. For Campion, Lovelace and Marlowe.'

Manfred was not surprised. He had spotted that the girl was a person of significance. But the evening was not going as well as he had hoped. Miss Rossetti was quite forthcoming in her replies but there was a faintly mocking note about them. And the old man showed no inclination to retire. On the contrary he seemed quite keen on having another flask of wine ordered, though not at his own expense. Manfred began to suspect that the proceedings might not end in the way he had hoped. The girl might be too complicated for him.

As he studied her face, Manfred came slowly to the conclusion that there was a certain estranging bitterness about her unusual eyes. She was not at all like his cheerful sisters, Erika and Petra, always so active in the house and dairy. And the old man had a disconcerting stare too, as if he had seen things which should not be seen. Manfred began to think of an excuse for getting away. Tomorrow night he would choose a different bar.

'Have some more of the Spanish stuff,' said Sir Marcus Stewart-Stibbs. 'Almost as good as French champagne and much cheaper. Felicity used to serve it in the embassy in Paris. With a big napkin round the bottle to cover the label.'

'It will be whisky in Washington,' said Amaryllis Gilbert.

'Are you reconciled to the idea?'

'It's worth it, to see Bernard so fulfilled. And the children are coming. That will be bliss.'

His knighthood would be announced in the New Years Honours. This Christmas party in the Office, given traditionally by the Permanent Under-Secretary for his closest collaborators, was one of her last semi-public appearances as a Mrs. Bernard would need his *K* in the States. Like most professed egalitarians, they were extremely status-conscious over there.

'You must be up to your eyes,' said Sir Marcus.

'There's a lot to do,' agreed Amaryllis happily. 'Ordering the visiting cards and all that. And we've found wonderful tenants for our house. Japanese.'

'Oh, good. Japanese are so clean.'

'Camilla is bringing her Finn,' continued Amaryllis. 'Now that we're going to the States, everyone suddenly wants to be with us.'

'I shall miss Bernard. He has been a tremendous help to me. It won't seem the same here without his ingenious postings chains and nifty little ladders of promotion.'

'He nipped up the last one himself,' said Amaryllis cheerfully.

'I suppose you might put it like that,' agreed Sir Marcus. 'It is all change and decay around here. My own retirement is only a few months away.'

'You will be greatly missed,' said Amaryllis.

'Oh, do you think so? Nobody is irreplaceable. And, before then, we have transfers from my office here. Jasper Tenby has got himself posted to Rome. A reward for putting up with me for so long, I suppose. Though he won't use much of his Arabic there. And Lucinda is heading for some place in the Far East where she believes there will be lots of ardent young men.'

'Is Lucinda that rather fat girl with spots who is taking round the food?'

This seemed to Sir Marcus a quite inadequate description of Lucinda, whose opulent torso and curly head appealed to him as the acme of female loveliness. But then he had noticed before that women sometimes failed to appreciate each other.

Bernard approached, exuding the good fellowship of the season.

'Jolly fine party, Marcus,' he said. 'So kind of you to invite my secretary, Penelope Johnson-Boswell. She leads rather a quiet life, I understand. Outside the office, I mean.'

'She worked for me once in Paris,' said Sir Marcus. 'That's why I invited her. Used to get palpitations in the hour of crisis.'

'She still does, poor dear. The only thing to do is to clap her smartly on the back.'

'I never thought of that,' said Sir Marcus. 'But then you are so resourceful, Bernard. I'm sure you will be splendid in Washington.'

'Thank you.'

'No news, I suppose, from the disappointed candidates? Poor old James and that amazing Mr Craxton?'

'They are both writing books, I believe. Sounds harmless enough.'

'Don't be too sure,' said Sir Marcus. 'Books can be time bombs. I promise not to write one.'

'You'll be far too busy,' said Bernard. 'United Biscuits have asked me to approach you. They hunger to secure you for their Board.'

'I'll see if I can fit them in,' said Sir Marcus cheerfully. The directorships were rolling in rather nicely now. He would be busier than ever after so-called retirement. And much richer. Felicity, as now, would only be seeing him in the evening and at weekends.

'But I'm not leaving you yet,' continued Sir Marcus. 'I hope to visit you in Washington before my retirement.'

'Oh, good. Bring Felicity, too.'

Sir Marcus did not appear to have heard this last friendly suggestion.

'Elmer Stigwood wants me to go over,' he said, 'for talks at the State Department. And I may be asked to give a lecture or two. Georgetown, perhaps, or Princeton. It's splendid to think that you and Amaryllis will be there.'

'I feel the same,' agreed Bernard with his usual hearty laugh. 'It all worked out rather well, didn't it?'

'I hope so,' said Sir Marcus.

'You only hope so? That sounds rather tepid.'

'I didn't want to tempt the gods.' Somewhere, at the back of his mind, lay the old adage. Was it Solon of Athens? Call no man happy until he is dead.

Banishing these sad thoughts, Sir Marcus started to visualize the pleasures of the Washington trip. He would make it in the spring. Bernard would be very busy but perhaps his wife could take him out for a day on the Blue Ridge. There was an evocative line in Milton. To sport with Amaryllis in the shade. It was better to be an old fool than to have lost the love of life, and the life of love.

'We have to go now,' said Bernard. 'Back to Blackheath. Amaryllis is expecting a telephone call from Timothy's house-master.'

'Never mind,' said Sir Marcus. 'We shall meet soon. Have a good Christmas and then a nice trip out.'

'I'll be seeing you,' agreed Bernard cheerfully. 'State-side, as they say.'

In fact, Sir Marcus never saw him again.

Sir Dominic Trowbridge had been shaken by his talk with Major Glossop. The old Plum officer had sat rigid at attention, his back straight, his moustache bristling, his eyes flashing with martial fire. It was difficult to believe that this magnificent product of the Royal Halberdiers could have acted incorrectly. And yet the evidence was there. Fortunately Major Glossop's contract was only for a limited duration. The way had been clear for Sir Dominic to propose politely that it need not be renewed when it elapsed at Easter. The old Plum had taken it on the chin. But it was not a pleasant way to start the New Year. It was particularly disturbing to think that these difficulties should have arisen in the very heart of the moon-pool. First young Fiona Hopkins had been found wanting, then Jonathan Fieldhouse and now the impeccable Major Val himself. Who was going to guard the guardians now?

It was thus a weary and disillusioned Sir Dominic who crossed the Horseguards on that blustery afternoon in mid-January to call at the Foreign Office on Sir Marcus Stewart-Stibbs. Nor was that dignified official in one of his sweeter moods.

'I'm booked for the Mansion House tonight,' he said. 'They seat you next to your own wife. So tiresome for her, I mean.'

'I wanted to talk,' said Sir Dominic, 'about the moon-pool.'

'Your idea, I seem to remember.'

'And a good one too,' opined Sir Dominic defensively. 'It saved you from making a dreadful mistake over that Washington appointment.'

'Us,' snapped Sir Marcus. 'It saved us.'

'However,' continued Sir Dominic, 'even the best ideas have their limitations. Nothing is for ever. One has to change one's perspective as the many facets of truth are slowly revealed to our imperfect human intellect.'

'You seem to be leading up to something, Dominic.'

'It's about the moon-pool. I've changed my mind. I want to abolish it.'

A playful smile had begun to play around the mobile mouth of the Foreign Office mandarin. Sir Marcus was by no means sorry to see the powerful Head of the Security Service looking so uncharacteristically defensive. In the jungle of Whitehall in-fighting, one could only rejoice at any sign of weakness among the feasting panthers.

'Abolish it, Dominic?' echoed Sir Marcus in feigned surprise. 'But I thought it was one of your most creative innovations.'

'It was. And we have achieved a lot in the moon-pool, using the laser-beam of the deep probe to sniff out human weakness in the public service. It was necessary. The positive vetting system had become too lax before I took over. But there were always certain inherent dangers in the experiment. After all, we are not a police state. I remember pointing that out at the time.'

'It was I who pointed it out,' said Sir Marcus. 'There *is* such a thing as personal privacy.'

'Well, that's the trouble. From the standpoint of state security, we need to discover all there is to know about our people. For that end, the moon-pool is a potent instrument. Too potent, perhaps. I'm afraid it's now telling us too much.'

'How can we know too much? At least for your purposes.'

'The material is too massive. Now that we really do know about the private life of government servants, the effect is mind-boggling. I had never realized before that people are so feeble and corrupt.'

'I had always realized that,' said Sir Marcus cheerfully. 'Right from the start. It's the basis of diplomatic method. The technique of the carrot and the stick.'

'I'm only a sort of policeman,' remarked Sir Dominic. 'I suppose it's been a sheltered life. Anyhow, I can't stand the moon-pool any longer. It exposes too much. The shady side of human nature. The recesses of the heart. The dark half of the moon.'

'What will you rely on then?'

'We will go back to the old system. Checking up on people's

references. Analysis of the known facts. But no more of those deep probes. There's too much crawling underneath the stone.'

'Does this have to be made public?'

'Oh no. The moon-pool was always a secret.'

'Ministers will be relieved,' said Sir Marcus. 'The public doesn't want to have its simple faith shaken.'

'*Sancta simplicitas.*'

'But tell me, my dear Dominic. This new line of yours is something of a volte-face. It must surely have been inspired by some specific incident. Have you had a shock, perhaps?'

He seemed so kindly that Sir Dominic felt rashly tempted to confide.

'I launched a moon-pool drive, you see, within the Security Service itself. I called it Operation Calpurnia. Caesar's wife, you know. It turned up some disturbing news about one of my key operatives, a Major Glossop. He had been using inside information to dabble on the stock exchange. Something complicated to do with the rate of the yen and the time differential with Tokyo. Of course he has had to go.'

'Quite shocking,' muttered Sir Marcus. 'I suppose every man has his little secrets.'

'Some have more than others,' said Sir Dominic. 'But we are all vulnerable.'

Sir Marcus gave him a swift gaze of appraisal. It occurred to him that perhaps old Dominic too had something to conceal. If so, he would have to go too. His premature retirement could open up a cosy niche for a senior diplomat from the Foreign Office stable.

'Oh, do you think so?' asked Sir Marcus hopefully. He waited, in the expectation that Sir Dominic might say more. But the Security Supremo had apparently relapsed into melancholy introspection. He looked like a small priest who had heard too many confessions and felt stunned by the sheer weight of human sin.

'I don't feel at all vulnerable,' continued Sir Marcus robustly. 'My career has been far too demanding to allow time for peccadillos.' How true, he added to himself, but also how sad.

'You agree then, Marcus?'

'To what exactly?'

'We scrap the moon-pool. Cement in the sides.'

'Willingly. I always thought the whole idea was rather silly.'

With the perfect courtesy for which he was noted in Whitehall, he escorted Sir Dominic all the way down to the park door. Sir Marcus had always been magnanimous in the hour of victory. Especially when it was handed to him on a plate.

It was drizzling on the Wall. And the February afternoon was short and dark. Perhaps he would have done better, thought Jonathan Fieldhouse, to spend it in the more hospitable valleys of north Yorkshire, inspecting those crumbling Cistercian monastic ruins. But that was too near to Otley. He didn't want the folk talking there. Besides, he had to get round the huge area of his ancient monuments assignment. In the bleak mid-winter, it would all be damp and dark. Regretfully he thought of his vain hope to dance under the chandeliers of the Paris Embassy. It seemed a far cry from there to Housesteads, as he looked out from the high Roman fort over the sinister dank marshes of what had once been no man's land, to the inhospitable terrain of the Picts and Scots. How miserably the Roman soldiers must have huddled here in their cloaks, dreaming of the warm south, the cypresses and the Samian wine. It was still a ghastly place as the winter night began to fall.

Two heavily muffled figures approached him, puffing upwards from the car park below, as he himself had done. To his surprise, they addressed him by name. It might have been the weird sisters hailing Macbeth.

'Who is that?' he asked tentatively.

'George Craxton,' riposted a mellow voice. 'And this is Sally. You remember her?'

'What a coincidence,' said Jonathan.

'I don't believe in coincidence,' retorted the politician. 'It is all somehow planned. Isn't it, Sally?'

'I don't know, George. I've given up thinking about those things.'

'It's wonderful to have Sally with me,' said Craxton. 'In a mist, I mean. She knows every stone around here.'

'I ought to. It's my country.'

'And what a grand country,' said George in his political baritone. 'So noble and so bare. This is where they held the barbarians back. It's still the task today. You know of course that I'm in the Lords.

The Prime Minister couldn't take me any longer in the Commons. I was too dangerous.'

'So you're an elder statesman,' said Jonathan politely.

'Not all that elder,' riposted Craxton hastily, not entirely pleased. 'If my country ever needs me, I shall be available. Meanwhile, I confine myself to the big issues. World poverty; the future of the race. It's the place in history that counts. I aim to echo down the centuries.'

'It sounds quite a nice life,' said Jonathan.

'It's a life,' said George. 'Though not what I had planned.'

'Nor is mine,' pointed out Jonathan. He intended this as an encouragement to George to ask him about his own misfortunes. But the statesman failed to take the hint. Perhaps he was still brooding over the big issues, thought Jonathan, a trifle nastily.

'I am on the box a good deal,' added George. 'Especially when the government make one of their numerous mistakes. I suppose I speak for the exiles.'

'Come on, George,' said Sally. 'We shall get soaked.'

'And they want me in the Third World,' added George. 'I plan a series of seminars. And I'm dictating my book now. *Failure of a Government.*'

'But you were in the government yourself.'

'That's how it failed. Booting me out. But I put it more delicately.'

'It's all right for you, George,' said Sally. 'You've got those thick boots.'

She was reasserting herself, thought Jonathan. Perhaps that was all to the good. They might be getting together again. Sally might not be inspiring but at least she was probably better for George than Martha had been.

'You're right,' agreed George. 'Poor young Vince will be getting bored. Even with the car tapes to play with.'

'Vince is with you?' asked Jonathan.

'In the car park,' said Sally, a trifle waspishly. 'He was too lazy to climb the hill for the sake of a lot of old ruins.'

'I can't say I blame him,' said George tolerantly. 'It is a bit of a pull-up.'

'You're too kind to that boy,' snapped Sally.

'This is a ghastly thing,' said Sir Marcus. His first reaction, on hearing the terrible news, had been to send for Sir Dominic Trowbridge. After all, it *was* a security situation. Summer had come round again and it was a delicious London evening in early July. But there was no time to enjoy that now.

'Poor old Bernard,' agreed Sir Dominic sympathetically. 'He was so happy about going to Washington.'

Sir Bernard Gilbert had been assassinated in his embassy residence an hour before. Owing to the time difference, it had been the lunch-hour on the eastern seaboard. He had walked out on the mellow Lutyens portico for drinks with his guests and there had been shot by a professional gunman concealed in the garden. He had died instantly.

'It's awful for Amaryllis and those children,' said Sir Marcus. 'I was planning to visit them, you know.'

His overriding, though secret, feeling was of relief, that he had not been there too. He at least was still alive. If one of them had to go prematurely, it was better that it should be Bernard. Sir Marcus was not proud of this feeling. But he recognized it to be entirely natural and human. It would be most people's real reaction, though encased in the usual hypocrisy.

'She's bearing up pretty well,' continued Sir Marcus. 'Or so they tell me. The British Government is not exactly generous in such cases. She'll be on a small widow's pension from now on. Quite a drop.'

'Where will she go?'

'Helsinki, perhaps. The daughter is marrying a Finn.'

'Poor woman.'

'It's not much fun now,' said Sir Marcus, 'being a British Ambassador. We have too many enemies. Who was it this time?'

'My people don't know yet. The Americans have promised us an urgent report.'

'That won't bring Bernard back. I shall miss him, you know. He was good fun.'

Sir Dominic Trowbridge had never considered Bernard to be good fun. In fact, he had always regarded him as rather a nuisance. Beneath that self-satisfied manner, and that air of faintly patronizing benevolence, there had lurked a streak of fairly ruthless ambition. Well, it had not done him much good in the end. But it would not have been quite correct to say so at the moment. There were certain decencies to be observed.

'Bernard was a very genuine character,' remarked Sir Dominic cautiously. 'Not the kind of person you could ever forget.' He remembered only too well his tussles with Bernard, which had not always resulted in victory for the Security Service.

'And now you will need a new ambassador in Washington,' continued Sir Dominic. 'And there's no moon-pool left to filter the candidates.'

'A new Permanent Under-Secretary too,' said Sir Marcus. 'I go after the summer.'

The competition for the two posts would be intense, in spite of the physical danger in Washington. He himself would take only an objective interest. Already, thought Sir Marcus, he was beginning to relax his hold. His own Private Office had changed with the departure of Jasper and Lucinda. The new girl was skinny but she had a winsome smile. What was her name again? Mary, Martha, Marianne? That was the trouble about getting old. Perhaps it was just as well to be leaving the Foreign Office. As a non-executive director, you were not expected to know so much about the detail. They valued your advice on the broad lines of policy.

The Foreign Secretary was calling for him now. He would want to talk about a new man for Washington. It seemed heartless but the job had to be filled. It would be important to avoid another attempt to make a political appointment. That would not be popular with the Service. And Sir Marcus wanted to go out on a high note. Hopefully, to the well-padded benches of the Lords. It was a bit sad, though, to have to discuss senior appointments, today of all days, without Bernard's smiling support. Human ambition was so tiring to cope with, and so short-sighted against the background of eternity. The old Arab proverb had it about right. The dogs bark but the caravan passes on.